"I do not wish yo
make a show for
watching," Will said simply.

Oh. Dangerous.

"Why not?" Plenty of men would have taken the kiss without worrying about such niceties.

"Because I would not like you to imagine that I am only kissing you for that reason."

Psyché opened the door and cold air slid in. "Can we agree, then, sir, that we are taking mutual advantage of the situation to do something we both wish to do?"

She reached up, brushed back that errant lock of hair and stepped into him.

"We can do that," he said huskily as his arms closed about her.

His lips were warm, smooth, soft. Tentative at first, not shy precisely, but wondering what she liked, finding out, moving in slow, gentle rhythms that lured her closer, had her relaxing even as tension coiled lightly in her belly.

He released her. Slowly. Stepped back. Slowly. And let out an audible, shaky breath that told her stepping back was the last thing he'd wanted to do.

Psyché returned inside, and closing the door, she leaned against it. After a moment, she remembered to flip the key in the lock. What in God's name had she done?

Author Note

Those who have read my last two books will recognize some familiar faces. James, Earl of Cambourne, and his young brother-in-law, Fitch, first appeared in *In Debt to the Earl*. Huntercombe also appeared in that book but got his own story in *His Convenient Marchioness*.

When I finished *His Convenient Marchioness*, I fully intended to write Kit and Martin's story immediately. In fact, I started on it. However, I'd run across the story of the intriguing, real-life Dido Belle, and before I knew it, this story with Psyché and Will had started to form in my mind, and because of the time line I had for Kit's story, I had to write Psyché's first.

I scribbled ideas down for the hero, but looking back, I have to wonder what I was thinking. Will Barclay was right under my nose all along. As Huntercombe's private secretary, he appeared in *His Convenient Marchioness*, so I went back to see what I'd already written about him. There wasn't a great deal—always useful because it leaves room to play!—but it was clear that he was kind and courageous.

In writing Will and Psyché's story, I have deliberately taken a step away from my usual Regency milieu of the aristocracy. I hope you enjoy seeing another side of London.

ELIZABETH ROLLS

—

A Marriage of Equals

HARLEQUIN
HISTORICAL

HARLEQUIN®
HISTORICAL™

Recycling programs
for this product may
not exist in your area.

ISBN-13: 978-1-335-50617-7

A Marriage of Equals

Copyright © 2021 by Elizabeth Rolls

This edition published by arrangement with Harlequin Books S.A.

For questions and comments about the quality of this book,
please contact us at CustomerService@Harlequin.com.

Harlequin Enterprises ULC
22 Adelaide St. West, 40th Floor
Toronto, Ontario M5H 4E3, Canada
www.Harlequin.com

Printed in U.S.A.

Elizabeth Rolls lives in the Adelaide Hills of South Australia with her husband, two sons, several dogs and cats, and a number of chickens. She has a well-known love of tea and coffee, far too many books and an overgrown garden. Currently Elizabeth is wondering if she should train the dogs to put her sons' dishes in the dishwasher rather than continuing to ask the boys. She can be found on Facebook and readers are invited to contact her at books@elizabethrolls.com.

Books by Elizabeth Rolls

Harlequin Historical

A Regency Invitation
"The Prodigal Bride"
The Unexpected Bride
The Chivalrous Rake
His Lady Mistress
The Dutiful Rake
Mistress or Marriage?
The Unruly Chaperon
Lord Braybrook's Penniless Bride
Royal Weddings
"A Princely Dilemma"
A Marriage of Equals

Lords at the Altar

In Debt to the Earl
His Convenient Marchioness

Visit the Author Profile page
at Harlequin.com for more titles.

For Philip, with thanks not only for the informative and entertaining walks around Soho but for over forty years of friendship and laughter.

Chapter One

Soho, London—Christmas Eve 1803

'Goodnight, John. Merry Christmas!'

Psyché Winthrop-Abeni stepped from the carriage to the pavement.

'Merry Christmas, Miss Psyché.' The old coachman grinned at her. 'Bert's got his orders. He'll see you in safe.'

The footman had already jumped down from his perch behind the coach. Psyché didn't bother arguing. She knew perfectly well that Uncle Theo had given those orders and she could hardly countermand them. Besides, it wasn't as if either man would take a blind bit of notice anyway. They'd been told to see her safe home and they would do precisely that.

She raised her lantern and led the way to the front door of the coffee house. Although at eight o'clock it had been full dark for hours, the carriage lamps cast light to see by and a few stragglers were still hurrying home carrying lanterns. Christmas Eve, and the bite in the air promised snow before morning.

She slipped the key into her front door and unlocked it. 'Thank you, Bert. Don't wait. I promise I'll lock up immediately. Merry Christmas.'

He just looked at her.

She let out a laugh. 'Oh, very well.' She went inside, closed the door, locked it, shot the bolts and set the bar in place. Then she unbolted the little shutter in the door, flipped it up and looked out. 'Happy?'

'Merry Christmas, miss!'

'Merry Christmas, Bert.'

Psyché watched as he leapt up behind the coach and it rumbled off. Bolting the shutter, she stifled a sigh, then threaded past the tidily stacked tables and chairs of the coffee house, through the kitchen and into the back corridor and storage area. A narrow set of stairs led upwards.

She shouldn't be sighing. She had been blessed, right from the day the terrified mulatta child had arrived on the London docks over a dozen years ago, to now, when, as an independent woman of twenty-four, she climbed the stairs leading to her private apartments over her own shop. The lantern threw dancing gilded shadows before her. The only sounds were those of the building creaking as it settled for the night.

Blessed. Privileged, even. Because although she worked hard to earn her living from the coffee house she owned and had christened The Phoenix Rising, she had been given the chance to do so. It could all have been very different.

Christmas was one of the times of the year she made herself remember that and count her blessings.

Blessing—the first? Her freedom. That, she knew, some would consider the greatest of those blessings because everything hinged on that.

Second? She was independent and that was important, too. Because while freedom and independence were related, they were not quite the same thing.

And third? Encompassing all the rest? She had family and she was loved unconditionally. Without that love none of the rest could have happened. And even before she was brought to London, there had been Mam. Mam who had loved her with everything she had. Without Mam…

Thank you, Mam. For everything.

So now, climbing the stairs to her apartment, she thought of love and family. And counted her present blessings.

Christmas Day she would spend with her elderly friend and neighbour from the bookshop across the road, Ignatius Selbourne. Ignatius, she knew, hoped to see his own great-niece on Christmas Day, but he didn't expect it. Catherine's father was unlikely to permit it. Ignatius had said very little, but she knew he was worried about the girl. Her betrothal had recently ended in scandal. Some said she had broken it, others claimed that Lord Martin Lacy, youngest scion of a ducal house, had finally spurned a *mésalliance* with the daughter of trade. If the latter was true, she considered Catherine well rid of the connection. A man who considered you beneath him was not a man at all.

She set the lantern on the table. By the fire her ginger cat, Fiddle, yawned and rolled over invitingly. She bent down and stirred up the fire, adding more coals. Fiddle *mrowped* his approval, stretching to expose his furry belly to the warmth.

'Pleased to be of service, Your Deityship.' Psyché rubbed his head, felt the rumble of his deep-throated purr. She suspected that in Fiddle's view of the world their relationship was not that of cat and mistress, but of beneficent god and humble acolyte.

She swung the kettle over the fire. It was too late to drink coffee, no matter how tempting. She'd never sleep if she did. A chamomile tisane was a much better idea. Her thoughts drifted to Ignatius as she spooned the dried flowers into the pot.

He'd worried about Catherine's betrothal at first, disgusted by what he'd described as Carshalton's 'medieval matchmaking'. But Lord Martin had brought Catherine to visit him… *Should have known better than to judge without meeting the fellow. He's the right sort. She'll be safe with him. And happy.* A week or so later the betrothal ended.

Psyché had delivered a pot of coffee to the bookshop while Catherine and Lord Martin were there and if he'd broken the betrothal then he was a fool. It had been so obvious that Catherine cared for him. She didn't know Catherine well, but she knew the girl feared her father, and loved her great-uncle, so she was predisposed to like her and think that if she'd broken the betrothal, then she'd had a damn good reason for it.

So instead of spending the day with her own family, Psyché would visit Ignatius. Attend church with him at St Anne's and dine afterwards. There would be other waifs and strays in the cosy, book-strewn apartment above his shop.

Uncle Theo had understood and not pressed her to stay the night and spend Christmas Day. Today it had been just the two of them in the library of his Mayfair mansion. Tomorrow—well, tomorrow her cousin Hetty and her husband, Lord Harbury, as well as Hetty's father would be there along with assorted other relatives, some of whom merely tolerated her. And while she and Hetty were as close as ever, it was awkward when Harbury was there.

As children they had spent Christmas at Uncle Theo's house on Hampstead Heath, with its views back down to London and the dome of St Paul's reaching into the cold, bright sky. Aunt Grace had turned a blind eye to two little girls shrieking in glee as their sled tore down the hill in a whirl of snow and laughter.

But Highwood House was no longer her home, although she still visited whenever she could. This comfortable apartment was home now. It might not be as luxurious as Highwood or the Mayfair house, or any of Uncle Theo's other properties, but it was hers. And little touches spoke of home. Aunt Grace's worktable and her silver brushes—utterly useless with Psyché's unruly curls—the Turkey carpet from her dressing room at Highwood, part of the pretty tea service from the Mayfair house and other items that Uncle Theo had insisted must be hers after Aunt Grace's death.

'She'd like to think of you using them and you'll remember to visit me from time to time, heh?'

She did not need reminding to visit, but over the past three years this had become her home. Little things like the book she was reading left on the table, her shawl thrown over the back of a chair that had once been in Uncle Theo's study and Fiddle curled by the fire where Nyx, the spaniel, had left such a gap when she died two years ago.

With the kettle not quite at the boil, she poured the water into the pot to steep. Wandering to the window, she twitched the curtain aside. Snow drifted down to the quiet street and at the familiar rise of delight, she remembered her first Christmas with Aunt Grace and Uncle Theo.

The cold had shocked her; it still did—but the snow… To the little girl from Jamaica it had been something out of a fairy tale. Until it actually began to fall she had not believed that such a thing was possible. Now she knew that slush would follow, but she had never lost her stunned delight at snow tumbling from a leaden sky to lie in soft, tempting drifts, inviting a small girl to make it into a ball and throw it at someone. How many snowball fights had she and Hetty fought with Uncle Theo? There could have never been too many before the snow's fairy tale turned to slush.

Now she pulled out the letter that Hetty had left for her with Uncle Theo and began to read it again.

Dearest Psyché…

She could enjoy her letter, drink her tisane and think back on a lovely day while she counted the blessing to come of spending a snowy Christmas Day with a lonely old man who loved her as a sort of second-best great-niece. They would eat a good dinner, play piquet and no doubt she would borrow yet another book.

Their sled tore down the slope below Highwood House, with Psyché and Hetty laughing and shrieking as the bells of St Paul's called across the valley and echoed in the bright, crisp air.

Funny, she'd never noticed them from up here on the Heath before. They must have come closer in the night...

Hetty turned, smiling, and somehow it was the Hetty of now, not the child. 'It's for you...'

Psyché rolled over and sat up. Far from hearing the bells of St Paul's, or indeed any other church, it was the jangling bell at the back door of her own shop that had woken her.

She flung back the bedcovers, smothering Fiddle's indignant *mrowp*, shoved her feet into slippers and snatched up her heavy shawl. She used a taper to light the lamp on the table from the glowing coals of the living room fire before hurrying down the stairs to the door.

'Who is it?'

'Ignatius. Quickly, Psyché!'

She dragged the bolts back and lifted the bar, then turned the key. The door opened before she could do it herself and Ignatius and a smaller, slighter someone were inside with a flurry of snow and the door banged shut behind them.

'What on—?'

'I need your help, Psyché. You have to hide her until I can get her out of London.'

The fear in the old man's voice stopped her heart. 'Hide who?'

'Kit—that is, Catherine.' He spoke fast and low. 'She's

run from her father. She can't stay with me. It's the first place he'll look. There's no time. I have to get back before he arrives.'

'I told you, Uncle, I left that handkerchief and the note. He'll think I fled with—'

'He may or may not believe that, child,' said Ignatius. 'He's a scoundrel, no question, but he's not stupid. We won't chance underestimating him.'

He gripped Psyché's wrist with startling strength and his voice shook. 'Please. I know what I'm asking of you, but there's no one else I can trust with this.'

Catherine Carshalton was under twenty-one, an heiress. And her father… Psyché knew exactly who and what Carshalton was. Chills that had nothing to do with the icy night skittered along her nerves. Hiding *this* girl of all the girls in London could see her arrested, gaoled…and none of that mattered in the least.

'She won't be safe here indefinitely.'

'I know.' Ignatius sounded steadier. 'I'm going to write to Huntercombe. And I'll spend the day rushing around London supposedly looking for Kit. Draw Carshalton off.'

'All right. Go back.' She nearly shoved him out the door. 'Get a message to me if you can, but don't come yourself. It may not be safe.' She slammed the door shut on his thanks and shot the bolts again. She set the bar back in place, turned the key and then peered in the dark at her unexpected guest.

Her eyes had adjusted to the faint light from upstairs and Catherine Carshalton was a white shadow in the darkness. Psyché could hear her teeth chattering.

'Here. Take my hand and mind your step.'

A gloved hand slid trembling into hers and she led Catherine to the stairs. 'First step.'

'Thank you. I… I can s-see enough.'

Upstairs, she gestured Catherine to the chair by the fire. 'Sit, Miss Carshalton. I'll make you a hot drink, then—'

'Kit. Please, call me Kit. I will *never* be Miss Carshalton again.'

Psyché, stirring up the fire, sat back on her heels and stared.

Miss—Kit sat there wrapped in an ermine cloak that must have cost several small fortunes, shivering. Her face was blue with cold under the hood, but her mouth was set flat and her grey eyes blazed in utter resolution.

'You've run away.'

The chin lifted. 'Yes. I'm… I'm s-sorry if I've put you in danger. I didn't think and I h-had nowhere else to go but to Uncle Ignatius.'

Psyché nodded. 'Do you mind telling me why you left?' *She* might loathe and abhor everything Carshalton stood for, but that didn't mean his daughter felt the same way necessarily.

Kit met her eyes. 'I planned to leave anyway when I turn twenty-one. But tonight—I overheard them.'

'Them?'

'My—that is, Carshalton.'

Psyché blinked at Kit's clear disavowing of her father.

Kit went on. 'Carshalton and the man he wants me to marry.' She swallowed. 'They had the wedding arranged for later today. But first he…he was going to force me. He… they thought that way I couldn't refuse.'

'Force you?' Psyché realised it was not only cold that made Kit's voice shake and rage flooded her own throat as understanding sleeted through her. 'Force his attentions on you? Lord Martin was—'

'No! Not him!' Kit's voice broke. 'He—Martin would never, *never*—anyway, that's over. Done. Martin will never marry me now. He can't. Carshalton made another choice for me—Lucius Winthrop. He's—'

'I know who Lucius Winthrop is.' Psyché heard her own voice from a distance, each word like an icicle breaking. 'And your—' She broke off.

I will never be Miss Carshalton again.

Carshalton had forfeited all right to be called a father. 'Carshalton *agreed* to this?'

'He suggested it.'

Psyché's gorge rose. 'No wonder you ran. How did you throw the bastard off your trail?'

For the first time a tear slid down Kit's cheek. 'I had a handkerchief Martin lent me. I left that along with a forged note telling me where to meet him tonight.' Another tear followed the first.

Psyché stared. 'Does Carshalton really think you're that stupid?'

Kit nodded. 'I'm a girl. We're not supposed to think.'

Chapter Two

Soho, London—January 1804

Will Barclay considered himself among the luckiest of men. Some of the fellows he'd known at Oxford wouldn't see it that way, of course. He was a mere second son, and with two younger brothers to boot, so relatively speaking his patrimony was negligible. Naturally their father's estate had passed to his eldest brother, Robert. Rob was married now with two sons and a little girl in the nursery. Will thought his nephews jolly little rascals and considered it his duty to teach them the finer elements of cricket, but he secretly doted on his niece and goddaughter, Lily. He wished he saw more of them.

He and Rob disagreed on political matters, but everyone disagreed over something from time to time. Politics should not be allowed to destroy family ties.

They were all scattered now, of course. His mother lived with Rob and Margaret, enjoying her grandchildren and writing affectionate weekly letters to her other sons; himself, James in the navy, and Reg—of all of them!— ensconced as a curate in Northumberland.

And, even though his family disapproved, Will considered himself blessed in his employment. While the church had not appealed as a career, he'd been giving it consideration in preference to the very advantageous position his mother's second cousin—his own godfather, Edward Long—had arranged for him.

Then, a chance remark made by Reg to the much older half-brother of a school friend had dropped Will straight into the sort of position he'd never even dared to dream about.

The Marquess of Huntercombe had taken Reg's cheeky suggestion that his sobersides older brother William would make his lordship a capital secretary perfectly seriously and made the time to meet him. To Will's disbelief, Huntercombe had offered him the position. It was beyond anything he could have hoped for. He had accepted on the spot, then dashed off a diplomatic letter to his godfather, declining the other position. The letter to his mother had been far more difficult, because he had felt obliged to be honest. Reading the letter she sent in response had been worse.

But here he was at thirty-two, very well paid—some of his peers were not half so lucky—with board and lodging thrown in and the kindest, most sympathetic of employers. An employer, moreover, who had discerned his young secretary's growing interest in politics and government, and encouraged it. In fact, before Christmas, the Marquess had said that when Will was ready and opportunity arose, he would use his influence on Will's behalf to find him a position at Whitehall.

He hadn't mentioned that while he was at home over Christmas. Not wishing to throw a very unwelcome cat among the family pigeons, he'd thought to mention it immediately before his planned departure to rejoin Huntercombe's household at the end of January. But Mama and Rob, for reasons best known to themselves, had reopened the argument about his political leanings on New Year's Day.

Their reaction to his weary refusal to consider his godfather's latest offer had been predictable and cataclysmic. He'd held out a couple of days before making an excuse to leave for London, wondering how the hell he could patch things up this time. And if he should even make the attempt.

Huntercombe House was closed up, but there was a skeleton staff there and he'd taken the opportunity to check his lordship's correspondence. Most of the letters were easily dealt with, sent on to the Marquess, or requiring a quick response from himself. But one had puzzled him.

So here he was, that odd letter from Ignatius Selbourne in his pocket, riding into Soho to find out what it was all about. That Selbourne indicated he'd written to all three of Huntercombe's primary residences suggested that something was very wrong.

There was the reference in Selbourne's letter to burnt feathers. And his lordship already possessed a copy of the 1633 edition of John Donne's poetry Selbourne was offering for sale—an edition the fellow had actually sold to Huntercombe ten years ago, which was even more puzzling. Ordering the catalogue of Huntercombe's considerable collection of antiquarian books and manuscripts was part of Will's brief and that catalogue included sources.

The book was code for something else and Will, who was more than happy to listen to servants' gossip over his breakfast, had a fair suspicion of what that *something else* might be. But with Huntercombe in Cornwall it would take days for a letter to reach him and even longer for him to get back to London.

Will stabled his mare, Circe, at the Red Lion Inn and strolled back towards Selbourne's. A chill wind hunted along the street, whipping around corners and snapping at his heels. He hadn't been here for several years. Until Huntercombe's remarriage late last year, the Marquess had preferred to use his Isleworth house when he had to be in

London, rather than the Grosvenor Square mansion. Most of his interaction with Selbourne had been in writing during that period.

Little had changed. The street was still busy, crowded and noisy with people, stray dogs, cats, delivery wagons and smells. The smells could be especially noisome...but on a bright winter's day with that brisk wind it wasn't very bad.

One thing had changed. The coffee house he remembered diagonally across from Selbourne's had a new name. A brilliantly painted crimson bird, tail feathers and wings aflame, announced it as The Phoenix Rising. Will frowned. *'Burnt feathers are quite a useful commodity should your lady wife require a restorative.'*

The name itself was familiar. Huntercombe owned a number of London properties—this was one of them. He frowned. Huntercombe's agent, Foxworthy, dealt directly with the London tenants, but he was familiar with the listings—P. W.-Abeni, that was it. Sure enough, writ small in the bottom right of the sign was the confirmation: *P. W.-Abeni, Proprietor.*

He let out a breath. A cup of coffee would not go astray before he called on Selbourne. He noted the small sign in the bay window assuring patrons that only non-slave-produced sugar and coffee from the Dutch East Indies was served. In his heart he wondered if the Dutch use of indentured labour was very much better than chattel slavery, but one did what one could.

A bell jangled above Will's head as he pushed open the door of The Phoenix. Warmth greeted him and he stepped into a masculine world of chatter, redolent of roasting coffee, damp wool and leather and laced with the spicy hint of chocolate. Staff, male and female, scurried about with trays bearing cups and pots wafting fragrant steam. Will drew the fragrances deep, more than coffee and chocolate— vanilla, cinnamon, ginger, cardamom and other scents he could not identify hummed in the air. An open fire simmered on one side of the room with several dogs snoozing beside it.

Men crowded at small tables sipping their coffee, tea or chocolate. A mixture of languages wove a babel tapestry. Several Frenchmen chatted in the corner, worn, tired-looking men in once grand, now outmoded clothes—Will knew a number of men like them, friends of Huntercombe's, who had fled the turmoil in France, lucky to escape with their lives, let alone a change of clothes.

A group of Africans sat in the bay window, all wearing the little medallions Mr Wedgwood had created to promote the Abolition cause—a white porcelain plaque on which a chained Black man knelt, pleading his cause as a man and a brother. They spoke in Portuguese, Will was reasonably certain, although he didn't speak it himself. Probably members of the Sons of Africa.

He noted that a number of other customers wore the medallion, so presumably The Phoenix with its Dutch sugar and coffee aligned with the Abolition cause. Talk of politics, books, horses and sex—four young idiots loudly discussed the previous evening's adventures in lurid and unlikely detail—filled the shop.

Possibly the mysterious P. W.-Abeni, owner of The Phoenix Rising, could explain the burning feathers…

He glanced about. A couple of men younger than himself, a curvaceous blonde woman and a Black lad wove paths through the shop, balancing trays and clearing tables. The proprietor would be older, probably middle-aged, and…his gaze fell on the young Black woman at the counter and simply stopped, along with his breath and his heart.

She measured beans from an earthenware jar, scooping them out and depositing them in the scales with an easy rhythm while chatting with the liveried Black servant standing at the counter. Her high-necked gown was plain, a soft grey-blue wool, the sleeves well clear of her wrists, and only the smallest of ruffles to adorn them. Her only jewellery was the anti-slavery medallion suspended on a crimson ribbon around her neck. Her black hair was arranged in an elegant complication of braids woven with crimson ribbons.

A gentleman strolled up to settle his bill and she broke off to deal with that swiftly, a friendly smile crinkling the corners of her eyes. A quick note in a ledger and she turned back to the beans and footman.

'There.' She secured the bag as Will approached the counter. 'I'll be interested to know what Sir Peter thinks of this roast. Please tender my regards to him.'

'Aye. I'll be sure to tell him.' The servant touched his hat. 'Good day to you, Miss Psyché.'

'Good day, Lucas.'

Will stepped back to give the footman room, and the woman inclined her head politely.

'Good day, sir. How may I help you?'

Her low, musical voice slid into him, somehow mingling with the exotic spiciness of the shop, and those dark, liquid eyes that held a faint, questioning smile.

Psyché—the beloved of Eros. If any mortal woman could enchant the god of love it would be this one...

His brain scrambled for coherent thought, let alone words. 'Ah, a pot of coffee, please. For myself, that is.'

'Certainly, sir.' She smiled and his lungs wondered where all the air had gone. 'Would you like to pay now or when you leave?'

'Oh, I think now.' His mind was so dazed he would not have cared to wager a groat on remembering to pay later. He scrabbled about for a mental foothold...there'd been something else... 'Ah... I'm looking for Mr Abeni.'

Arched brows rose. 'Are you, sir? Is there some problem?' Cool suspicion crystallised in that honeyed voice now.

Will flushed. 'No. Er… I'm his landlord's secretary.'

The wariness in the dark eyes deepened. 'Are you now? And how does his lordship go on, Mr Barker?'

'Barclay,' he said automatically. 'Very well to the best of my knowledge.' It was done so smoothly he didn't even feel the hook. But then— 'You did that deliberately. You knew my name.'

'Huntercombe has mentioned you, Mr Barclay.'

Will floundered. Why would Huntercombe have mentioned his secretary to a girl—woman, really—working in a Soho coffee house? Huntercombe was unfailingly courteous. No doubt if this woman had waited on him at some time he would have spoken to her politely, perhaps even remembered her, but—

'I am Psyché Winthrop-Abeni, Mr Barclay.'

Shock, Will knew, came in packages of varying size. This one dropped on him like a hundredweight. *This* was P. W.-Abeni? How in Hades—?

'But you're—' He broke off, uncomfortably aware that he teetered on the edge of rudeness, or at the very least, indiscretion.

'Black?' She finished his sentence anyway.

He gazed dumbfounded at her. The slightly tilted dark eyes, the full, sensuous mouth, just now with a cynical twist, and the dark bronze silken complexion. Her eyes were narrowed now, the slender figure braced with her chin up.

He let out a breath, fully aware that his cheeks were burning. 'I could deny that I was going to say anything of the sort—say instead that you are very young to be the proprietor. And that women do not commonly run coffee houses.'

Cool amusement edged the lush mouth now. 'That's true enough. I am both of those things, too.'

'But it would be a lie,' he said. 'And worse, it would suggest that I thought you stupid enough to be fooled.'

Her gaze softened. 'Which I'm not. But I would have pretended had you chosen that path. Why didn't you?'

Good question. 'God knows.' He held out his hand across the counter. 'Will Barclay at your service, ma'am. Selbourne wrote to his lordship and I believe he mentioned your shop.'

She stared at him in surprise, then gave him her hand briefly. A warm, firm grip, with surprising strength in the slender fingers. 'You *believe*?'

Will hesitated. 'A passing reference to the convenience of burnt feathers.'

He could have sworn that amusement danced in those dark, deep eyes.

'How very cryptic, sir.'

'Does that mean anything to you?'

She didn't answer immediately, but he couldn't have said she hesitated. Rather, he had the impression he was being summed up. In stages. And that she was withholding final judgement.

'Take a table, Mr Barclay, and I'll have your coffee brought over. Would you like a second pot to take over to Mr Selbourne when you go? I can put it on his account.'

He blinked. 'If you think he would like it, certainly, but I'll pay for it.' He could hardly show up unannounced on Selbourne's doorstep with a pot of coffee and tell the man he was paying.

'Very well, sir.'

'And will you forgive me?'

She looked coolly amused. 'For informing me that I'm Black? My looking glass tells me the same every morning. You've hardly insulted me, sir.'

The deuce he hadn't. 'Implying, even accidentally, that

the colour of your skin somehow makes you less competent is definitely an insult. My apologies.'

Some of the fire banked. 'Many think precisely that, Mr Barclay. I am glad that you do not.'

Psyché watched as Will Barclay threaded his way through the hum of chatter and outright gossip to a small table in the corner.

So *that* was Huntercombe's secretary. Or was it? It seemed odd that the Marquess would send his secretary to deal with something like this… But when she'd asked how his lordship went on…

Very well to the best of my knowledge.

Ignatius had written to Huntercombe in Cornwall, as well as Isleworth and Mayfair because he didn't know where Huntercombe might be. If Barclay had received the letter sent to Grosvenor Square, then as his lordship's secretary he might have thought it his duty to investigate. But could he be trusted?

And what on earth had possessed her to challenge him like that? It wasn't as though she didn't meet that attitude regularly. He was hardly the first to express surprise that a Black woman could run a successful anything, let alone a coffee house. And when he'd caught himself—pulled back from actually saying it—she'd had to go and rub his nose in it!

It was a nice nose, although it looked as though it had been broken at some point, set in a quiet, kind face. Oh, for heaven's sake! How could a face be kind? It was a collection of features, wasn't it? Only, she'd known Uncle Theo was kind from the moment she'd met him in that inn by the docks, even before he spoke to her. Just as she'd known that her father's brother, Lucius, was not. She'd learned young to judge people accurately and most people were kind enough in their way. But most people didn't really *see* her, not as a person in her own right, a human being who could be insulted or hurt. But Will Barclay…

She wiped the counter, rubbing fiercely at a spot of dried milk. An impression. She'd had the impression he was kind. Very well. Perhaps he was. Perhaps he wasn't. *Kind* people could still make your teeth grate with well-meant insensitivity. Nor did *kind* mean a man was willing to break the law and she had still to make his coffee. What did it matter if he were one of the few who possessed the ability to see her, acknowledge that she was Black and *still* see her humanity? More important to notice that Mr Wilkes and Mr Barnes were nearly ready for their second pot. She pulled forward a grinder, poured the roasted beans into the top with broken-up sugar, and turned the handle.

But Will Barclay, sitting peaceably in the corner by the window, refused to be dismissed from her mind. He'd spoken politely, requesting his coffee, not giving an order. He'd neither leered at her nor ogled her breasts. Old Mr Wilkes always stared at her breasts when she brought their coffee over and as she walked away told Mr Barnes that she was '*a pretty little thing, and clever enough, for a darkie*'. He leered at the other girls working here, too, of course, even pinched the occasional bottom. The girls took it in their stride, especially Sally who had a very pretty bottom and generally got a penny out of it. Psyché doubted Mr Wilkes had the least idea he was known as the Penny Pincher. And he was rather deaf and probably had no idea that half the shop could hear his remarks.

She couldn't imagine Will Barclay saying anything of the sort whether he could be overheard or not. She doubted he was a bottom pincher either. Glancing over, she saw that he'd pulled out a book and was reading. She registered his reading glasses with a jolt. A stray lock of brown hair fell over his brow and she caught herself wondering if he had someone to smooth it back. As if he felt her scrutiny, he looked up and their eyes met. She wanted to look away, but something in his gaze held her trapped. And then he smiled below those ridiculously attractive reading glasses. Not a lascivious smile, nor a seductive smile accompanied by a suggestive wink and a smacking of lips. A friendly smile that crinkled his eyes and invited her to smile right back.

Her wrist turning the handle slowed and her breath shortened as an odd fizzing sensation invaded her belly. Annoyed with herself, she jerked her attention back to what she was doing. The handle was turning without resistance which meant all the coffee and sugar had gone through. She tipped them into a pot, added cardamom pods and a cinnamon quill, poured water on them and set the pot on the stove to brew beside one that was nearly ready. Swiftly she set up the trays and beckoned to Sally.

Sally cleared a table, nodded to the occupants and swirled up to the counter. 'Who's the new boy, then? Got an eye for you, he has.'

'Nonsense. Of course he hasn't.' Curse it! Her cheeks were heating. 'He's Lord Huntercombe's secretary. He brought a message.' If she was going to stretch the truth a little…

'Now *Lord Huntercombe's* a nice one.' Sally tucked a stray curl behind her ear. 'Always got a kind word for a body, nor he don't pinch no bums neither.' She heaved a gusty sigh. 'More's the pity.'

'For heaven's sake, Sally!' Smothering a laugh, Psyché snatched the first pot off the heat and poured it into the waiting cups. 'Lord Huntercombe must be fifty!'

Sally gave a low chuckle. 'He's still a handsome one. And he's only married a couple of months back, you said. Saw him with his lady when he called on Mr Selbourne. I'll wager he pinches *her* bum.'

'You just said he wouldn't do that.' Psyché added a small jug of hot milk to the tray for Mr Wilkes and Mr Barnes.

'His *own* lady's bum.' Sally took up the tray. 'Watch me get tuppence out of this. You taking the new boy's tray over?'

'Yes.' Psyché made that decision on the spot. Really, if she'd had any doubts about Will Barclay, knowing he was Huntercombe's secretary ought to have settled them. It was a wonder she hadn't met him before.

'Thought you might.' Sally grinned knowingly and strolled off, hips swaying in good-humoured invitation.

Psyché stared after her. Sally couldn't have known what she'd only just decided.

Got an eye for you, he has...

Whether he did or not, she should take his tray over personally. When challenged, he hadn't backed away. He'd deliberately acknowledged a mistake and refused to smooth it over with a polite lie. Very like Lord Huntercombe, in fact. She set cream and hot milk on the tray, not knowing which he liked. How odd that she hadn't asked. That was what came of allowing herself to be distracted by a customer. With a muttered curse, she added a small custard tart. The fragrance rose as the coffee frothed up the pot and she took it off and set it on the tray.

Lifting the tray, she began to weave a path through the tables, exchanging quick greetings as she went.

'I say, Miss Psyché! Did you say that was Huntercombe's secretary? Has Selbourne got something special for his lordship?'

Mr Phelps, seated near the counter, also collected books, although not on the scale of Lord Huntercombe. Psyché sidled around his question. 'I couldn't say, sir.'

She'd known Huntercombe for years, meeting him often as a child in her great-uncle's house. He and his first wife had been among the few to engage her in ordinary, sensible conversation when she and Hetty were brought down to the drawing room by their governess after dinner. She was more than happy to keep his secrets, along with those of Ignatius Selbourne.

Mr Barclay looked up from his book as she approached and his friendly, disarming smile set off warning bells and more of that wretched fizzing.

'Your coffee, sir.'

He drew an appreciative breath as she set the pot before him and his smile deepened. 'That smells excellent.'

'Thank you, sir.' She couldn't help smiling back. 'I didn't know if you preferred cream or milk.'

'Neither,' he said. *'Am* I forgiven? You didn't really say.'

She gave a rueful smile. 'I think I owe you an apology.'

His gaze narrowed. 'We might have to agree to disagree on that. Huntercombe would have cuffed me around the ears, metaphorically speaking, for being a clumsy lout. However, I'll admit to curiosity. How does any young woman come to be running a coffee house?'

'By having a great-uncle who is friendly with Lord Huntercombe.'

'I see.'

He didn't ask who her great-uncle might be. She had to give him credit for that when the question had to be burning a hole in the tip of his tongue.

'Viscount Staverton.'

His jaw dropped, for which she really couldn't blame him.

Slowly he said, 'Then…you're Staverton's Folly.'

Psyché inclined her head. 'I see you know the story, Mr Barclay. The pot for Mr Selbourne will be ready when you are.'

She walked away. Thirteen years ago, London had buzzed with the scandal of Viscount Staverton's perverse attitude towards the mulatta child the Polite World had unanimously dubbed Staverton's Folly.

Chapter Three

London—July 1791

The noisy, smelly inn stood close to the docks. Most of the luggage and Nyx had gone somewhere else, but the sailors had refused to carry the father any further. The innkeeper had been willing enough to take the money offered, but put them in this tiny, dark room, well away from other customers.

'God only knows what he's got! Is the darkie wench with him?'

The sailors had said she was, a servant of some sort.

'Right. Saves one of my servants having to look after him.'

Psyché didn't argue about being a servant. It didn't matter. The father was sick and *someone* had to look after him. He'd started with stomach pains and vomiting a few days before they'd sighted the English coast. Even so, he'd insisted on coming up from the cabin to see and had pointed out landmarks to her.

'That's the Cornish coast... There's the Lizard...'

She thought he pointed things out more to taste the names on his tongue than to inform her, but she listened, shivering in the bitter wind that hurled the ship through the leaping waves, striving to learn about this strange new land. Green, she could see how green it was, but it was a different green to Jamaica, and instead of the blue skies she was used to, it was all grey and dull, and there was rain, more cold grey rain, sweeping towards them.

'Better get below. You'll need warmer clothes when we reach London.'

Cold wind and rain had lashed them all the way up what the father called the Channel. She remembered from her lessons that while England lay to port, France lay to starboard. The French called this stretch of water La Manche. And as the ship beat its way up the Channel against the wind, the father became sicker and sicker, until he could no longer leave the cabin, could barely stand to void himself in the bucket, or vomit.

Psyché emptied the buckets, walking Nyx on the deck at the same time. She brought food the father couldn't keep down and held his hand when he cried out against the agony tearing him apart.

In a rare moment of lucidity he ordered her to write a letter for him to his uncle. Gave her an address to send it to.

'Uncle Theo. He's a viscount. Send it as soon as we reach London. He'll find a place for you if I can't. Tell him...'

But the pain seized him again before he could tell her what to write. But she had the address. So she wrote what she thought was right and then signed the letter with the only name she had ever used: Psyché Black, because Mam had been Black Bess on the plantation records, although the father had only ever called her Bess.

Black Bess—house slave
Psyché Black—house slave, her daughter

She ran into the captain when she was returning from emptying the bucket. One of the sailors had been kind, emptying it for her and tying a rope to duck it in the water and cleanse it.

The captain stopped her. 'How is your master?'

She didn't really know. 'Bad, sir. He...he can't keep anything down and he doesn't know where he is.' Or when for that matter.

The captain frowned. 'Do you know where he planned to go when we reach London? We'll dock on tomorrow morning's tide.'

Her stomach flip-flopped. 'I...he had me write a letter. To his uncle, a viscount. I have the address.'

The captain looked relieved. 'I'll have him carried to an inn. You can send the letter from there.'

So here she was, still emptying buckets and holding the father's hand while he drifted and tossed in a sea of pain, and his skin burned like a thousand suns. Jamaican suns, not the pale watery thing that passed for a sun in this England of his. She had sent the letter, asking the landlord how to do it. The landlord had glanced at the direction on the letter and his brows had shot straight up.

'I'll have one of the grooms take this at once.'

She hoped he hadn't stolen it, although there'd been nothing of value in it, and the landlord had sounded impressed—even intimidated. But it had been hours now. Although she didn't know how far Highwood House in Hampstead—that was the address—might be. It might be a day's ride. More.

Darkness pressed against the tiny window and she was nearly asleep in her chair when she heard voices and footsteps in the corridor.

'He's in here, my lord. Had to keep him away from the

other guests, you understand.' The landlord sounded oily, not at all like when he spoke to her. 'There's no telling what might be ailing him.'

'Of course, my good man. Here. Something for your trouble.'

She straightened in the hard wooden chair. Patted the father's hand.

He roused. 'Bess?'

'It's Psyché. Your uncle is here.'

Awareness crept into the fever-bright eyes. 'Thank God!'

The door opened and two men walked in. Psyché gasped. The second, the younger of the two, looked like the father. He had the same golden hair, the same features and tawny eyes.

His gaze fell on her. 'Who the hell are you? Get away from him, wench!'

The father struggled to sit up, gripping her hand. 'No. Leave her, Lucius. She's…mine.'

Lucius—this man who could be the father's double was his brother, then. He'd told her a little on the voyage before he fell ill.

Lucius gave a short laugh. 'The hell she is, Jack. Not now you've been fool enough to bring her here. No slavery in England.'

No slavery? Could that be true after all?

'My daughter. She's my daughter.'

'Your—' His brother gave a bark of laughter. 'Good God, man! You've come home to marry Maria Hempleworth and brought your mulatta by-blow?'

Psyché flinched. She hadn't heard 'by-blow' before, but she could guess at the meaning easily enough.

'Enough, Lucius.' The older, silver-haired man glanced at her. 'The child is right there.'

Lucius shrugged that off. 'What of it? It's what she is and she probably doesn't understand one word in ten anyway.'

'I speak French, too,' she blurted out, stung.

She quailed as he whipped around, eyes blazing, and took a step towards her. 'Watch your tone, wench! You're in—'

'Do you, child?' The older man was somehow between them. *'Tu es très intelligent, petite. Quel âge as-tu?'*

'Merci, monseiur. J'ai onze ans. Êtes-vous Français?'

He laughed. 'Are you, now? No, I'm not French, child. But I know France well enough. Speaking her language well is the mark of a gentleman. Or...' he bowed slightly '...a lady.'

'The brat is irrelevant, Uncle!' The younger man was scowling as he bent over the father. He glared at Psyché. 'Where the hell is this Psyché Black?'

Swallowing her fear, she answered. 'I'm Psyché.' He hadn't liked her speaking before, but he'd asked her a direct question now.

He snorted. 'Rubbish! She wrote to summon us. You may speak better than the average parrot, but—'

'You wrote that note, child?'

She looked to the older man, the uncle. 'Yes, sir—my lord.' The father had said his uncle was a viscount. That meant he was *my lord*.

He smiled. 'Told you that, did he? Sir will do.'

'For God's sake, Uncle Theo!'

He glanced at the younger man in mild reproof. 'She speaks French. Her English is excellent and she writes a good, even hand. I'll warrant *you* could not do as much at eleven.'

Lucius stared. 'How do you know she's eleven? Did you *know* about this?'

My lord winked at Psyché. 'She told me a moment ago, Lucius. In French.'

The younger man's mouth and eyes hardened as colour rose on his cheeks and he stared at her. From that moment Psyché knew that Lucius Winthrop hated her.

The father spoke. 'Uncle—'

'I'm here, lad.' The old man bent over the bed and Psyché scrambled up to give him her place. 'Thank you, my dear.'

He sat down. 'Gently now, Jack. We'll get you home.'

'Listen,' the father got out. 'The child—'

'Jack!' Lucius spoke sharply. 'You can't waste your strength worrying about some mulatta brat you sired! God knows why you brought her home, but if anyone finds out she's your spawn—'

'She's my daughter!' The father's pain-racked gaze wandered, then settled on Psyché. He beckoned to her.

She obeyed, hesitant, keeping an eye on Lucius.

My lord took the father's hand, patted it. 'What would you have me do, Jack?'

'I was going to find her a place. A safe place. She could be a…companion. Run errands for Aunt Grace. Will you do it?'

He brought their hands together, placed hers in my lord's. The old man stared down at their joined hands. She wondered what he saw. Hers was so much smaller, so much darker. She made to pull away—no white man ever touched a mulatta willingly except to punish or take his pleasure— but his fingers, cool and dry, closed strongly on hers.

He let out a breath. 'Very well. My word on it, Jack.'

The father fell back, as if he had reached the uttermost end of strength. 'Thank you, Uncle.' He looked at Psyché. 'You will be safe.' He shut his eyes.

Jack Winthrop died three days later in his uncle's house at Hampstead, clinging to Psyché's small hand. His uncle sat beside her, his brother on the other side of the bed holding the father's other hand. Tears tracked down Lucius Winthrop's cheeks and Psyché knew he had loved the father. His wet, grieving eyes met those of his uncle. 'He's gone.'

Fear choked her, but she said quietly. 'I'm sorry...sir.'

He stared at her. 'Hold your insolent tongue!' He released the father's hand, rose and strode from the room.

'He grieves, child,' said my lord. He bent forward and closed the father's sightless eyes. 'Be at peace, lad,' he murmured. Then, to her amazement, he lifted Psyché into his lap. 'There. We'll sit for a little. Keep him company.'

So she sat, exhausted with the endless fear devouring her. Tired to the bone, she slept cradled in his arms, her cheek resting on his shoulder.

She woke to fear and loneliness in a strange bed the next day and discovered herself to be in the care of the servants. Lucius had gone back to some place they called town and my lord had gone, too. They would return for the funeral. The servants had told her that.

She had been given a room in the nursery. Much bigger than the nursery she had been used to in Jamaica, it was a whole set of rooms, with a schoolroom that held a single small desk, but she had only peeked in there. There were also several other bedrooms, including those for a maid and nurse, although they were all empty. There was also a bigger room just called the Nursery. She was very unsure of what she was supposed to be doing. The room was empty except for a couple of chairs.

A maid sat with her after assisting her to dress. But there was nothing to do now that the father was dead. Nothing to do, nothing to read. The maid sat and mended, her needle flashing in and out as she worked. At first Psyché looked out of the window. They were very high up, both in the house and high on a hill. The world beyond the treetops fell away in rolling greens, down to where she could see buildings, misty with distance. One fascinated her—she thought it must be enormous, although all she could see was the great, rounded roof with a sort of tower on top, reaching towards the sky.

On the second day she asked the maid, Sarah, what it was.

Sarah looked up. 'That's St Paul's in the City, child. Went right up there once on my day off and, if you know where to look, you can see this house all the way up here on the Heath.'

'Oh.' That would be an adventure. To climb right up to the top of the building and hunt for this window. And imagine someone waving back to her. She waved. Perhaps there was someone up there right now looking this way. She waved again to her unknown friend. It was better than nothing and she'd never had a real friend. The house slaves in Jamaica had not allowed her to play with the younger slave children, the older slave children were working, and the white children had not been allowed to play with *her*.

Sarah was mending again.

'May I help you?'

Sarah started. 'Help me?'

'Yes. Help you sew.' She wasn't fond of sewing, but she liked to help and it would be something to do.

Sarah spoke stiffly. 'I'm sure that's very kind of you, but—'

'I'm bored.' It was out before she had thought and terrified guilt swamped her. She was living in this beautiful house, eating good food every day, although some of it was strange to her after Jamaica. But she ate it all without a fuss and said thank you as Mam had taught her. Only now she'd been insolent and ungrateful.

But Sarah smiled. 'You must be bored if you want to mend sheets! And I'm thinking you might be lonely, too, with no other children about. All right, let's see what you can do.' She pointed to a chair. 'Bring that over and sit beside me.' Rummaging in the basket of mending, she brought out a pair of stockings. 'Can you darn?'

'Oh, yes!'

Psyché took the stockings, threaded the darning needle and bent her head in utter concentration, feeling a ridiculous burst of delight when Sarah approved her efforts.

'Someone taught you proper.'

Warmth spread through her. 'My mam taught me.'

Sarah nodded. 'Did she, now? Well, you're a credit to her.'

She thought of Mam, her needle flashing as she worked on some piece of mending, telling stories of her childhood in her soft voice as they sewed. The knowledge of being a credit to Mam glowed inside her.

After that it was better. She had something to do and over the next two days some of the fear left her. She was useful. If she kept being useful, did her very best, perhaps she might be allowed to stay and mend the clothes and sheets. She might even, although she scarcely dared to hope, be paid.

Sarah, she had known at once, was not a slave. She was white. But when asked about slaves, Sarah had stared. According to her, no one was a slave. You couldn't be a slave in England. All the servants were paid and they could leave if they wished. She learned from Sarah that Lord Staverton's employ was enviable. That he was a kind master and no one wished to leave. So she allowed herself to hope a tiny bit.

'Hard to find a better place,' Sarah declared, snipping off a thread. 'And the mistress is a good soul, too. Why—'

'Thank you, Sarah.'

The quiet voice was a new one—a woman—and Psyché looked up from the sheet she was turning sides-to-middle. The silver-haired lady—Psyché knew she must be a lady from the fine clothes she wore—came further into the room, Lord Staverton behind her.

She had not seen him since the night the father died and she had fallen asleep on his lap. Sometimes she had fallen asleep in Mam's lap, but she doubted such a thing was permitted with *my lord*.

Perhaps she should apologise? But he smiled at her and she found herself beaming back.

'Carried you up himself, the master did.'

Sarah had told her that when she asked how she'd got to bed that night. So perhaps he hadn't really minded or he would have handed her to one of the servants, or woken her up to walk.

'This is Psyché, my dear. Jack's daughter.' He smiled again. 'Psyché, this is your Great-Aunt Grace—'

'That is yet to be decided, sir!' the lady snapped. 'Good God, Theodore! Have you lost your mind? Have you any idea what will be *said* if you insist on this course? She is *Black.*'

Fear crawled inside her. 'Only…only mulatto, my lady. Or…or mulatta, the governess said. Because I am a girl.'

There was a sharp intake of breath. Psyché gulped. She should have held her tongue. If my lady was like Lucius—

'I think we will simply acknowledge that you are a *girl*, child.' There was something odd in my lord's voice and he held out his hand to her. 'Would you like to come downstairs with us for a little, my dear?'

She hesitated. 'I am helping Sarah, you see. There is a very great deal of mending. I promised.'

He nodded. 'And a promise must always be kept. But I think Sarah will spare you for an hour.'

Sarah nodded. 'Of course, my lord. And—if I might speak?'

'Certainly you may, Sarah.'

'The child—Miss Psyché—she's been right helpful.

Mends and darns beautifully, she does.' Sarah took a deep breath. 'And, if I might make so bold, she's very nicely spoken. Ladylike.'

My lord nodded. 'Thank you, Sarah. You confirm my own observation.' He still held his hand out. 'Come, Psyché. I promise you shall come back later to help Sarah.

Sarah gave her a little push. 'Go on now, Miss Psyché.'

Slowly, Psyché laid her hand in my lord's.

Miss. She was *Miss* Psyché. Hope, so long choked, dared to whisper in her heart.

Her hand lost in my lord's bigger one, Psyché went downstairs in my lady's wake. My lord chatted cheerfully, pointing out pictures to her. 'Your namesake,' he said, indicating a painting of a beautiful, white-skinned girl with golden hair leaning over a dark-haired but equally beautiful white-skinned young man asleep in a bed. The candle she held tilted dangerously and the painter had caught a drop of wax in the instant before it fell on the young man's arm.

'She couldn't resist finding out what her lover looked like, so—'

'Theodore!' My lady turned with a quelling glare. 'The child is *far* too young for that story!'

My lord looked stricken. 'So she is, my dear.' But he squeezed Psyché's hand and smiled down at her. 'When you are older.'

This lower corridor was impossibly grand. She'd barely seen it when she arrived, so focused was she on the father who clutched her hand and demanded her presence every waking moment. She stared in wonder. All the picture frames and looking glasses were made of gold. Even some of the furniture had gold on it. And the walls—her fingers itched to touch and find out—were covered in what she was quite sure was silk. Silk of the softest, clearest blue, like the sea in the very early morning before the wind woke up.

Tables held vases of strange flowers—their fragrance swam in the air. My lord saw her staring, reached out and plucked one of the flowers, giving it to her. Awestruck, she took it.

'You like roses, eh?'

'Is that what they are called?' She cradled the crimson flower gently. 'They're very pretty.' She sniffed the bloom and smiled at him as the fragrance poured through her. 'Thank you, my lord.'

'You've not seen one before?' He cleared his throat as she shook her head. 'Well, I'm a lucky fellow to have given you your first rose. Here we are.' They had halted before a door of white and gold. 'There is someone in there waiting to see you.'

A manservant, in the uniform Sarah called livery, opened the door.

'After you, my dear.' My lord stood back for my lady, then led Psyché in.

The room was huge and she could see no one. Just the room soaring into a curve of pale pink and blue, with clouds and people in robes. Little fat, pink babies peeped from behind the clouds, apparently spying on everyone.

A sharp bark was followed by a scurrying of paws and Psyché dropped to her knees with a cry of delight, releasing my lord's hand.

'Nyx! Oh, Nyx!'

The little black spaniel scrambled straight into her lap, tail awhirl with joy, and covered her face with damp affection. She buried her face in the silky coat to hide the rush of tears.

'You are glad to see her, then?'

She nodded, still with her face hidden.

'Well, then. Well.' My lord cleared his throat. 'Come over by the fire—ah, when you are quite ready, child. London is a great deal colder than Jamaica as I recall.'

She looked up, forgetting her tears. 'Have you been there, my lord?'

'Briefly, many years ago.' He lowered himself to a sofa and patted the space beside him. *'Viens, ma chère. Assieds-toi avec moi.'*

Obediently she went to sit beside him. *'Voulez-vous parler en Français, monsieur?'*

He chuckled. 'No. We'll speak in English. I was merely demonstrating to your great-aunt that *you* can converse in French.'

My lady spoke. 'Look at me, if you please, child.'

Fighting against every rule that had ever been drummed into her about keeping her gaze lowered, Psyché swallowed, and looked timidly at my lady, who she didn't think was entirely convinced that she wished to be any sort of aunt to her.

Please. Oh, please! I promise I will be good! Please let me stay here where there is no slavery! Please.

She kept silent and fought to meet the ice-blue gaze that bored into her. Her lip wobbled; she bit it. Hard. More tears threatened and she blinked them back. A frown creased my lady's delicate white brow and Psyché scarce dared to breathe.

That blue gaze softened. 'Theo, if the child—if *Psyché*— remains with us, what is to happen with Henrietta?'

My lord frowned. Then he glanced down at Psyché. 'Henrietta, my dear, is your cousin. The daughter of your uncle—'

'Theo, is that quite wise?'

He sighed. 'Grace, she may be too young for the tale of Eros and Psyché, but she needs to know about her family.'

Family? She was to be *family*?

He continued. 'Henrietta is your cousin, the daughter of your Uncle Lucius, a little older than you. Her mama has just died.'

'I'm sorry.' She had cried and cried and cried when Mam died. Terrified, lost and numbed by the overwhelming guilt…the knowledge that if only she had been quiet, and unresisting…

'Of course you are. We have agreed to take Henrietta into our household to raise for Lucius. However, that… may not happen now.'

She nodded. 'He doesn't like me. He wouldn't want his little girl raised with me. Not…unless I was her servant.' She looked up questioningly. It wouldn't be family, but… 'I wouldn't be a slave, would I?'

A shocked gasp came from my lady. 'Certainly *not.*' My lady leaned forward, speaking earnestly. 'As you grow older, you will have household duties to help me, as will Henrietta if she comes to us, as *any* young lady would. How else is she to learn to manage her husband's house one day?' She glanced at my lord.

He nodded. 'You are not a servant, Psyché, and certainly not a slave. You are our great-niece.' He glanced at my lady. 'Lucius must do with Henrietta as he thinks fit, Grace. There will be any number of relatives happy to take her.' He patted Psyché's hand. 'You had better stop my lording me and call me Uncle Theo.'

She looked across at my lady, who nodded. 'And I am Aunt Grace.'

This time the tears would not be stopped. At first Uncle Theo just put his arm around her and let her cry, but after a moment he lifted her into his lap where she sobbed. All the pent-up terror since the father had died washed away in the outpouring of relief.

'Theo, surely—'

'She needs to cry, Grace,' Uncle Theo said softly. 'And soon she'll be far too big to sit in my lap with propriety. I'm going to indulge myself while it lasts.' And he held her while she wept and patted her back as he had the other night, murmuring comfort and reassurance. There was a snuffle and an insistent paw, as Nyx, worried by her crying, shoved her head under Psyché's elbow. Uncle Theo laughed. 'Here is your little dog come to comfort you. Would you like her to sleep in your room at night?'

Psyché sat up. 'May she?'

'Oh, I think so. Best place for one's dog to sleep, *I've* always thought.' He chuckled. 'Your aunt doesn't agree. At least, not when it's *her* bedchamber!'

Aunt Grace sighed. 'There can be no harm in it.'

In that moment Psyché vowed to herself that she would always be good. That she would try her very hardest to be no trouble at all so that they might not send her away. That she would learn her lessons, mend and do whatever she could to repay them for giving her, and Nyx, a place.

Chapter Four

Soho, London—January 1804

'*Then…you're Staverton's Folly.*'

Will could have kicked himself for blurting that out. It had been the summer after that first revelatory year at Oxford and his mother had been full of the scandal… '*That poor little girl!*' By which she'd meant Lord Staverton's *real* great-niece… '*Being brought up with a blackamoor! Staverton's Folly, they're calling the wretched creature!*'

Disgusted with himself, Will nudged open the door of Selbourne Books and a bell jangled overhead. All around the walls bookshelves rose to the ceiling. Shoulder-high shelves created bays and in one back corner a couple of sagging leather chairs provided seating by a crackling fire. Beside the fire, a shaggy grey puppy snoozed, its oversized paws twitching occasionally. A large, spectacularly untidy desk stood in the other rear corner with a curtained doorway behind it. Steep, narrow stairs led up to what Will assumed must be living quarters.

Selbourne was seated behind the desk. He looked up at Will from under his heavy, untidy brows. 'What's this? I didn't order coffee.'

'No, sir. Miss Winthrop-Abeni sent it over. It's paid for. She was going to put it on your account, but I said I'd deal with it.'

The brows lifted. 'Obliging of you. Why would a chap I don't know from Adam be buying me coffee?'

'You might not remember me, sir, but I'm Barclay— Lord Huntercombe's secretary.'

The old man took off his spectacles and squinted. 'So you are. Eyes aren't what they were. And where's Huntercombe?'

'Cornwall, sir.'

Ignatius Selbourne gave an abrupt nod. 'Right. Put the coffee here, Barclay.' He shoved some papers aside, clearing a dusty space and producing a cork mat.

Will set the pot down on the mat. 'You do remember my name, then?'

Selbourne snorted. 'Fat chance I'd have to forget since he sings your praises. What brings you here, boy? A message?'

'Not exactly. I read your letter, sir. It sounded as though you were quite eager for his lordship to examine that *particular* volume.'

Ignatius poured coffee into cups he produced from some fastness in the desk and passed one to Will. 'I believe you've met my niece, eh?'

Will accepted the coffee and sipped while he considered how to answer that. It sounded innocent enough, but—

'Very briefly, sir. I doubt she would remember me.' At the time Miss Carshalton had been confronted with the fact that her father and projected mother-in-law had connived at the attempted murder of Huntercombe's ten-year-old stepson. Miss Carshalton had been too busy breaking her engagement to Lord Martin Lacy to notice the secretary taking notes in the corner.

'Discreet, aren't you? Heard the rumours?'

Will took a deep breath. 'There is servants' gossip to the effect that Miss Carshalton has either run away or been abducted from her father's house.'

'And what do *you* think?'

'That you are concerned either way for your niece's safety and that you are requesting Huntercombe's help.'

He gave Will a considering look which Will returned blandly. Selbourne snorted. 'I've no doubt you're as—'

The doorbell jangled and Selbourne broke off to look at the newcomer. His eyes narrowed and Will had the impression that he was summing the man up. He'd noticed the fellow with his obviously expensive, but ill-fitting, clothes in The Phoenix.

Selbourne looked back at Will. 'We'll talk on that volume further.' He rose to his feet and went to greet his customer.

'Good afternoon, sir. Is there something with which I can help you?' After the summing up Selbourne had subjected the man to, Will found his tone surprisingly unctuous.

'Oh, well, ah—that is, I was after Mrs Radcliffe's ah, *Romance of the Forest*.' The man's tones were painfully refined. 'A present for my…er…wife, you know.'

Selbourne raised his brows. 'And you are happy with a used set, sir?'

'Used?' The man looked shocked. 'Oh, well—'

'This *is* an antiquarian bookshop, sir. I do not stock new books. But I have several of Mrs Radcliffe's works including an autographed set of that one. This way, sir.'

He led the man to the front of the shop and began taking volumes down. 'It is in fine condition, sir, and see? All three volumes are signed by the authoress. Your lady wife will like that, I make no doubt.'

Will browsed, noting that Selbourne's stock was extensive and catholic. In the background Selbourne continued to show his customer other novels—'that your lady wife might enjoy, sir.' Will noted with some amusement that Selbourne made great play with that phrase *'your lady wife'*. It seemed oddly out of character—he'd never thought the bookseller to be obsequious.

A memory flickered. Sitting by the library fire with Huntercombe once, his lordship reminiscing about a diplomatic mission years back to the Court of Portugal.

'Whenever one of us wanted to warn the others to be particularly careful about what we said, the words "lady wives" would be casually mentioned.'

Huntercombe still used it occasionally if he wanted to warn Will to be careful…

The grey puppy by the fire had woken up. Selbourne glanced over.

'Damn. Excuse me, sir.' He started towards the pup.

'Shall I take him out for you?' Will waved at the pup. He knew exactly what happened when a puppy woke up.

Selbourne frowned. 'Kind of you. She. Answers to Moth. There's a yard at the back. Go through the curtain and you'll see your way.'

Will nodded. 'Lady wife?' he murmured.

Selbourne's eyes narrowed. 'Exactly so. My thanks.'

The puppy rose, stretched.

Will clicked his fingers. 'Moth. Come along.'

The puppy cocked her head and followed him out through a kitchen area and into the snowy yard. Will watched as she sniffed around, squatted and did what puppies do. She came back, wagging her tail, clearly pleased with herself.

'Good girl.' He bent down and scratched her ears, wondering where Selbourne had acquired the pup and just what, precisely, had gone into her ancestry. Whatever it had been—and it had been large, judging by the paws—the tail lashed. 'That's exactly right. Now, have a bit of a run.' He moved off the step and clicked his fingers to encourage the pup to follow.

So Selbourne knew Huntercombe's code for discretion. And he'd used it, assuming Will would recognise the warning. But what about that little man had bothered him? Moth scampered around, rushing with a high-pitched bark at a sparrow. The fellow was dressed as a gentleman, his clothes were of excellent quality…he frowned, bringing the man into his mind's eye…and those clothes didn't fit. Who spent a large amount of money on clothes and didn't have them made to fit? The puppy scratched and snuffled in the rubbish pile with obvious pleasure while Will continued to mull over the oddly dressed man. Even if he'd bought them second-hand, clothes could be altered to fit easily enough…unless of course they had been hastily assembled as some sort of disguise. Which meant Selbourne thought he was being watched.

And perhaps he was simply being paranoid.

'Come on, Moth. Back inside.'

He opened the door and the puppy trotted back in with him.

Selbourne had sold the set to the little man. 'Thank you, sir. Come back again. Bring your lady wife next time.' He handed the man his change.

'Ah, thank you, sir. Most kind. I fear she does not go about much. An invalid, you know.'

'Quite so.' Selbourne strolled ahead to open the door. 'I hope she enjoys the books.'

He stood in the open doorway watching his customer hurry away. 'Thank you for that, Barclay.'

Will joined him. 'Do you think he was a spy, sir?'

Selbourne smiled. 'Oh, yes. Carshalton is furious. He's convinced I'm hiding his property.'

'His *property*?' Will stared. 'I thought—'

'That's all she is to him.'

'*Are* you hiding her?'

Selbourne's eyes narrowed and Will braced for a blistering set down.

'*Oh, God!*' For an instant Selbourne gripped the door as if it were the only thing holding him up.

'Sir! Are you unwell?' Will set a supportive hand under his elbow and followed his gaze down the street.

Several men in blue greatcoats had entered at the far end, moving purposefully.

'Bow Street Runners.' Selbourne hurried across the shop to his desk.

The Runners knocked on the door of the first house. Even above the street racket, Will thought he could hear the pounding. Imagination only, but he could *see* the confident, rhythmic pounding. '*Open in the King's name!*' And people hurrying by slowed, stared, then hurried on, heads lowered, shoulders hunched.

Nothing to do with me. I'm not even here.

A second group of Runners on the opposite side, entering a shop, and another group coming around the corner behind him and entering the Red Lion. Three remained outside, one going into the yard, the others watching the street.

Selbourne was back, the coffee pot in his hands. 'I have to—'

Will grabbed the old man's wrist. 'No. Not you. Where is she?' Even as he asked he knew… *Burnt feathers.* 'Never mind. Stay here.'

'What? But—'

'They're watching you. If you go, it will alert them.'

Selbourne let out a breath. 'Take this.' He shoved the coffee pot into Will's hands. 'Tell her I asked you to return it.'

Psyché glanced across as the doorbell jangled. Her foolish heart did a little skip and dance as she saw that it was Will Barclay and she couldn't help the smile.

Then she saw the coffee pot, the grim expression as his gaze met hers…

Her smile still firmly in place, she strolled back, weaving through the tables, to meet him at the counter.

Heart hammering, she forced herself to sound unconcerned. 'Mr Barclay. Back so soon?'

He held up the coffee pot. 'Mr Selbourne asked me to return your pot.' His voice lowered. 'Urgently.'

Her brows rose. 'Thank you, sir.' She turned slightly to present her back to most of the shop and lowered her own voice. 'What is it?'

He put the pot in her hands, murmured, 'Runners.'

A quick intake of breath, a swift glance around and she drew him back behind the counter. 'A moment, sir.'

She reached up, tugged on a cord and heard the faint chime of the bell.

She led him further back, still in sight of the shop and the front door. 'Tell me.'

'They're searching the street,' he said. 'I can try to get her out the back, but—'

'No.' She shook her head. 'They'll be watching the yards.'

'Listen! If they take her here, you'll be—'

She brushed her fingers over his lips to still his arguments. She already knew the risk she ran, but that he would worry touched her to the core.

'Trust me. I can hide her.' She gave him a little push. 'Go up to my apartment. Tell her you brought the coffee pot.' Despite the fear hammering in every vein, she smiled. 'Make yourself comfortable. Suggestively so.'

His eyes widened. 'Suggestive?'

She nodded. 'It will explain any impression that more than one person has been living there.'

'You want them to think we're—?' He actually blushed.

'Don't be too shocked, Mr Barclay. We're just playing pretend.'

He couldn't believe he was blushing, but then he wasn't entirely sure he wanted to risk playing pretend with this woman. He might want it to be all too real…his lips tingled from the light touch of her fingers.

Her smile turned wicked. 'Rolled back shirtsleeves are always…indicative and—' one finger slid along the edge of his cravat '—you might want to loosen this.'

He swallowed. 'Right,' he said, then shook himself mentally and headed for the stairs.

He nearly mowed Miss Carshalton down as she came out of the apartment clutching a valise and a knife.

She recoiled with a startled gasp, but the knife stayed steady in her hand about a foot from his belly. 'Don't move!' A fierce, low command.

He stayed absolutely still. 'It's all right. I'm a friend.'

The knife didn't waver.

'I brought the coffee pot.'

To his relief the knife was withdrawn. 'Go down. She's waiting for you.'

'Is it Carshalton?'

'Runners. Go.'

She went past him like a ghost, silent as she raced down the steps barefoot.

He stared after her. The bell. Psyché's calm as she swung into action. Miss Carshalton's readiness…

They planned and they were ready. They've probably rehearsed this.

Now it was up to him to improvise on the theme she had given him.

Psyché controlled her slightly laboured breathing, shut the storeroom door and strolled back to the counter. She smiled at Caleb as if she had been up to nothing more nefarious than a visit to the storeroom. She had to behave normally, not as if she expected to be raided by Bow Street in short order. Her staff knew nothing. None of them would intentionally betray her, but unthinking gossip, Ignatius had warned, little things that added up to something significant, could sink a battle fleet. Besides that, she had to protect them from the potential consequences of her actions. She had scrupulously avoided taking too much food upstairs in front of them, been wary about when she brought crockery down for washing up and Kit moved about as little as possible during shop hours—and always on bare or stockinged feet.

She glanced at the slate board, where orders were scrawled, and began grinding coffee beans. The servers memorised the orders at the tables, then noted them on the board for her in varying ways. Caleb could write, but most of the others used symbols and pictographs. She focused on the coffee grinder. Normal.

Caleb handed a pot and cups to Sally, who whisked them off to a table near the door. 'You right, Miss Psyché?'

Damn. Clearly she wasn't doing a good job with normal.

'Perfectly, Caleb. Why shouldn't I be?'

If normal wasn't working, then she'd try for flustered, perfectly plausible given that she had just sent a man up to her apartment... She let a glance slide towards the back corridor and up towards the apartment, to where Will Barclay should be by now.

Caleb hesitated. 'It's only…that chap. He was in earlier, wasn't he?'

'Yes.'

'Know him, do you?'

'He's a friend.' She hoped.

'Well, you don't usually let anyone up to your apartment like that.'

Psyché went for very flustered, avoiding his bright gaze. 'No. So when I do you may assume the person is a very good friend. Now, if we've quite exhausted that subject, let's make some coffee.'

Caleb turned away, but not before she saw colour stain his cheeks. 'Yes, ma'am.'

There was apparently such a thing as too much success. Now Caleb's adolescent male mind was going to be filled with quite the wrong thoughts for a boy his age. Then again, what did she know about boys? For all she knew they were the right thoughts. It was girls, young ladies, who were supposed to pretend they didn't know sex existed. Which, she thought as she ground a pile of defenceless cacao nibs, cardamom seeds and a soupçon of sugar to a fine powder, had actually been true of Hetty. Uncle Theo had realised very early that she herself was aware of certain facts of which most young girls were kept in ignorance.

'You cannot un-know things, child.'

He had asked only that she keep her knowledge to herself.

Out of love for him she had obeyed, although she thought on reflection that ignorance of any sort was dangerous for a young girl.

A pot of chocolate, several of coffee and two pots of tea later, Bow Street made its unceremonious entrance.

'Everyone to remain right where 'e is, *if* you please, gentlemen.'

The tone made it very clear that the *if you please* was a mere sop tossed in the general direction of diplomacy. The lead Runner brandished an official-looking piece of paper, embellished with an even more official-looking seal.

He came forward, looking about him with a frown, his gaze scarcely registering Psyché. Eventually he beckoned to Caleb. 'Where's your master, boy?'

Caleb, looking utterly petrified, said, 'Um, Miss Psyché's mistress, sir.'

The man scowled. 'Are you deaf or stupid, boy? I said your master, not your mistress.'

Psyché nudged the boy aside. 'I'm in charge, Officer.' She spoke over the scandalised mutterings of her customers. 'What may I do for you?'

He gave her a suggestive leer. 'I'll speak to your master first, wench.' He looked her up and down, then swaggered a little. 'Then we might have a little chat about what you can do for me.'

Behind him, his men sniggered.

Caleb surged forward and she grabbed his elbow, holding him back. 'Don't be a fool,' she said sharply.

Returning the Runner's assessing gaze, she allowed her lip to curl. 'I *am* the owner, Officer. The warrant.' She held out her hand with a snap of her fingers. '*If* you please.'

Or even if you don't.

'Owner.' He goggled at her, apparently having trouble with the concept in this context.

'Yes. Owner.' She smiled with deceptive sweetness. 'A noun. Deriving from the verb *to own*, signifying possession of an object. In this case, The Phoenix.'

Not me.

The fellow did a more than passable imitation of a landed trout, but he handed the warrant over.

Psyché took her time, reading it carefully.

'A young lady, a Miss Catherine Carshalton?' she said

at last. 'Why on earth would she be here? You're welcome to look, but you're wasting your time, Officer.'

He shrugged. 'That's as maybe. We've to search every house, every shop along here.'

She had no choice. 'Very well. This way.'

It took fifteen minutes for them to poke into every corner, every nook and every cranny downstairs, including the storerooms and the little closet where a servant occasionally slept, asking questions of all the staff if they had seen a young woman thereabouts—grey eyes, brown hair, wearing a white fur cloak. Psyché barely resisted an eye roll. Lord! Did they think Kit such a fool she wouldn't have got rid of something as identifiable as an ermine cloak?

The staff looked suitably blank as well they might. Sally did roll her eyes. 'Women don't come in 'ere, guv. Saving the mistress and meself. It's a coffee 'ouse, ain't it? Gents only.'

Sally took them down to the cellars and gave it as her opinion that they'd be lucky to find as much as a rat down there. They came back empty-handed, the senior officer very red-faced and puffed after, from the scraping and banging that had echoed up the stairs, moving everything around to check for trapdoors and hidey holes.

'We'll see up there, missy,' he announced, waving at the stairs leading up to Psyché's apartment.

She scowled and placed herself in front of the stairs. 'Don't be ridiculous! Those are my private apartments up there! No one is—'

A muffled thud filtered down and the man's eyes narrowed. 'Going to say no one's up there, weren't you, my fine wench?'

She shrugged. 'I do own a cat, Officer. The occasional thud is to be expected.'

He pushed past her and went up rapidly, making no effort to keep his footsteps quiet.

He threw open the door and Psyché winced at the crash as it hit the wall. 'I hope you are going to make good any damage,' she said.

Fiddle, sprawled exposing his belly to the fire, stretched lazily and looked over with a lazy *mrowp*.

'Doesn't look to me as that cat's moved in the last couple of hours,' the officer remarked. He pointed to the bedroom door. 'What's back there, eh, missy?'

He strode across, his boots clunking on the floorboards.

'Is that you already, darling?'

The very masculine voice was muffled by the door and the officer, his hand already on the door knob, stopped dead and glanced back at Psyché in patent outrage.

Taller than he by half a head, she looked down her nose at him and shrugged.

The Runner flung open the door and Psyché, looking over his shoulder, felt her jaw drop.

Will Barclay was a very good-looking man. She knew that. He had a lovely smile and kind eyes, and there was that wretched buzzing of attraction.

That was when he was clothed.

Chapter Five

She'd told the man to make himself comfortable, but she had to admit he'd exceeded expectations. Naked to the waist, sitting up reading in her bed, his half-moon reading glasses perched on his slightly crooked nose and that wretched lock of hair hanging over his eye, the buzz became a roar in her blood. Clearly, to have a chest like that, Mr Barclay did rather more than merely scribe letters. And his arms, not heavily muscled, were exactly right, wiry and strong.

But the glasses, and the tousled lock of hair, topped the whole thing off. She wanted to remove the glasses, brush his hair back and— She pulled herself together.

'Mr Barclay is a friend,' she said coldly to the Runner. 'I trust you are now satisfied?'

'A *friend*, is he?' sneered the man.

'Yes.' Will—how was she supposed to think in formal terms of a man half-naked in her bed?—kept his tone crisp and cold. 'I am Miss Winthrop-Abeni's *very* good friend and you would be ill advised to offer her any insult whatsoever. Perhaps you would care to explain this intrusion?'

The Runner straightened. 'We have a warrant to search properties in the area for a kidnapped heiress. A Miss Catherine Carshalton.'

Will snorted. 'Well, I'm not hiding her, as you can see.'

The man stood his ground. 'Dare say, but I got to make a note of everyone we speak to for my report.'

'Report?'

The officer nodded. 'For Mr Carshalton. He's employing us for this job and he wants a full report.' He produced a pencil and notebook. 'Your name, sir?

'William Barclay,' he said shortly.

The man noted that down. 'Address, sir?'

Psyché kept her face expressionless. *Damn.* A lie would bring the Runners back here hotfoot if it were discovered, but Huntercombe's name—

'Moresby House, Grosvenor Square.'

Psyché breathed a mental sigh of relief. She'd forgotten that Huntercombe used the family name rather than the title for his London house.

The man scribbled that down. 'And your connection there, sir?'

Double damn! Moresby might slip past Carshalton; Huntercombe's private secretary would not.

'His lordship's private secretary!' he retorted. 'I trust this information will not be made public!'

Shrewd hazel eyes considered him. 'Nice goings on, I must say. Well, it's none of our business. Only the magistrate, and the young lady's father, will see my report.' He snapped the book shut and shoved it back in his pocket.

Bloomsbury—that evening

'Blast the wench!' Josiah Carshalton slammed a fist on his desk as he set down the brief message advising him that the search had failed. The search he'd been utterly convinced would flush Catherine out. 'Nigh on two weeks and they've not found hide or hair of her!'

The fact that a mere girl, his own daughter, had so far

evaded his efforts to hunt her down was an insult he was not prepared to accept.

Lucius Winthrop, the man he intended to be Catherine's husband, scowled. 'May I?' He held out his hand for the message.

'Doesn't say much.' Carshalton passed it across. 'They'll send the full report in a couple of days, but they found nothing.'

Winthrop nodded, his lips pursed. Silence, apart from the crackle of the fire, held as he scanned the single page. He handed it back. 'Unbelievable that a chit of twenty has evaded Bow Street and all the other men you've got out searching for her.' He frowned. 'Have you considered that she may not be in London?'

'Of course I have!' snapped Carshalton. Did the man think him a fool? 'But I've had the posting inns covered since Christmas morning. The stage coaches, the mail—all checked daily. It's costing me a damn fortune! No, she's still here.'

'Lord Martin Lacy? He may be—'

'No.' Carshalton shook his head. 'He's left the country. Sailed from Portsmouth for Portugal over a week ago. She wasn't with him. I had him watched so damn closely he couldn't have hidden a mouse in his luggage, let alone smuggled a girl aboard.'

He ground his teeth. 'That's not to say he wasn't involved—I'll wager he was! But it's that sly old bastard Selbourne hiding her now.'

Winthrop took a swallow of brandy. 'She hasn't got some friend—a married friend, perhaps, who might be hiding her? I mean, Selbourne didn't seem to know anything when we—'

'Sly,' Carshalton repeated between his teeth. 'He knows something. He must. He was the most obvious person for her to have gone to. But like a fool I tried Lacy first because the little bitch threw me off the scent with that damn handkerchief of his and the note.'

'You're quite sure she would have gone to Selbourne?'

'Yes. There's no one else she could have gone to.' He'd made sure of that over the years, controlling the girl's acquaintances and cutting off any friendship that looked set to become too close. That was the best way to keep a woman in her place. That and the occasional thrashing. He'd done his best to break her link to Selbourne, but he hadn't bothered with any beatings in the past two years. Hadn't thought they were needed any longer.

His fist clenched. She'd fooled him with that meek and mild façade, and in the last year or so he'd permitted occasional visits to Selbourne, just to have a carrot to dangle that could be taken away if she displeased him. He'd thought her cowed, but he'd underestimated her duplicity. In going after Lacy first he'd given the bitch time to get to cover. She'd earned a good thrashing when he did find her. Then Winthrop could finish taming the little shrew.

'If Selbourne's shop is watched, he'll lead us to her,' Winthrop insisted. 'He must have her hidden in one of the inns nearby.'

Carshalton shook his head. 'No. All the inns were searched top to bottom along with every other building in the street. And right now? I wouldn't care to wager a groat on him leading us to her. He's fully alerted. He won't go anywhere near her. I've had at least one man in that blasted bookshop every day and there's no sign that she's been there at all. The place is watched day and night, as are all the inns in the area. He's barely stirred from the shop since Christmas except to stroll down to the Red Lion to eat his dinner, or get a coffee over the road.'

He let out a vicious curse and took a gulp of his brandy. 'We've got less than two months to find her. Once she's twenty-one, it will be damn near impossible to take her back.'

Winthrop drummed his fingers. 'The threat of a lunatic asylum might bring her to heel.'

Carshalton shook his head. 'No. Once you're married, the last thing you want is gossip she's been locked up in Bedlam. Besides—' he shot Winthrop a savage glance '—Selbourne has powerful friends. Including your own damned uncle.'

Winthrop snorted. 'My saintly Uncle Theo. However, I take your point about the gossip. What about Selbourne's friends? Could one of them be hiding her?'

'To oblige Selbourne?' Carshalton stared at him. 'It's possible. She lived with Selbourne after her mother died, so she'd know his friends. Though how we're to find her in that—'

'Servants' gossip.'

Carshalton couldn't blame Winthrop for the smug smile. Should have thought of it himself.

The fellow continued. 'Servants always gossip. Make a list of likely households. We'll divide it and set men in the local taverns to pick up if someone has a mysterious young lady in residence. Dangle the reward. Someone will talk if there's money in it.' He tossed off the last of his brandy. 'Once we've got the house, they won't dare refuse to hand her over. Kidnapping an heiress still carries the death penalty.'

He rose. 'I must be off. I'll be out of town for a few days doing the pretty with my uncle at Hampstead. Send me a note if there's anything interesting in the full reports.'

Carshalton shrugged. 'I'll have one of my scribes make a copy and send it out to you.'

Lucius inclined his head. 'Excellent idea.'

'There is one thing,' Carshalton said slowly. 'One of my men was in Selbourne's shop this afternoon. He was still around on the street when the Runners arrived. According to him Selbourne didn't leave the shop at all, but another fellow did. He went across the road to the coffee house there.'

Lucius shrugged. 'What of it? Men go in and out of coffee houses all the time. I do myself.'

Carshalton scowled. 'I dare say you're right. Anyway, the coffee house would have been searched along with the rest. The full report may tell us more. Still, it might be worth keeping an eye on the place.'

With the exception of Caleb, Psyché let her serving staff out of the front door and shut it behind them. Naturally the news that the Runners had found Will Barclay naked in her bed had amused all of them. Sally in particular had been pleased.

'No point livin' like a nun, an' that's a fact. You got everything you need? Don't want no surprises down the road.'

Which Psyché understood to be an expression of womanly concern that Sally's mistress would not be left holding the baby, either figuratively or literally.

Caleb was the last as usual, waiting to help her with the shutters. He'd got into that habit soon after he came to her. What wasn't usual was the scowl.

'What's bothering you, Caleb?' she asked.

The scowl deepened. 'Seems odd is all.'

'Odd? What's odd?'

He hesitated. 'None of my business, is it?'

Her turn to hesitate. But this was not a case of an overbearing male attempting to rule her life. This was a young man she had encouraged to think of her like a sister. Eighteen months ago Caleb had been a groom in Lord Callington's household, riding out with the young ladies. But the elder Miss Callington had become too obviously interested in him and he'd been dismissed without a character.

'I didn't do anything, Miss Psyché. Didn't even look at the girl, let alone lay a finger on her beyond helping her into the saddle! And they knew it! But I'd tempted her, they said.'

Caleb had ended up on the streets, begging, stealing, surviving on his wits and speed. She'd found him one evening in the yard at the back, searching the dustbins, and offered him a meal. He'd told her his story and she'd offered him a job. In return he'd offered unspoken and unstinting loyalty.

'You're worried because he's white.'

Caleb had probably not looked sideways at the Callington girl, but it was always the servant who took the blame. And in the case of a Black male servant accused of dallying with or *tempting* the white daughter of the house? Caleb had been lucky to get away with only being dismissed.

'Yeah.' He heaved the shutter bar into place. 'Look at me. Tossed out after six years because a white girl looked sideways at me.' He bit his lip. 'You say Mr Barclay's a *friend*. But—' he shoved his hands in his pockets '—what if his lordship doesn't like his secretary having a bit of—?' He cleared his throat.

'Having an affair?' she suggested.

He nodded. 'That. What if he doesn't like it? He's your landlord. He could make trouble.'

She touched his shoulder lightly. 'Lord Huntercombe is not like that, believe me.'

He looked unconvinced. 'They never are until they are.' He shuffled his feet. 'You sure?'

'I'm sure, Caleb.' She gave his shoulder a friendly shake.

'There's other stuff you're not telling us. You haven't had Mrs Archer in to clean and tidy recently.'

She returned his direct gaze. Apart from renting Caleb a room, Jenny Archer also cleaned for her and Ignatius, and Jenny was the only other person he'd told about Kit, but her little boy usually came with her and could not be relied upon for silence. 'No, I've been doing it myself. But for the rest, nonsense. Unless you mean the details of my... friendship with Mr Barclay.'

He shook his head. 'Not that. Look, I won't say anything to anyone. You know that. Just...you'll be careful, won't you? Whatever it is. It's different for us.'

She wanted so much to trust him. Another ally would be invaluable, but— 'I'm always careful, Caleb. You'd best be off or Mrs Archer will lock you out for the night and you'll be back here cadging a bed.' She couldn't afford that tonight of all nights. The less he knew the safer he was.

'Right. Night, then.'

'Goodnight.'

She'd already locked the back door and bolted it, but she did a final check that no one had slipped in while they cleaned up. At last she considered it safe to retrieve Kit.

The crates in the storage room scraped loudly as she hauled them aside and her arms protested the weight. She would have to shove them back, too. But in a few moments she had the cupboard exposed again as it had been when the Runners searched earlier. After checking the cupboard and finding it full of extra crockery, they had concluded that it was no more than a cupboard. Then they'd moved all the crates about, searching for a trapdoor. Which they'd duly found. Great excitement all around. Followed by disappointment when they found only an empty cellar.

Psyché lifted out the contents of both the floor and the bottom shelf of the cupboard, and the bottom shelf itself. The leather tab at the back blended in with the wood, barely visible. She pulled on it and the floor of the cupboard lifted out to reveal utter blackness.

'It's Psyché. You can come out now.'

There was a shuddering gasp and Kit's face, bone-white,

appeared. Her hands shook as she clambered out of the hole. She blinked in the soft glow of the lantern and flinched as Psyché reached for her.

'Kit. What is it?'

She seemed to struggle for words, for breath. 'The...the dark. I... I kept *seeing* things. I started to wonder if I was still there, or...or if I'd disintegrated.'

Five hours. She'd been down there five hours.

'Let's get you upstairs.'

Will, dressed again, sprang up, dropping his book, as Psyché, half carrying Miss Carshalton, came through the door.

'Here, let me help.' He got an arm around the other side of the trembling girl, taking most of the weight. 'What happened?'

'The cellar,' Psyché said. 'I should have thought. Should have warned her what it would be like. By the fire. Come along, Kit.'

Together they got Kit to the fire, settling her in the chair he had vacated.

'Stay with her.' Psyché reached for the shawl draped over the back of the chair and wrapped it around the girl. 'She'll be all right in a moment. I'll make tea.'

She rose and moved about, all quick, efficient competence as she swung a kettle over the fire, set a teapot to warm on the hearth and spooned tea into it.

She talked quietly the whole time to Kit, her voice low and gentle, as if she spoke to a wounded creature. Will listened, himself insensibly soothed by that soft voice. Nothing important was said, but the sound of the words, the promise of a cup of tea, that she was safe now, breathed comfort and kindness. And he could see it working. Slowly

Kit responded, her pallor easing, her breathing less jerky and her eyes seeming to see again.

When Psyché poured the tea her hands reached for it, closing about it.

'Th…thank you.'

'You're welcome.' Psyché's hands remained there a moment, then she stepped back as Kit raised the cup to her lips.

'I… I'm better now.' She looked at Will. 'I didn't realise before. You're Lord Huntercombe's secretary.'

He nodded. 'Yes. Your uncle sent for him.'

'And he sent you?'

Will smiled. 'Not exactly. I sent myself.'

'You might like to explain how that came about, Mr Barclay.' Psyché poured another cup and handed it to him. 'There was no time earlier for explanations and I wouldn't mind knowing how I came to have a man I've only just met occupying my bed.'

'Your bed?' Kit stared from one to the other.

Will found himself blushing. 'You wanted a distraction, didn't you?'

Psyché snorted. 'I had in mind that you might loosen your cravat, maybe remove your coat and sit about in your waistcoat and shirtsleeves. I didn't expect to find you naked—'

'*Naked?*'

'In my bed.'

'I wasn't naked!' Will's ears were close to combustion. 'I had my breeches on!' Mostly. He'd unbuttoned the falls and shoved them down a little so they wouldn't show above the bedding, but he suspected this was one of those times that explaining would be far more dangerous than not. And he was trying very hard not to remember the expression on Psyché's face when she'd seen him, seemingly naked, in her bed. It had confirmed his suspicion that he would very much like to be fully naked in her bed. With her.

'Oh, well.' Psyché grinned at Kit who was now spluttering into her tea. 'Breeches make all the difference, don't you think, Kit?' She poured her own cup.

Will took a restorative gulp of tea. 'So. As to *why* I decided to find out what was going on—'

Chapter Six

It didn't take him long to explain and at the end of it Kit set her teacup down with a steady hand. 'Thank you, Mr Barclay. I'm… I'm very grateful. But this makes something very clear.'

'What would that be?' he asked.

Kit looked straight at Psyché. 'We were extraordinarily lucky this afternoon. From now on I should be in that cellar during the day.'

'No.' Psyché's response was swift and uncompromising.

Will looked up, surprised at the vehemence. 'She has a point. If—'

'*No.*' Psyché looked sick. 'You didn't see her straight after she came out. It's something they do to slaves in Jamaica—locking them alone in the dark not just for hours, but days sometimes to break them. It breaks their minds.' She reached out and touched Kit's wrist. 'I'm sorry. It never occurred to me to warn you.'

He tried again. 'But surely now she knows—'

She rounded on him, suddenly furious. 'You know nothing about it! Warning her might have helped. But it's not something you get used to. It gets worse every time. If she had snapped and started screaming, that would have finished it.'

He opened his mouth and shut it again. He knew more than she thought. But this was not the moment to admit it. The point was—she was right.

Kit flushed. 'I don't think I would have screamed, but—'

'You can't know, Kit.' Psyché spoke gently to the girl. 'I've seen grown men come out of a cellar like that close to insane, weeping in terror. It's not your fault.'

Will's stomach clenched. He knew nothing of her life before she came to England. Had *she* ever been locked up like that? Isolated in the dark?

'But it's too dangerous for you having me up here!' Kit gripped Psyché's wrist. 'He'd have you arrested for abduction.'

'She's right,' Will said quietly. 'You were lucky today. What if you don't get a warning next time?'

Psyché grimaced. 'Ignatius—'

'Was being watched,' he said bluntly. 'If he'd come across himself, they would have torn this building to pieces and found her.'

Psyché let out a frustrated breath. 'I know you're right. But that means we can't wait for a next time.'

Will looked up sharply and she met his gaze. 'We have to get her out quickly. Before Carshalton is sent the report from today's search.'

Will frowned. 'Won't he have that already?'

She shook her head. 'Unlikely. My Uncle Theo used to sit as a magistrate. Full reports from Bow Street take a little longer than that. Carshalton has hired the Runners privately, so he will have been told the search failed. But the officer in charge will have to write up a full report. Then his commander will read and approve it. After that copies will be made and one sent to Carshalton. That's when we're in real trouble.'

'Because I had to give my name? I don't think Carshalton will realise—'

'It's *my* name that's the problem,' she said. 'They'll put my name in the report as well as yours.'

Kit shook her head. 'Why should Carshalton recognise your name?'

'He might not,' Psyché said quietly. 'But Lucius will. And I'm afraid he will also know who lives at Moresby House'

'Oh.' Kit paled.

Will frowned. 'Lucius?'

Psyché nodded. 'Staverton's heir. My uncle, Lucius Winthrop. He's the man Carshalton was selling Kit to.'

'Selling?' He hadn't thought of it quite like that—

She shrugged. 'What else would you call it when she had no say in the matter? And even if she does have a say in it, once a woman is married, she no longer owns her own body, let alone anything else. She has no rights beyond what her husband chooses to grant.'

Will stared at her. Good lord! The woman was a radical!

He forced himself to concentrate on the main issue. 'So your uncle intends to marry Kit.'

Her mouth twisted.

'I can assure you Lucius does not acknowledge that connection. He hates me.' Her voice was calm, but beneath the surface Will sensed—fear? One hand gripped the arm of the sofa so hard the knuckles showed pale.

He reached out and covered that hand with his own. 'Why?'

For a moment she just stared. At him, then at their hands. And slowly, under his, he felt the tension in her fingers ease.

She let a breath. 'For a start, because Uncle Theo brought me up as a member of the family, which meant I was immediately a very visible stain on the family name. An embarrassment. That alone would be enough, would it not?' She tugged gently on her hand, but he held on. It felt absolutely right exactly where it was.

'No.' There was no reason sufficient for hating a child.

She sighed. 'Apart from that, I cost him the inheritance he would have had from my father.'

'Life is full of disappointments,' he said mildly.

The small choke of laughter charmed him. 'True,' she said. 'But for someone like Lucius to lose an inheritance he'd counted his own to the Black, illegitimate daughter of a slave?'

Kit made a small, distressed sound.

Psyché glanced over. 'I was born a slave, Kit, and that is how Lucius sees me.'

Despite the lightness of her tone, Will heard the core of pain and his fingers tightened. 'The way I'm seeing it you are also his *brother's* acknowledged daughter.'

'Perspective is all,' she said quietly. 'One may approach any object from several directions and I am afraid Lucius has always seen that particular object from the other side.'

'He's looking in the wrong direction then,' Will said simply, releasing her hand. 'However, we do need to find somewhere else to hide Miss Carshalton.'

'But where?' Psyché demanded.

He turned to Kit. 'Do you have no friend, no relative beyond Selbourne who would agree to hide you?'

She shook her head. 'No. There's no one. That's why he's so sure I must be close by.'

Will looked at Psyché questioningly.

She shook her head. 'No. Uncle Theo might be willing, but the risk of servants' talk is too great. And there is no one else I could call upon. What about Huntercombe's Isleworth house?'

Will let out a breath. 'I thought of that. He keeps it lightly staffed. But for me to appear there and install a young lady—'

'The gossip would beat you back to London,' Psyché

said. 'If he were here himself it might be possible—he could pass her off as a poor relation, or a potential governess.'

Will considered. 'That's an idea. Look, the Runners won't come back tonight. And tomorrow is Sunday. We have time to think on it. I'll leave you two and—'

Psyché shook her head.

'No?'

'No,' she said. 'It's barely an hour since I shut the shop. You'd better stay for supper. Otherwise your early departure might raise questions—'

'My—? Oh.' Heat crept up his throat. 'You do know that this is an extraordinarily improper sort of conversation to be having?'

'It is, isn't it?' Psyché didn't seem bothered in the slightest. 'But since they know you were eagerly awaiting me in my bed, it would be very odd if you left quite so soon.'

He wondered if it was safe to breathe. The truth was that if indeed he *had* been waiting for Psyché to join him in that bed he would be unlikely to leave it willingly before dawn. And, since tomorrow was Sunday, even dawn would have been a push.

He swallowed. 'In the interests of authenticity then, why don't I go down to the Red Lion and buy a jug of wine?'

Psyché laughed. 'That will make it quite a party. Very well.' She rose. 'I'll let you out the front and see to supper.'

Psyché picked up the lamp and walked back downstairs, fiercely aware of Will on her heels. What had she been thinking to tease him like that—and in front of Kit—about being in her bed? Now he would be thinking...

He'd be thinking the truth: that she was attracted to him, that she'd been flirting with him. It was folly! They had far more important things to occupy their minds. Like where they could hide Kit and how to get her there. There was no time for frivolities such as attraction, or flirting!

'Whatever is on the range does smell very good.'

She glanced back at his shadowed face. 'I had to learn when I decided to come here. Believe me, my first efforts were rather hit-and-miss.'

'But you learned.'

'Yes.' After Uncle Theo had reluctantly agreed to what he'd termed her *'insane plan'* she'd invaded his kitchens and begged the cook to teach her.

'Not the fancy things. Good, plain cooking that I can do myself. Soups, stews, rice dishes.'

She had wanted recipes that could largely look after themselves on the back of the range while she ran the shop. She had also learned how to bake bread. The cook had insisted.

'Easy enough, Miss Psyché, to do between other jobs. Rises all by itself while you're doing something else, then twenty minutes in the oven and you're done.'

She had a loaf rising now.

Reaching the kitchen area, she whipped the cloth off the dough risen in its tin, opened the oven and shot it in.

'Bread, too?'

She shrugged. 'Why not?'

'But—you've no servants,' he pointed out. 'How do you do it all?'

She laughed. 'That's a man talking. Who is going to do it for me? Why should I not do these things for myself?'

'I'm not saying you shouldn't,' he replied slowly as she walked with him to the front door. 'But—you said you inherited your father's fortune. Could you not live on the income of that?'

'I prefer not to do so.'

She shot back the top and bottom bolts, turned the key—and her pulse skipped as she found herself very gently nudged aside when she reached for the heavy bar.

He set it down and regarded her with a half-smile, one

hand resting just above her elbow. 'Yes. I know you can do that for yourself, too. But I'd like to do it for you.'

That smile did shocking things to her heart, to her mind. The gentle touch on her arm seared through the wool of her sleeve.

'I find myself in a quandary, Miss Winthrop.'

Her voice was likely to come out as a squeak, so she waited.

'The thing is, after waiting all that time for you in your bed, and then strolling down to the tavern to fetch wine for our supper—presumably before repairing to your bed again—I have to wonder… Would you be likely to kiss me at the door?'

She would definitely be likely to kiss him, but—'And that puts you in a quandary, Mr Barclay?'

'Will. If I'm thinking about kissing a woman, I'd rather she called me Will.'

'Will, then. How is that a quandary?'

'Because I do not wish to take advantage of the situation,' he said simply, 'if you would rather *not* kiss me.' She heard his indrawn breath. 'Nor do I wish you to kiss me merely to make a show for anyone who may be watching.'

Oh. Dangerous.

'Why not?' She was amazed that she could find breath enough for the question. Her heart tripped and pounded as if she'd had far too much coffee. Plenty of men would have taken the kiss without worrying about such niceties.

'Because I should not like you to imagine that I am only kissing you for those reasons.'

She opened the door and cold air slid in. 'Can we agree then, sir, that we are taking mutual advantage of the situation to do something we both wish to do?'

She reached up, brushed back that errant lock of hair and stepped into him.

'We can do that,' he said huskily as his arms closed about her.

His lips were warm, smooth, soft. Tentative at first, not shy precisely, but wondering what she liked, finding out, moving in slow, gentle rhythms that lured her closer, had her relaxing even as tension coiled lightly in her belly and lit sparks under her skin. The promise of heat, of *more*, should *more* be wanted. And in the tension she felt in *his* body, the promise of demand, when demand was right. But now there was this whisper of a kiss and his arms that cradled her in complete joy and utter safety.

He released her. Slowly. Stepped back. Slowly. And let out an audible, shaky breath that told her stepping back was the last thing he'd wanted to do.

Feeling as if she tempted a simmering volcano, she reached up and touched his face lightly, tracing the line of his cheek, his jaw. Under her fingertips his jaw was slightly scratchy. Her breath caught, as she imagined how it might feel on her body.

'Wine.' His voice was definitely husky.

'Wine.' Her own voice trembled.

Psyché stepped back inside and closing the door, leaned against it, forcing her lungs to do their job properly. After a moment, she remembered to flip the key in the lock. What in God's name had she done?

It took Will a moment to orient himself and remember that the Red Lion was to the left. He walked down, glad of the bite of the wind, even the more than a hint of horse manure that wafted from the inn's yard. Something had to reorder his wits after that sweetly chaste kiss had scattered them completely.

Kissing her at all had been completely unfair. She was a woman in a very dangerous situation. If Kit had been found in that cellar this afternoon, it was probable that Psyché would have been dragged off charged with the abduction of an heiress. Kit's testimony would have been useless—in fact, her father would have refused to allow her to testify.

He walked into the spill of light from the tavern windows and became aware of footsteps hurrying behind him.

He whirled, hand on his sword, ready for the shadowy figure.

'It's Selbourne. Ease up, boy.'

'Your pardon, sir.'

'No problem. Best to be alert around here, especially at night. I'm just off for my dinner. Care to join me?'

'I have another engagement, sir.' Will wondered if the old bookseller would put it together. 'I'm fetching a jug of wine.'

Selbourne's brows shot up. 'Are you indeed? Well, well, well. My compliments, boy. She's a tasty piece.'

Fury welled up and Will's fists clenched themselves. 'I—'

'Play the game out.'

It was barely audible, muttered out of the side of Selbourne's mouth, but it jerked Will back to his senses.

He clapped Selbourne on the back. 'She is that.' He opened the door of the tavern and noise and light spilled out. 'An ale with you, Selbourne? I've time enough for that.'

In undertones, covered by the noise in the tap, Will made his report.

'Move her?' Selbourne frowned. 'The question is—where?'

'I'll think,' Will said. 'The answer may be one of Huntercombe's properties, but I suspect he's too closely linked. Any whiff of his involvement and they'll have Grosvenor Square watched and the Isleworth house as well. We might get her in, but we'd never keep it secret. I'll look through his holdings and see if anything else—'

'Taking a bit on yourself, aren't you?' Selbourne's voice was cool. 'You scarcely know the chit. Or is it her fortune?'

Will dragged in a steadying breath against the surge of anger at the implication. 'Have you considered the danger in which Miss Winthrop-Abeni stands?' He didn't bother to hide his fury, but kept his voice low. 'Danger which *you* have brought upon her.'

Selbourne let out a breath. 'Stand down, lad. Yes, I'm deeply aware of that and I'd hoped to have Kit out of there much sooner, but—' He grimaced. 'I underestimated how closely Carshalton would watch me. Very well. Do what you can. With luck Hunt will be in London before the situation becomes critical. He's the only other person I can trust in this.'

Will tossed back the last of his ale and set the tankard down. 'It's critical now. We can't wait for Huntercombe to reach town.' He leaned forward. 'Psyché believes, and I agree, that if Lucius Winthrop sees the Runners' report he'll suspect her involvement.'

Selbourne cursed softly. 'Staverton has been a customer of mine for decades. Winthrop would know that. And since Psyché acted as Staverton's amanuensis for some years, he would be aware that I know her.' He smiled. 'It's one reason Staverton and Huntercombe settled on that particular property for her—I was across the street to keep an eye on things.'

Will looked at him. 'She says that Winthrop hates her.'

Selbourne grimaced. 'He does. Hates and resents her. Not only because she inherited her father's personal fortune, but he believes that Staverton made a laughing stock of him by acknowledging her. Staverton took extensive legal action in order to ensure Psyché and her fortune would be protected even after his death. He said he wouldn't trust Winthrop over Psyché's well-being as far as he could spit.'

Will rose. 'Huntercombe knows all this?'

Selbourne nodded. 'He's one of her trustees, boy. Didn't you know?'

He hadn't. But now Will saw that the situation was a great deal more complicated than he'd understood.

Chapter Seven

Psyché sat quietly on a sofa in the drawing room attending to her needlework, with Nyx curled up beside her. Aunt Grace, she thought, was very kind. She did like dogs, but she preferred them to remain outside. Yet she permitted Nyx inside and even on the sofa—as long as she remained on the carefully folded blanket placed there for her.

So Psyché stitched and listened to the ladies' conversation without appearing to do so. She had learned long ago that if you didn't look up, or so much as flick an eyelid no matter what was said, adults assumed you either weren't listening or didn't understand what was being said. One or two of Aunt Grace's visitors had resorted to very bad French this afternoon as an added safeguard. Aunt Grace had not bothered to inform them that Psyché spoke French. Mam had spoken French, just as well as the governess. Sometimes they had sat quietly together speaking in French, mending the father's clothes, Mam showing her, teaching her the stitches. And sometimes, if there was no one close by, they might speak in the language of Mam's childhood and, instead of being Psyché, she could be Abeni.

'Tell me your day name again, Mam.'

'Afua—because I was born on a Friday. And you are Abeni because God gave you to me on a Tuesday.'

Names they kept secret, just for themselves because the father would not like it. But Uncle Theo and Aunt Grace did not mind. She could write *Psyché Abeni Winthrop* and not be afraid.

'My dear Lady Staverton, I'm sure it is a very Christian thing that you do—but one cannot know where such things may lead. Is it wise?' The question was accompanied by a sideways glance at the sofa where Psyché sat sewing.

'So far,' Aunt Grace said drily, 'it has led to a dog on the sofa and a new handkerchief apiece for Staverton and myself.'

The ladies tittered.

'How very droll, Lady Staverton,' one lady cooed. 'Still, I vow I should put my foot down should Mr Kidderburn suggest such a thing.'

'Naturally one would not dream of questioning your judgement, Mrs Kidderburn.' Aunt Grace sounded as though the fire poker had been stitched into her spine.

'But is not your *niece*—your great-niece, that is—dear Lucius's little girl to live with you?' asked a long-nosed lady in deep purple. She turned to Mrs Kidderburn. 'I dare say the creature will be an acceptable companion and later a lady's maid.' Another glance at the sofa. 'She seems biddable enough.'

Psyché clamped her lips together and concentrated on the needle sliding in and out, trailing rose-pink silk. Uncle Theo had given her a rose. He'd liked the red rose on his first new handkerchief. She hoped he would like a pink one.

'I understand,' continued Madam Purple Gown, 'that Mr Lucius Winthrop is not at all sure of the wisdom of such a *connection*.'

She made *connection* sound like something one of the peacocks left on the terrace.

'My nephew,' stated Aunt Grace, as she crooked her finger at Psyché, 'is very free with his opinions. Psyché, dear child—would you be a good girl and carry the cups for me, please?'

'Yes, Aunt.' Psyché set her work down and slid off the sofa. She understood that Aunt Grace was not treating her as a servant, but showing her to be a good daughter of the house. In addition, she was showing the ladies that she had excellent hearing and understood English. And that she was not a *creature*.

Nyx came off the sofa and followed her as, one by one, Psyché distributed the cups, Aunt Grace murmuring each name and indicating which lady was which. Three ladies murmured their thanks, four, including Mrs Long in the purple gown, gave stiff little nods and were careful their fingers should not touch hers.

The last, Lady Huntercombe, smiled and said, 'I like your little dog. Did she come with you from Jamaica?'

'Yes, my lady. Nyx was the papa's dog, but Uncle Theo says she must be mine now.'

Lady Huntercombe took her cup. 'Thank you, Psyché. A dog makes a very good friend. They see always with the eyes of love, do they not?'

'Yes, my lady.' She was not sure exactly what my lady meant, but it sounded nice and her eyes were friendly.

'Thank you, Psyché.' Aunt Grace spoke gently. 'Perhaps you would like to take dear Nyx into the gardens for a time. You may leave your embroidery here.'

'Yes, Aunt.' Psyché tried not to show the relief she felt and dropped the little curtsy she had been taught before moving decorously to the door.

Madame Purple Gown spoke. 'I do think—'

'Such an exhausting venture for you, Mrs Long.' That was Lady Huntercombe of the smiling eyes, only now her

voice had iced over. 'Should you put yourself to so great
an effort?'

Psyché whisked herself through the door and got it shut
before the bubble of laughter burst free.

The grounds stretched, if not quite for ever, at least half
that far. She had to stay within sight of the house and not
go out on to the Heath. Not that she needed to go out on to
the Heath—which sounded so wild and exotic—to have an
adventure. There were deer right in the park and, if you
moved slowly and quietly, you could get quite close—one
big stag lay always in the shade by the outer wall every afternoon, quite hidden in the undergrowth unless you knew
where to look. Uncle Theo had shown her. And once at dusk
they had seen a fox. She had clutched Uncle Theo's hand
in speechless delight.

'Oh, dear,' he'd murmured, smiling down at her. 'I
should mention that to the groundsmen, but he is a very
fine fellow, is he not? And his ancestors were very likely
here long before the house.'

The fox trotted on unmolested and, Psyché thought now,
unreported. Uncle Theo had a kind heart for persecuted,
unwanted creatures, human or otherwise.

She ran on, coming to the spot where the stag might
be and peered into the undergrowth. He wasn't there yet.
A glance at the sun and she knew it was too early. What
now? Her gaze slid to a great tree—Uncle Theo had called
it a scarlet oak, pointing out the convenient lower branches
'…that two young boys called Jack and Lucius found very
useful for climbing.'

She looked up, considering. It would be easy for boys
wearing breeches… But if she tucked her skirts up into her
sash, she suited the action to the thought…she was hidden
from the house just here by the bottom branches of the tree
which dipped nearly to the ground, making a dappled green

cave. Nyx couldn't come up, but she didn't think the little dog would run off very far and, if she did, then she could always call her back.

Skirts out of the way, she jumped for the lowest branch and caught it, swinging her leg over. Nyx stared up at her. 'Sit.' Nyx sat. 'Stay.' Nyx cocked her head to one side, then lay down, curling up with a gusty sigh. Satisfied, Psyché kept climbing.

Higher and higher she went and the world stretched and fell away beneath her. On the ship the sailors had climbed the rigging like this, even on the wildest days, to set sails. One had perched high in the crow's nest with a spyglass to watch for land or other ships. She wondered if Uncle Theo might have a spyglass and, if he did, if she might borrow it. And…there—she shaded her eyes—there *was* Uncle Theo coming in through the gate out on to the Heath.

She drew breath to call out—and recognised the man with him.

Uncle Lucius.

Uncle Lucius didn't like her and even from up here she could see that he was angry. Still, she should say something in case it was a private conversation. Arguments nearly always *were* private things. Uncle Theo looked…not angry, but *something*.

She didn't want to call out and let them know she was there, but she should climb down and slip away to give them their privacy.

Nyx barked. Horrified, Psyché peered down through the spreading green to see the spaniel shake herself and trot out to greet the two men.

'Where did that dog come from?' demanded Uncle Lucius.

'I dare say she's been chasing rabbits.' Uncle Theo bent to pat Nyx.

'There wouldn't *be* any rabbits if you'd set a few traps,' said Uncle Lucius irritably.

'I don't like trapping creatures.' Uncle Theo continued to pat Nyx, but Psyché could see he was glancing around. She froze, trying not to breathe. He straightened. 'We'll take her back to the house and have this out there.' He started to walk and Psyché breathed again.

'No, sir. We'll talk here where there are no damned eavesdropping servants.'

Psyché's breath lodged in her throat as Uncle Theo turned back to him.

'Damn it, Uncle! I've been cheated!'

Psyché felt a little sorry for Uncle Lucius. The father had once lost a great deal of money at cards and he'd said some other man had cheated. Cheating, she knew, was very bad. You couldn't be a gentleman if you cheated.

'How can this be possible? That brat is entitled to *nothing* by law. *Filius nullius*—child of no one, in case you are not—'

'Thank you, Lucius.' She had never heard that tone, hard and angry, from Uncle Theo. 'I am fully aware of what that term means and what it signifies, but an illegitimate child *can* inherit if the parent specifically names said child in the will.'

'How *can* you have persuaded Jack to leave her his fortune? It should have been *mine*. It *was* mine!'

She was shivering now, despite the heat of the day, as if a cloud had blotted out the sun and sucked all the warmth from the world. The fear stalked in with the chill as if it had been awaiting its chance to pounce.

'He cannot have been of sound mind! He was delirious!'

'Part of the time, yes.' Uncle Theo was crouched down again, petting Nyx. 'But when the doctor came, and the solicitors, he rallied. They all agreed he was in his right mind and knew what he was saying. Distressed, certainly.

But he was of sound mind and could make a new will to provide for the child.'

Uncle Lucius's fists clenched and Psyché drew breath to cry out a warning. But Uncle Theo glanced up and Uncle Lucius turned away.

'Why? Why did you persuade him to do it?'

'Because it was the right thing for the child. Lucius, you are my heir now. You cannot begrudge Psyché the relatively small amount Jack could leave her.'

'All London is talking,' Lucius said bitterly. 'You know that, do you not?'

'I am aware.' Uncle Theo continued petting Nyx. 'I can do nothing about idle gossip, only act in accordance with my conscience.'

'And protecting your family does not accord with your conscience?'

'I was not aware you needed protecting. Lucius—she is my great-niece. My blood.'

'For God's sake! She's not even *white*! She is the spawn of a *slave*, a slave herself if only Jack had retained the sense not to bring her to England! She is not a member of our *family*. She should be sent back before it's too late. Ship her to Freetown, and—'

'*No!*'

Uncle Theo's furious refusal masked her own choked whimper. Even a child in Jamaica knew of Freetown on the west coast of Africa. Freetown, and Bunce Island, the slave fortress a few miles upstream on the Sierra Leone River. Slaves spoke of it in despair and loathing, and Mam had wept when she'd asked.

'Never, Abeni. Never will I speak of that cursed place to you. Don't ask! Don't ask!'

'I will do no such thing.' It sounded as though his teeth were gritted together and his expression was a stone mask.

'I would not do that to any living soul, let alone a child, and my own blood.'

Uncle Lucius scowled. 'I'll contest the will! There is every chance that the courts would overturn it. A substantial fortune left to an illegitimate Negress? Why, it's—'

'You may do that.' Uncle Theo gave Nyx a final pat and rose to face the angry younger man. 'And if you are successful, then I shall make up the deficit from my own fortune.'

'*What?* Do you think I wouldn't—?'

'Challenge *my* will when the time comes?' Uncle Theo sounded so weary that even with fear clawing at it her heart broke a little. 'I am in the process of setting up a trust to safeguard her inheritance when there can be no question of *my* fitness to do so. She will have use of the income when she reaches her majority, otherwise it will be untouchable until she reaches thirty, and I have been extremely selective in my choice of trustees and in the terms for the appointment of new trustees should the need arise. However, should you contest Jack's will successfully, I will more than make up that deficit from my own fortune.'

Lucius snarled a curse.

'You might break a will, boy. You won't break a trust. Not the way I've set it up.'

The silence burned with rage. 'And Henrietta, my *daughter*, is to be raised with this…this child of sin?'

Uncle Theo's crack of laughter startled Psyché. 'So puritanical, Lucius? At last count you were providing for two illegitimate children.'

This silence echoed with shock. 'I'm not bringing up my daughter with them, sir.'

'No. You are asking myself and your aunt to bring her up. Henrietta is welcome in our home as long as you understand that she and Psyché will be treated as cousins.'

'Cousins?' Uncle Lucius spat the word out. 'Damn it! What choice have I?'

'To bring up Henrietta in your own home, or find another relative to bring her up who won't expect you to pay board for her.'

Lucius swung on his heel and stalked away towards the house. Psyché remained frozen on her perch. The swaying crow's nest had become a refuge above a sea of loathing. There was no slavery in England. Even Lucius had said it and she had heard the servants say so. But there was still hatred and contempt for those who were marked *other*. As she was marked.

The ladies in Aunt Grace's drawing room had been less outspoken than Lucius, but the undertow was as dangerous. And Lucius? No longer did she tag *Uncle* before his name—he would have seen her sent to the auction block on Bunce Island. He had denied all kinship, so he was not her uncle. Anyway, Mam had always said their relationship with the father was only by spirit, *not* by blood. She was *Mam's* daughter. That was the Akan way. Except Uncle Theo said she *was* his blood. Apparently things were different here in England. She took a soft, trembling breath. It was all too hard and confusing.

'Are you staying up there much longer, child?'

He knew she was there.

She clambered down, shaking. She'd climbed a tree. She'd eavesdropped. She jumped off the bottom branch and stood before him. 'I'm… I'm sorry I climbed the tree, Uncle.' Calling *him* that felt right. She desperately wanted it to be right. And not only because of Bunce Island. Mam was gone and she wanted someone to *belong* to, someone to love and who cared for her a tiny bit.

He looked down at her. 'Are you? Why?'

'I promised myself that I'd be good. Always. That I wouldn't ever be naughty.'

'Hmm.' He didn't sound terribly upset. 'Your aunt might have something to say about a little girl climbing a tree, but I did show it to you. I even pointed out what an excellent specimen it is for climbing. Why do you imagine I did that?'

Oh. 'I eavesdropped.'

'Hmmm.' This one sounded a great deal more serious. 'Eavesdropped, to my mind, signifies intent.'

'I beg your pardon?'

He chuckled. 'My apologies, sweetheart.' He held out his hand and she took it. 'Did you climb up there and deliberately hide, intending to listen to that conversation?' He began walking towards the house.

'I didn't know you were coming!'

'Exactly. You climbed to the top of the mast—was it a ship? It was always a ship when I was a lad and climbed a tree—and then Lucius and I came along and had an argument that I am deeply ashamed you had to hear.'

'I should have called out.'

'Why did you not?'

Shame flooded her. 'I was afraid.'

His hand tightened. 'Not of *me*, I hope.' They had reached a garden bench and Uncle Theo lowered himself to it.

She stood before him. 'You might send me to—' She couldn't say it. To say it aloud might make it happen. 'Away,' she whispered. 'If I was naughty you might send me away.' It would be so easy. No one would care, or query a child, a Black child, being taken to a ship.

He looked as though she had struck him. After a moment he reached out and drew her down beside him. 'No, Psyché. Never that. One day, when you are a woman, you may perhaps leave my house. To marry, or for some other adventure God has not yet revealed. But you will *never* be sent away.' His voice rang clear. 'For as long as I live, and after, I will protect you.'

He took out the handkerchief she had made for him and blew his nose. 'Bone of my bone, blood of my blood. My word on it, child. Even if you're occasionally naughty.' He laid his arm along the back of the bench and Psyché felt the last knot of fear unravel and dissolve as she leaned against him in the summer heat.

She was still going to be a very good girl, but no longer out of fear that she might be sent away. Now love and gratitude burned bright in her heart, banishing fear to a tiny dark corner where it could starve, hidden and unremarked.

Chapter Eight

Soho, London—January 1804

Will spent a very uncomfortable night in the little servant's sleeping closet next to the downstairs storeroom.

He blamed Kit for that. If the wretched girl hadn't asked without a blush what would be a convincing time for him to leave—she'd actually *asked* what might be a believable period of time for a man to spend in a woman's bed—and then expressed concern about his safety on the streets so late when Psyché said several hours… Coming from the girl who had escorted herself here from Bloomsbury in a snowstorm—

But Psyché had agreed and suggested the closet.

'I'm sorry there's no second bedchamber upstairs,' she said as he followed her down with a candle, escorted by the orange cat. 'But the sofa is far too small and Kit and I are sharing my bed.'

Looking into the sleeping closet, Will was not convinced that the sofa was so very much smaller. But the more he thought about it, the less he liked the idea of leaving the two women unprotected at night. And he now had the perfect cover for being here.

'This will be fine,' he said.

She frowned at the space. 'It's not very big, is it?'

He smiled. 'I can always leave the door open. Don't worry.'

She smiled back. 'If you do that, you'll have Fiddle in with you.'

He glanced at the cat, who returned his gaze with an unblinking golden stare. 'I'll survive.'

Will settled down with a sheet, a couple of blankets and a spare counterpane. He had to draw his legs up—the space was far too short for his length of leg—but he was comfortable enough. He'd left the door open and, sure enough, a few minutes after he'd blown out the candle a heavy weight landed beside him, purring approval.

'You do know there's another, probably more comfortable bed upstairs, don't you?'

The cat curled up right beside him and continued to purr contentedly.

He woke in utter darkness, but not to utter silence.

Something was growling.

After an instant's confusion he realised it was the cat. He could still feel the creature's weight beside him, but it felt different somehow. He reached out a cautious hand and discovered that Fiddle was not only standing up, he was fluffed up and his considerable bulk quivered with the force of his deep-throated annoyance.

Surely he wouldn't react like this to a rat or a mouse? What sort of hunter—?

The faint metallic scrape brought him to his feet with a soft curse. Not a mouse or a rat, but someone picking the lock on the back door. For all the good it would do. Like the front, the back door was not only locked, but secured with bolts top and bottom, as well as a heavy bar. Even if they breached the lock, nothing short of a battering ram would breach the door. He'd slept in his shirt and drawers, but grabbed his breeches and hauled them on.

Fiercely aware of the chilly stone floor under his bare feet, Will felt his way along the rear wall to the door. Now, with his ear pressed to the timbers, he could hear voices, as he buttoned the falls of his breeches. Three men, he thought, but it was hard to be sure with the scraping of metal and the heavy door muffling other sound. After a moment he heard a distinct click.

'Got the bugger!'

His breath caught, despite knowing that the bolts and bar would hold them out.

'Ready, boys?'

More than two, then. He held utterly still, listening. And felt the slight movement as they pushed against the bolts.

'Damn.'

'Stuck?'

'Nah. Reckon there's bolts. Another bar as well likely. Sod it. Better *un*pick the bloody thing.'

The scraping sound came again and the click as the door was relocked.

'Right. Let's get out of this. He won't like it, but there's naught else we can do tonight.'

Who wouldn't like it?

Will lingered, hoping for more, but all he heard was the faint sound of footsteps receding. Then silence. The cat's growling had stopped. He stood for a moment, thinking. The darkness was no longer absolute as his eyes had adjusted to the very faint glow of the kitchen fire.

The cat wound once around his legs, then trotted off, a silent shadow heading for the stairs.

Will hesitated only a moment before following.

Psyché woke in a rush at the soft tapping. Beside her Kit didn't stir. In the dim light from the parlour fire she could see the tall shadow in the doorway.

A soft *mrowp* heralded the weighty arrival of Fiddle on her legs.

'Will?'

'Yes.' Very soft. 'I need to speak with you.'

'A moment. Could you stir up the fire? No other light.'

'Of course.'

He moved away, and Psyché shook Kit's shoulder. 'Something's happened.'

She frowned over Will's story.

'You're sure they picked the lock?'

He nodded. 'I heard it click.'

'And relocked it when they found the door bolted.' She thought about that.

'Wouldn't they have realised the back door was likely to be secured with more than a lock?' Kit asked.

Psyché nodded. 'It's possible they've been in the shop and seen the bolts and bar for the front, but—'

'They have.' Will scowled. 'How the hell did I miss that? One of them said there was likely *another* bar.'

That flash of irritation touched her. 'Don't blame yourself. Most men would have ignored a growling cat and gone back to sleep. We'd be none the wiser.'

'We're not much the wiser anyway,' he muttered.

She had to smile. 'Oh, yes, we are. We know it's unlikely to be Runners. So that tells us that in addition to them, Carshalton is using his own men.'

'And that he suspects I'm here,' Kit said quietly. 'I should—'

'*No.*' Psyché gripped her hand. 'Kit, you are not going to leave.'

'But—'

'Kit—you can't just leave.' Fear for the girl flooded her. 'He'd be on you in an instant!'

'Kit.' Will's voice was steady, calming. 'We'll think of something. Trust us.'

Trust us. Us.

Kit managed a faint smile. 'We haven't got very long.'

'No.' Psyché looked at Will. 'There's something else. If I go out through the back, supposedly leaving the place empty, and they try that door again...'

Understanding flashed in his eyes. 'If they find the door still bolted, they'll *know* beyond all doubt that there is someone inside.'

'Exactly.' Psyché gritted her teeth. 'Fortunately you didn't give away that they'd been overheard, so they don't know we're on the alert. But still...'

Kit bit her lip. 'If they came back—'

'It would take a battering ram,' Psyché assured her. 'Which would alert us and give us time to hide you again. It would also wake up the neighbours who would definitely take exception.'

Will cleared his throat. 'There's something else that would do it.'

The very quietness of his voice told Psyché she wasn't going to like it. 'What?'

'A fire right up against the door.'

Her stomach clutched. 'The whole row of buildings would catch. We'd have to—'

'Escape through the front, right into their hands,' Will finished for her, his face grim.

Psyché let Will out the front door with dawn brightening the east. The morning was clear and cold, sharp and crisp. Despite being Sunday, people were already hurrying by. Usually she would have gone out on such a glorious day. Swung a warm cloak about her shoulders and gone for a long walk. Sundays, with the shop closed, were almost the only chance she had to get out and enjoy a walk along the river. But now, knowing that someone had picked the lock on her back door, she was trapped.

'Be careful, Will,' she said softly.

He shook his head. 'That's my line. *I'm* not hiding a missing heiress. I'll be back tonight.'

'What?'

'I said, I'll be back tonight,' he repeated, as though she had merely misheard him. 'That way we'll have some warning should our enterprising friends return.'

'You don't think I'm capable—'

'Of sitting guard on the back door all night?' he suggested.

That was exactly what she'd intended.

'The problem with that is that you're planning on a full day's work tomorrow as well,' he said cheerfully. 'Whereas I can take a nap during the day. Besides which no one will think I'm warming the back door. They'll assume I'm warming your bed, which might make them think twice about burning you out anyway.'

There was absolutely nothing to be gained from arguing against logic of that calibre.

She changed the subject. 'And how do you propose to spend your day?'

'Checking Huntercombe's property ledger to see if there's somewhere better to hide Kit.' He removed his hat, bent and kissed her gently on the lips. 'Because I want to,' he murmured, lingering.

She kissed him back. Because, God help her, she wanted to do a very great deal more.

Except for the beat of his mare's hooves, Mayfair lay quiet as Will trotted along Grosvenor Street. Not only was it far too early for the Quality to be abroad, very few of them were even in town at this season. Circe's breath as well as his own smoked in the morning chill as he entered Grosvenor Square.

He took the mare around to the stables and entered the house through the back. And walked straight into the housekeeper, Mrs Bentham.

Will swallowed, aware of the appearance he presented. He'd washed, yes. But he was wearing yesterday's clothes and the entire staff would be fully aware that he had not come home the previous night. And he'd had to run straight into the very proper Mrs Bentham, who, judging by her expression, had arrived at her own conclusions.

'Good morning, Mr Will. Coffee, sir?'

He'd had coffee with Psyché and Kit, but given he'd spent the latter part of the night on guard rather than asleep— 'A very large pot of coffee, please,' he said. Otherwise he was going to nod off over the ledgers.

Three hours and two pots of coffee later, he rose from his desk in the library and stretched. So far he'd found nothing that could serve as even the most temporary refuge. Huntercombe's properties were all fully tenanted and there wasn't even a convenient brothel listed among them. Not that he had expected there to be, but it would have been helpful. He rolled his shoulders and walked to the window to stare out. Surely, out of all those properties, there must be somewhere to hide one slip of a girl. A walk around the Square might clear his head. Then he'd go through them again.

Will let himself into the central garden which was surrounded by the dwellings of the seriously wealthy and powerful. At least he had the place to himself. He doubted any of those wealthy families were actually in residence. They would still be in the country…except there, to prove the exception, on the opposite side of the Square to Moresby House, was an elegant sporting curricle with a pair of very familiar bays harnessed to it.

His jaw dropped as he recognised the man stepping down, strolling around to pat his horses and walking up the front steps of Cambourne House, accompanied by a gangly teenage boy. James, Earl of Cambourne, a close and trusted, albeit much younger, friend of Huntercombe, and his young brother-in-law, Philip Fitzjames.

He was debating the wisdom of charging straight across against at least giving Cambourne time to get inside, when Philip—more usually known as Fitch—spotted him and waved.

The boy gave his brother-in-law's arm a sharp tug and pointed.

The Earl stared, as well he might. But he raised a hand in friendly greeting and strolled back down the steps with Fitch, crossing the street to the iron railings.

'Good morning, Barclay. Surprising to see you in town at this season. Hunt with you?'

Will hesitated. This was a risk. And not *his* risk strictly speaking. He should probably discuss this with Psyché and Kit first. Hell, with Selbourne. Most men would look askance on hiding a girl from her father. Only…his gaze fell on Fitch—the Countess's adopted brother…perhaps not *this* man. As Huntercombe's secretary, he knew a little about the circumstances under which Cambourne had met his Countess, and the part Huntercombe had played in their courtship. Quite apart from the fact that Huntercombe trusted this man unreservedly, Cambourne was possibly the only person in London who could not only help, but would understand the need.

He took a deep breath. 'I need your help, my lord.'

Cambourne raised his brows. 'You'd better come in and tell me.'

* * *

Cambourne had dismissed his brother-in-law, but as Will finished his tale, and explained what he was asking the Earl to do, he said slowly, 'I think, with your permission, we'll have Fitch back in.'

Will sat back. He liked Fitch. The boy was refreshingly outspoken and highly intelligent. But…

'Fitch? Why, my lord?'

Cambourne smiled. 'Barclay, how long have you worked for Hunt?'

How that was relevant he couldn't imagine. 'About seven years, my lord.'

'So we've known each other that long. And we're about the same age,' said the Earl. 'Do you think you could call me Cambourne and be done with it?'

'I could do that, if you like.'

'Good,' Cambourne said with feeling. 'Because when a man engages me to compound a felony I do like to feel that we're upon terms of friendship.'

Will smiled, but felt obliged to say, 'You understand that I am *not* acting on Huntercombe's instructions, don't you, Cambourne?'

'You made that abundantly clear,' the Earl said calmly. 'However, it's also clear that if Hunt were in London he'd be in this right up to his neck.' He drummed his fingers on the arm of his chair. 'Hiding Miss Carshalton is the least of our concerns. From what you tell me, getting her out of that coffee house will be the tricky part. Which is where my brother-in-law comes in. How much did Hunt tell you about Lady Cambourne?'

Will considered that. 'Directly? Very little. Naturally I heard a certain amount of gossip.' Gossip over the Earl of Cambourne's startling marriage to a girl whose family had scarcely acknowledged her and whose father was— according to the gossip—a Captain Sharp had rocked society. Huntercombe had called privately on Cambourne one evening and returned hours later, dishevelled and stinking of opium and a particularly cheap scent. He'd said very little about the evening beyond he'd helped the Earl out of a nasty scrape. Since Cambourne's betrothal had been announced almost immediately and Huntercombe had gone to some lengths to throw his support behind the scandalous bride, Will had put two and two together and kept his mouth shut.

'You've never asked him about that business, have you?' Cambourne reached out and tugged on the bell pull.

'Certainly not,' Will said stiffly. 'If his lordship—' He caught Cambourne's amused glance. 'Very well, *Huntercombe*, then! Had he wished me to know anything about it he would have told me!'

Cambourne smiled. 'He thinks you a prince among secretaries, you know.'

Will was aware that his ears had turned pink as Cambourne continued. 'Anyway, that's beside the point. Part of the point is that Fitch grew up on the streets. He helped keep Lucy safe and I think he'll be able to help us.'

Will nodded. 'I was aware of his background.' He'd tutored Fitch in mathematics for a while as a favour to Huntercombe. While imparting the mysteries of Euclid, he'd also done his best to mould the boy's speech without sounding like his own Great-Aunt Maria. Fitch never bothered to hide his origins, but he was like a sponge, soaking up knowledge and a new way of speaking with ease.

Cambourne grinned. 'I thought you would be. The rest of the point is that apart from Hunt's opinion, I know I can trust your judgement and discretion from my own observation. I am also very slightly acquainted with Miss Winthrop-Abeni.' He grimaced. 'And somewhat better acquainted, to my sorrow, with Lucius Winthrop. Of the two, I prefer the lady. Which isn't saying much because Winthrop is a wart on the arse end of a toad and that's insulting warts, toads and possibly arses. And as for Carshalton—there is no creature or blemish on the face of the earth that deserves comparison to him.' He shot Will a keen glance. 'I am fully aware of his involvement in the attempts on Harry Lacy's life last year. Can't say I liked him before, but that rather put the topper on it.'

The door opened to admit a footman. 'Yes, my lord?'

'Ah. David.' He glanced at Will. 'Your permission? And, yes, I may lack Hunt's omniscience, but I know exactly what you are thinking about secrets.'

That a secret shared between more than two is no longer secret...

However, as Cambourne had put it, he'd asked the man to compound a felony.

'If you are going to trust my judgement, Cambourne, I'd best return the compliment.'

Cambourne turned back to the footman. 'Send Master Fitch in, if you please. And coffee. Milk and cake as well.'

The footman didn't precisely grin, but his mouth twitched. 'Master Fitch is already partaking of milk and biscuits in the kitchen, my lord.'

Cambourne snorted. 'Of course he is. I can only hope he's left enough biscuits for us.'

Chapter Nine

Psyché spent the day dusting, catching up on her accounts—
and incidentally teaching Kit how to read the accounts—
and checking stock. Kit, with all the ground-floor windows
shuttered, came downstairs to help with the stock check.

'You don't have to help, you know.' Psyché pushed a
stray curl out of her eyes as she scribbled a note for herself.

Kit scowled. 'It's the least I can do to make up for being
such a nuisance. I'm sorry.'

Psyché looked up. 'Stop right there. You do not apologise for being in trouble.'

'I *am* trouble for you.' Kit started to put back the coffee
cups she'd been counting. 'You're breaking the law for me.
If they find me here—'

'Just as bad for Ignatius,' Psyché said lightly.

'It's *not*.' Kit had a mulish look Psyché was coming to
know. She was keeping a strict accounting of every penny
spent on her, vowing to pay it back. 'It would be much
worse for you. Ignatius has powerful friends in high places
and he's not—' She broke off.

'Black?' Psyché smiled across at the girl she had taken
in out of pity and come to like very much.

'Yes. I… I don't mean to be offensive, but—'

'Why should I be offended?'

Kit bit her lip. 'That cloak I was wearing when I arrived.'

Psyché blinked. 'It's white. What of it? Handy in the snow. Very few would have seen you that night.'

'It probably cost a fortune,' Kit continued stacking cups. 'I wouldn't know how much, but you know *what* paid for it. What my father's ships carry.'

Ah. Psyché nodded. 'Yes. I know.' She didn't have to make the girl spell it out.

Kit swallowed. 'He's a slave trader. When I lived with Ignatius and Aunt Agatha I read the pamphlets Mr Wilberforce left in the shop and…and it was *vile*.'

Psyché nodded. Mr Wilberforce came into her shop occasionally, too, and left pamphlets about the horror of the slave trade.

Kit went on. 'After Agatha died, my—Carshalton decided I had to live with him again and I said something about the Middle Passage. He said it was all lies and exaggeration by do-gooders, but I…didn't believe him.' She dragged in a breath. 'I argued and he hit me. Told me if I knew what was good for me I'd shut my mouth and leave business to him and make sure I got a husband who could get brats on me because that was all I was good for.' She faced Psyché squarely. 'So I shut up because I was a coward.'

'You shut up because you were afraid,' said Psyché. She kept her voice calm, but her stomach churned at the flash of memory. Of being afraid so that it became a constant, something that was with you always, gnawing away inside your belly. And the knowledge that to other human souls you were a *nothing*, a commodity to be used and discarded.

'That's what I—'

'No.' Psyché reached out, laid a hand on Kit's and found it trembling. Somehow that eased the grip of her own memories. 'You said you were a coward. Being afraid does not mean you're a coward. It means you used your brains. You waited. You waited until you could make your actions and words count.' She squeezed the pale hand. 'In fact, you lulled him. He thought he'd broken you, didn't he?'

Kit nodded. 'Because he had.'

'No.' Psyché shook her head. 'If he'd broken you, you wouldn't be here. You'd be married to Lucius.'

Kit looked unconvinced. 'The thing is,' she went on, 'I've put you in danger. Carshalton will be howling for someone's blood over this. He's not stupid. He'll know Ignatius is protected. He may go after you if he ever realises you helped me. And because...because you're Black and he can't touch Ignatius, he'll be even angrier. You won't be safe.'

'Don't worry.' She patted Kit's hand, rose and went back to the window. 'I have friends, too. Such as Lord Huntercombe and my Uncle Theo, of course.'

'It still would have been safer for you if you'd refused to take me in. Why did you when my—Carshalton is a—'

'A complete brute who arranged the rape of his own daughter?'

For a moment, as Kit's mouth trembled, she wondered if she had spelt it out too brutally.

But Kit's mouth firmed and her chin lifted. 'I suppose that's my answer.'

'It is.' She wouldn't give a dog to Lucius, let alone a woman. Perhaps memory was more important than she was willing to acknowledge—memory and a soupçon of revenge to flavour it—but it was not only that. It was the knowledge that Kit's father had considered her as little more than a brood mare.

Kit scrubbed impatiently at her cheeks. 'The thing is, I never thought past escaping, but I need to *do* something. Like you do. Carshalton will disinherit me. I know that and I don't want his beastly money anyway. But I've been thinking that if I learned how to run a business, then I could actually help Ignatius and not just sponge off him. So, if you don't mind teaching me about the books and a budget? I've never had to think about anything like that before. But watching you, seeing how you manage the books and run The Phoenix, well, I want that, too. It never even occurred to me that a woman could do something like that.'

Psyché stared at her with new respect. 'You know you don't have to. Ignatius wouldn't think of it as *sponging*, you know.'

'Of course, he wouldn't.' Kit frowned. 'I know that. But it's what *I* think about it. And if I'm going to be independent, I want to create it for *myself*. As you have. Not just be given it. Can you—when you take coffee over—can you talk to him about it? Please?'

'Of course.'

'And we can be friends?'

The knocking on the front door froze Psyché in place. She flung up a hand to silence Kit.

'Who is it?'

'It's Will.'

Relief rolled through her and, more disconcertingly, a wave of delight. 'Wait a moment!'

She started for the door, then looked back at Kit, saw the shy diffidence in that sad, haunted face. *And we can be friends?*

Warmth flowed around her heart. 'I thought that was where we were already. Make sure you're out of sight from the door.'

She unlocked the door and swung it open part way. Will stood there smiling, gripping a large valise.

Psyché swallowed. 'Are you…are you moving in?'

'Not quite,' he said. 'Officially I've taken a room at the Lion. Unofficially…' He grinned at her. 'Are you going to let me in? I've got news.'

Shaking her head, she stepped back. 'Come in.'

* * *

The valise held wine, cheese, a very fine-looking pork pie and biscuits.

It also held a set of boy's clothes.

Psyché bit back a curse, wondering how to tell him kindly that this simply wouldn't work, that such a disguise would be seen through immediately.

Kit didn't bother to disguise her scepticism. 'You don't think dressing me as a boy is just a tiny bit obvious?'

He grinned. 'It is,' he agreed. 'Which is why it will work. Listen, if we simply tried to sneak you out dressed as a boy they'd be on you in a heartbeat—'

'Then—'

'But if they see one boy enter The Phoenix and what looks like the same boy—in identical clothing—leave a little later it won't raise suspicion.'

Psyché considered. That might actually work, but—

'Where do we find the first boy?' she demanded. 'And what do we do with him afterwards?'

'He slips out later. It won't matter if they stop him because he's a genuine boy with nothing to hide.'

'But we don't have a boy in the first place,' Kit pointed out. 'And where am I supposed to go?'

'We have a boy,' Will said. 'And I've found someone who can and will hide you.'

Psyché's blood iced. Fear, fury—all of that stormed through her. And edging it, the burn of hurt. And disappointment that she hadn't been able to trust him after all.

'*Someone?* Not *somewhere?*'

'That, too,' he said. 'But I had to—'

'You told someone else without discussing—'

'There was neither time, nor opportunity,' he said quietly. 'Believe me, I—'

'Did you simply dismiss what you must have known

would be our concerns because we're *women*?' she demanded.

She saw that strike, saw him flush and then pale. So he was upset—*good*! Then—

'That insults all of us.'

The formal, clipped tones doused her fury as nothing else could have. He was *angry*. Oh, he was hurt as well, but he was angry, equal to equal, and he wasn't bothering to hide it.

'I know there are those who would dismiss your opinions because you are female.' Those grey eyes were wintry. 'You aren't supposed to have opinions at all according to many. That wasn't why I acted independently.'

'Why then?' she demanded.

'Because I saw the best chance of success. A chance not only to get Kit out, but to hide her with someone who has no obvious connection to yourself or Selbourne.'

'Psyché?' Kit sounded apologetic. 'Sometimes you have to *act*. The opportunity or danger is right *then*. You either act, or you're lost. There's no time to discuss or take advice.' She gave Will a faint smile. 'Rather like myself on Christmas Eve. I had either to run then, or...or—'

Psyché's hand flashed out, gripped hers unthinkingly. 'Don't even think it. You'll give yourself nightmares.' She turned back to Will. 'I'm sorry. You had better tell us what you've arranged and who you've told.'

'Cambourne.'

'*Cambourne?* The Earl?'

'Yes, he's a friend—'

'Of Huntercombe's, I know.'

Kit shifted in her seat. 'I don't think I know him.'

'I do, a little,' Psyché admitted. 'Not well. But I know Huntercombe trusts him without reservation. Hasn't he got a rather unusual brother-in-law?'

Will's smile was disarming. 'He does. And that's how it's all going to work. Let me explain.'

He did, and Psyché had to admit it was a good plan, but—

'We can refine that a little,' she said thoughtfully.

'Refine?'

She could hardly blame Will for the suspicion in his voice. It was not just a good plan, it was brilliant in its simplicity. Too much gilding would make it top-heavy. However—

'A diversion,' she said.

He sipped his wine. 'What sort of diversion did you have in mind?'

Psyché smiled. 'If you want to distract someone properly, you give them what they're looking for.'

'They're looking for me,' said Kit.

Psyché refilled Kit's glass. 'More precisely, they're looking for a young woman.'

'What in Hades do you have in mind?' Will demanded.

She explained.

Will and Kit exchanged glances.

'No.'

Will's sharp veto didn't surprise her in the least.

She sipped her wine. 'It will work. That's all that matters.'

Chapter Ten

Walking down the darkening street towards the bookshop the following evening, Will had no idea how he'd lost that argument. Even with Kit's support, and Ignatius Selbourne turning the air blue with his opinion, he'd finally agreed.

She's right that the last thing the Runners are likely to do is fire. After all, they're being paid to recover Kit, not shoot her.

But still.

It was a damned brilliant plan and he hated it, couldn't rid himself of the leaden weight in his gut at the thought of Psyché, even with himself at her side, acting as decoy. He wanted to call a halt, beg her to reconsider, to stay out of the way, to stay *safe*. Any other woman he'd have had no hesitation in overriding her opinion and insisting she stay safely out of any hint of danger.

He couldn't do that with Psyché. She wouldn't permit it even if he attempted it.

Now everything was in place and it was too late to do anything but follow through. Ignoring the closed sign, he walked into Selbourne's and Ignatius glanced up from his desk.

'Barclay.'

The shop was empty except for the cat and pup snoozing by the fire.

Will nodded to the old man and pretended to browse the books near the window. It was nearly time. And sure enough, on the opposite pavement, a tall, well-dressed gentleman strolled along, accompanied by a gangly youth with his hat pulled low. They did not so much as glance toward Selbourne's, but walked into the still busy Phoenix.

Selbourne rose. 'Was that—?'

'Yes.' Will let out a relieved breath. 'Yes. Cambourne and the boy. They're in.'

Ignatius nodded. 'Everything is ready. The back door is unbolted.'

Will went back to his perusal of the books. As long as they timed it correctly. Ignatius was key there.

Ten minutes later the door of the coffee house opened and a slim, cloaked figure came out and strolled across the road.

Psyché whisked into the bookshop, carrying a coffee pot. 'There's a Runner in the shop.'

Ignatius's mouth tightened. 'Then we should abandon—'

'No.' She set the coffee on his desk. 'Kit looks exactly right in the boy's clothing. I warned Cambourne when he ordered coffee. He knows which man to watch and the light in the shop is poor because only half the lamps are lit. Also, I gave Caleb orders to make a lot of smoke in the kitchen with embers and hot water when you enter. He doesn't know why, but he'll yell fire. Cambourne should be able to walk straight out with her in the scramble for the door.'

'And his brother-in-law?' Ignatius demanded.

She smiled. 'Fitch? He'll slip out the back door. They'll stop him, but that should keep a few more occupied. No one knows who he is and who's to say he wasn't there all along?'

'Be sure, Psyché,' urged Ignatius.

She smiled, twitched back her dark cloak to reveal one of white velvet. 'With this? I guarantee they'll come after me. My uncle gave it to me several years ago for Christmas.'

Will's stomach iced. 'Damn it, Psyché! You didn't say anything about *that*. You're making yourself a target!' Quite literally.

'That's the whole point. They have to come after us to give Cambourne and Kit time to reach the carriage.'

With that she slipped through the curtain into the back room. Cursing under his breath, Will picked up the darkened lantern Ignatius had ready and made to follow.

Ignatius caught his sleeve. 'Keep her safe, boy.'

Will gripped his hand. 'My word on it.'

They went out the back door into a gentle flutter of snow.

Will looked at her. Psyché's face was set with determination, her eyes bright in the glow from the windows. 'No going back now.'

Her smile flashed white. 'There never was. Come on.'

His heart skipped as she slipped her gloved hand into his. Automatically his fingers tightened.

It's too late now.

They ran across the snowy yard and out into the back lane as he went through his strategy for the possibility of shots fired.

The Runners wouldn't deliberately fire at Psyché, but there was every likelihood that they would fire at *him* as the supposed abductor of an heiress. Ignatius had pointed that out, but Will had dismissed his concern. He wasn't worried about being hit. What terrified him was the knowledge that unless the person shooting was a damn good shot, pistols were notoriously inaccurate—they might aim at him and accidentally hit Psyché. But he had a plan for that...

A couple of turns and they reached the lane leading out on to Dean Street. Little more than a narrow passage between buildings, it gave excellent cover. Will stuck his head out and looked up and down the street. The windows of The Phoenix glowed fifty yards away across Compton Street. He stepped clear of the lane's shelter and opened one side of the lantern briefly. A moment later he saw the figure of Selbourne leave the bookshop and hurry across the road.

He took a deep breath and put his arm around Psyché, drawing her close. She settled against him, every curve fitting as if made for him. Together they watched as Ignatius entered The Phoenix.

He swallowed. 'Ready?'

She smiled up at him. 'Yes.'

He took another breath and the fragrance of coffee, chocolate and the deeper, warmer scent of Psyché herself wound through him. What the hell. He leaned down, brushed a swift kiss over her lips, wanted more, so much more, as her mouth softened under his and he tasted her.

There were things he needed to tell her. The truth. But not now. When this was over and they were safely back in her apartment... She needed to know. And he needed to tell her.

Later.

'Later,' she agreed and he realised he'd spoken aloud.

Then they heard it—the panicked uproar, followed by patrons spilling out of the coffee house on to the pavement.

Dark eyes laughed up at him. 'It's working. Let's go.'

They came out of the lane and set off at a brisk walk away from the fuss outside The Phoenix. Will glanced over his shoulder several times, making it as obvious as possible, and—

'Hoy! You two! *Halt!*'

'Our cue, I think,' muttered Psyché.

They broke into a dead run and Psyché let the dark cloak fall, revealing the white.

'Stop!' Footsteps pounded behind them and a whistle blew. 'In the name of the King!'

'The white cloak! It's her! Stop in the King's name!'

They ran all the harder. He'd thought he'd have to adjust his stride, but her long legs kept pace easily.

'By God, it *is* her! You stupid little bitch, Catherine! Stop or I'll shoot you myself!'

And that was *his* cue. 'Keep going!' He dropped back to cover her.

'Will! No!'

Hands on her shoulders, he kept her moving. 'Go!'

A shot roared, then a second, and his right side seared white-hot. He stumbled, his vision blurring… Didn't matter. All that mattered…get a little further. Once they saw her…

'Hit him, b'Gad!'

And Psyché's voice, breathless, cursing, and somehow she was beside him… *No, keep between her and—*

'Don't shoot again, sir! You'll hit the girl!'

Thank God!

A strong arm went around him. 'Will!' Everything was fading, whirling, turning to darkness shot through with searing pain. They weren't running any more… *Keep going…keep going…*

'No. Will.' Her voice shook. 'You're hurt. Stay still.'

Damn it. He was on the ground, someone's arms around him, but the pavement was so cold and hard.

'Stay with me, Will!'

'Got you, you little bitch!'

Pounding footsteps came closer, but all that mattered was Psyché's arms about him, her warm breath on his cheek…

Psyché sank to her knees on the cold, slush-mired pavement, supporting Will's limp weight against her. Her sleeve was soaked with blood and those pounding footsteps were close…too close. As soon as they saw her face they'd know. She turned away, hiding her face for as long as she could while tearing at his cravat, unwinding it and wadding it up, pressing it to the wound…he was losing so much blood.

She swore.

He seemed to revive slightly. 'Not…that bad.'

Not that bad? Her stupid plan had got him shot.

'Got you, you little bitch!' A large powerful hand gripped her shoulder. 'You're coming with me, my girl, and—'

She flung him off. 'Get your hands off me!'

She tossed back the hood of the velvet cloak and stared up into the furious craggy face. Shock and outrage stared back.

'What the—?'

'*This* is your daughter, sir?' The Runners came up, gasping for breath, and doing quite a bit of staring themselves as Psyché blinked in the lantern light. Her braids had slipped from their pins and hung around her face.

Carshalton. This was Carshalton. Her stomach threatened to heave at the sight of the man who had sold God only knew how many souls into the hell of slavery.

'Of course this isn't my bloody daughter,' he growled. 'But the bitch is wearing her cloak, so—'

'This is my cloak!' Psyché said. She pulled it off, wrapping it around Will, trying to keep him warm. 'Will! Will!' She could see his chest rising and falling, but his eyes remained closed.

'Yours?' Carshalton sneered. 'Where does a Black whore get the blunt for an ermine cloak?'

'Ermine? It's *velvet*,' she said. 'Is there a law against wearing a velvet cloak?'

One of the Runners took a fold of the cloak between thumb and forefinger. He rubbed it and swore. 'She's right, sir.' He straightened up. 'She's not your daughter and I don't know who this chap is, but you've made a serious mistake shooting without being sure of your man.'

His side was on fire and everything was grey and blurry. When it wasn't outright black, that was. Psyché kept pushing the dark back, demanding that he stay with them. Stay with her. He wanted to float off into the beckoning void, but she anchored him, refusing to let him go.

'Put him in my bed, Officer.'

Psyché's bed. Again. That was all he wanted...except not like this...something he needed to tell her...

'I'll have my daughter! Officer, leave that rubbish alone! Do your duty and tear the place apart! They're hiding her here somewhere!'

He tried to sit up, to tell Carshalton to go to hell, but he was held down and his brain couldn't find words through the pain, the unrelenting pressure on his side.

'Get out! Who let you up here?' Psyché's voice. Fire and ice splintered off every word. 'Caleb, keep pressure on that!'

'Who do you think you are, wench, to tell *me* to get out?'

'Psyché Winthrop-Abeni!' Every word rang clear and bright. 'This is my home, my place, and you will leave!'

'Winthrop?'

Will found the strength to force his eyes open. Psyché stood between him and Carshalton, blocking the man from coming any nearer, her hands covered in blood. Caleb knelt beside him on the bed, holding something firmly against his side. It hurt like hell, but he had a fuzzy idea any argument about it would be ignored. He forced his mind to focus through the pain.

Carshalton looked as if an exploding shell had landed at his feet. *'Winthrop?'* he repeated. 'You're...you're Staverton's—'

'Lord Staverton is my great-uncle, yes.' Psyché's head

turned slightly and Will caught the edge of the fury blazing off her. 'Officer, why the devil aren't you arresting this man for attempted murder?'

'Ah, miss, I've got to ask why you two were running.'

'What? Why we were—oh, for God's sake! Poor Mr Barclay wagered I couldn't run as fast as he!'

Will kept his mouth shut.

The Runner looked dubious. 'Seems odd, miss, but—'

'Odd?' Carshalton roared. 'Damn her for a lying poxy whore! This man is a fortune hunter and he's paid off his doxy to help abduct my daughter!'

'Ah, Mr Carshalton, sir...' the Runner sounded as though he had a wolf by the tail '...we've got no evidence for any of that.'

'Does a man with a bullet in his side not constitute evidence?' Psyché demanded in a blistering voice. 'Get him out of here, Officer, before my complaint to Sir Richard involves you and your men.'

'Sir... Sir Richard, miss?'

'Sir Richard Ford, Officer. The Chief Magistrate.'

'You...you *know* him?'

'He is a friend of my great-uncle, so certainly I know him. Get this oaf out of here!'

'*Oaf?* Why, you—!'

'Out, sir!' Apparently the mere threat of Ford had made the Runner a great deal more certain of his ground. He actually caught Carshalton's arm and hustled him out of the room.

Will started to laugh, but it hurt too damn much.

He must have made some sort of sound because Psyché turned to him, all the fury draining to fear and worry.

'Will!' She came to him through the fog of pain, bending over him. 'Stay still. Please. And don't try to talk.'

'*Not tha' bad.*'

'Bleeding's slowing, Miss Psyché.'

'Let me see.'

For an instant the pressure lifted.

'Well done. I'll take it now.'

The pressure came right back along with the dizzying blackness.

Psyché's voice came from somewhere a long way away, snapping orders as though she stood on a quarterdeck. 'Caleb! Go for a doctor, a surgeon.'

Someone groaned and he realised, with a shock, that it was himself.

'Mr Selbourne went already.'

'Scissors, then, and help me lift him. I need to cut this coat off.'

What? Not his good coat! But his tongue wouldn't work, or maybe it was his brain, and he heard the snip, snip, felt the slide of cold metal against his side. Damn it. That was his shirt, too.

Finally, finally, they laid him down. God! He must be covered in blood. What about—?

'Shut up, Will. I can afford new bedding. The doctor will be here soon.'

He drifted in and out. Voices. Psyché's voice, soothing and gentle, then sharp with surprise—'What? He's *here*? Oh, thank God! Send him straight up.'

That would be the bloody surgeon, no doubt...

But there was another familiar, if unexpected, voice, deep and calm, telling him to drink something. A strong arm supported him and a cup was held to his lips. He sipped. Recognised the bitterness of opium and tried to shove it away. He'd be seeing pixies and pink elephants if not worse.

'Don't be an idiot, Will. Drink it.'

He so rarely heard that sharp a command from Huntercombe that he obeyed. Swallowed the entire disgusting draught and floated off again before he could really take in that Huntercombe was there.

The fires of hell in his side dragged him back as something dug around in there with merciless precision.

Another voice. 'Hold him very still, my lord. Blasted thing's lodged near his rib. Damned nuisance.'

Fair enough. He didn't much like that himself.

'Another cloth, girl. Thank you.'

More poking and digging… *Oh, hell!*

'Ah! Got you, you bugger. There we are. It's out.'

Thank you, God!

'He's been lucky, my lord. The ball didn't penetrate anything much…' *the hell it didn't!* '…and missed all the major blood vessels. Must have been right at the limit of its range. Just lodged near the bone. I'll have a look, but I don't think it's even chipped.'

Right. That was good. Especially if the damn butcher had finished with— Sod!

'Sorry about that, son. Need to make sure there's nothing left to cause infection. Little bits of cloth, or bone for that matter. Hold him, my lord.'

He gritted his teeth and endured until the black wave dragged him under again.

Psyché sat beside her bed, watching Will as Huntercombe saw the surgeon out with profuse thanks for his services. She let out a ragged breath. They were safe. At least she was. But Will… She fought to hold back tears. She could not think past this man who had deliberately taken a bullet for her.

He lay so still, so pale. The surgeon had strapped his side, lain him flat. Apart from the strapping and bandage, he was naked to the waist.

'Don't let him sit up unassisted. We'll hope there's no

infection, but call me back if there is. That's the main dan-
ger now. Call me sooner rather than later.'

Will's right hand lay limp on the counterpane. Or it
would have if she hadn't been holding it. She felt as though
she *had* to hold his hand. That only in that way could she
keep him there, stop him slipping away. This was her fault.
If she hadn't had that hare-brained plan to act as decoy…or
at least hadn't allowed Will to be her escort—

Huntercombe came in, looking grey and tired. Apparently he'd left Cornwall on horseback as soon as he received
Selbourne's letter, riding straight through, changing horses
constantly and only stopping when the light failed. He sat
down in the chair on the opposite side of the bed and released a breath. He gazed at Will's face for a moment, then
those sombre grey eyes lifted to her face.

'I'm sorry,' she whispered. 'It was my fault… I—'

'Stop.'

Even if his lordship hadn't used that firm voice that
brooked no argument, grief and fear choked her.

'Psyché. My dear. It wasn't your fault.'

She saw Huntercombe through a blur of tears. 'It was
my plan to act as a decoy.'

'It was a good plan,' he said quietly. 'Selbourne explained. You were right—the Runners wouldn't have fired.
It was Carshalton.'

'But, if I hadn't allowed Will to come with me, then—'

Huntercombe let out the ghost of a laugh. 'That would
have been quite an argument.' He laid a gentle hand on
Will's forehead. 'My dear, he'd be blaming himself if you'd
been shot. As it was Carshalton missed you and—'

'He didn't miss.' Her voice shook. She had gone over and
over it. 'He dropped back when Carshalton threatened to
shoot at Catherine—Kit. He—Will—put himself between
me and the pistol.' She couldn't stop the tears now. They
had been there all along, held back by the sheer necessity

of getting Will here, dealing with his wound and throwing Carshalton out when he forced his way in to threaten Will.

Huntercombe swore softly. 'My apologies. You're telling me Carshalton intended to shoot his own *daughter*?'

She could only nod.

'Sir?'

Will's eyes opened.

Huntercombe leaned forward. 'Rest easy, Will.'

'Psyché...where—?'

Her heart lurched. 'I'm here, Will.'

His cloudy gaze drifted to her face and a faint smile touched his lips. 'You're safe.' His voice strengthened and Psyché felt his fingers grip. 'Kit?'

Huntercombe's brows rose. 'Safely away.' He leaned forward and brushed a lock of hair back. 'You did well. But next time, try not to get shot.'

'I'll remember that. Bloody hurts.'

Psyché stared at him. Was that *amusement* in his voice? *Men!*

Huntercombe spoke again. 'The nature of bullet wounds. Go back to sleep, Will.'

'Yes, sir.' But Will's gaze remained on hers and his fingers tightened. 'You'll be here?'

'I promise.'

She watched as Will slid away into sleep again. They had done everything they could for now. All that was left was prayer.

'You should sleep, too, Psyché.'

She looked at Huntercombe over Will's sleeping form, then looked down at his hand, the fingers still curled loosely around hers.

'Not yet.'

He sighed. 'Believe me—short of tying him up, you could not have stopped Will going with you. He makes his own decisions. Always. Even when it would be easier and far safer to do what others want or expect.' A brief laugh shook him. 'In that he's very like yourself.'

She dozed off eventually, still in the chair, Will's hand safe in hers.

Huntercombe watched her with a troubled gaze. How was it that the child he had known had grown up so fast to become a beautiful and vibrant woman?

Well. Maybe not so fast. He did a small calculation. Thirteen years had passed since Staverton had shocked society by taking his illegitimate, slave-born great-niece into his home and raising her as a member of his family. Some had thought his actions admirable. Most had been horrified. Disgusted, even. Many had made it clear that they would never consider Psyché as anything but the bastard spawn of a slave woman. Something not quite human, that might be trained to ape—oh, and they'd used *that* word deliberately with titters behind fans, and sniggers over a brandy—her betters, but would never be accepted by them.

Knowing that, and desiring to protect the child, Staverton had ensured she was shielded from the worst of it. He himself had been among the few to see much of the child over the years. He'd watched her grow up and had only affection and respect for her character and intelligence. He'd become one of her trustees, determined to help Staverton protect her, when she had chosen to chart her own path rather than follow the conventional one Staverton had envisaged.

How the hell was he supposed to tell Staverton that the girl he was supposed to protect had acted on *his* behalf to save the daughter of Josiah Carshalton?

It shouldn't surprise him.

Psyché was *not* as other women. In choosing her path she had declined to accept a woman's usual restrictions. She made her own decisions and she had decided to help

Kit, no matter the cost. But that didn't mean he couldn't want her safe. And she was safe, thanks to Will's courage. But beyond her safety, he wanted her happiness. He looked at their hands linked in sleep and wondered.

What the devil had been unleashed here? It wouldn't have surprised him to learn that Will had fallen for Kit—he had a chivalrous streak and she was the classic damsel in distress. But Will's first concern just now had been for Psyché's safety. And Psyché? There was more here than horror that someone had been hurt protecting her.

He leaned forward, touched the boy's brow again. Still no fever and he was an idiot. Will was no boy. He was a man. Not even—he did another mental calculation—that young a man at thirty-two. He knew his own mind and held his course, no matter who disapproved.

Which reminded him—he should send for Will's mother in the morning. Please God, he was in no danger, but if anything went wrong... He would not think of that possibility. But regardless he still had to send for the boy's— for *Will's* mother.

He mentally outlined the gist of his intended letter— namely, informing a woman that while her son had been shot the wound was not immediately life-threatening. However, he thought it best to apprise—that was a good word— yes, apprise her of the situation and assure her of a welcome in his house should she decide to come up to town to see Will for herself. In fact, he should probably send the carriage.

He hoped it would be possible to move Will to Grosvenor Square *before* the lady arrived in London. If Mrs Helena Barclay could see her rebellious second son now—his head on the pillow turned to the girl he'd been shot for, his fingers loosely entwined with hers while they both slept—the bullet hole in his side would be of secondary concern to her.

How was he supposed to face Staverton if he exposed the man's great-niece to exactly the ugliness they had tried to protect her from?

Chapter Eleven

Psyché roused to mild cursing. Will was trying to sit up.

'Protect you…won't allow it…dangerous!'

'Will.' She set a gentle hand on his chest, restraining him. 'There's no danger. I'm here. We're both safe.'

He stared at her from fever-bright eyes. 'Psyché?'

Her throat swelled. 'Yes.'

He glanced down at their hands, still linked. Flushing, she tried to pull free, but his grip tightened. 'Stay. Stay.'

She needed the cloths to bathe his face, cool him, but his fingers gripped, hot and dry.

On the other side of the bed, Huntercombe blinked sleepily and straightened in his chair. 'He's feverish?'

'Yes.' The wound itself, now the ball was out, was nothing. Infection was always the danger.

Huntercombe bent over him. He glanced up at Psyché. 'We should get some more medicine into him.'

Fear choked her, but she nodded. 'If you help him sit up, I'll dose him.' She drew a deep breath, forcing herself to stay in the present, not to see another bed, her mother's pain-racked, feverish form. She focused on the willow bark extract the doctor had prescribed, measuring it into the spouted cup.

'Will.' Huntercombe's voice was gentle but firm. 'Sit up now.' He slipped an arm behind him.

Will's eyes opened again.

'There you are.' Huntercombe supported him and beckoned Psyché forward.

'Drink this, Will.' She slipped the spout between his lips and tilted. He swallowed, then made a face. 'It's not that bad,' she chided. 'And the rest. To please me.'

He obeyed, downing the entire dose.

'Well done.' Huntercombe made to lay him back down.

'Sir.' Psyché shook her head. 'We should check the wound again.'

He nodded. 'Very well.'

They unwound the bandage and Psyché's stomach lurched. The wound was an angry, red mess, oozing pus.

Huntercombe swore softly.

Will grimaced. 'That good?'

Psyché bit her lip. 'We'll clean it,' she said.

Several distressing minutes later the wound was as clean as brandy could make it. With the pus gone, it didn't look as bad, but the angry red spelled a warning. Will had lapsed back into unconsciousness.

Huntercombe was breathing hard. He looked up at her and she knew what he was going to say—that they should call the doctor back and they should, but... Psyché reached over to touch his arm lightly.

'Sir? We can try something extra with the dressing.'

He nodded slowly. 'What did you have in mind?'

She took a deep breath. It hadn't helped Mam, but Mam's injuries had been too horrific, the consequent fever too swift and devastating...she saw again—*No*. She could not, *would not*, go back there in her thoughts. 'Honey. My...in Kingston, when I was—' She broke off. Had to fight for breath, for sanity. *No*. Not even to Huntercombe could she speak of *that*. 'I got a burn and it became putrid. They used honey to draw out the infection. And…and cobwebs—fresh ones in the bandage.'

'Cobwebs?'

She couldn't blame him for the disbelief. 'I know it sounds mad, but—'

'Not entirely,' he said slowly. 'My head coachman swears by honey in the poultice if one of the horses cuts itself. Stay with Will. Your lad and I will see what we can find.'

Will drifted in strange byways, his mind fogged. There were voices always in the fog. A husky, musical voice reading quietly from Shakespeare. Occasionally that voice commanded him to sit up and take his medicine when the pain came back. He was glad the voice was there—it helped keep the snakes at bay. At least he supposed they were snakes—strange writhings of colour twisting around the bedposts. If he focused on the voice they kept their distance.

The doctor came again, did something to his side that hurt beyond all imagining, so that he either had to scream or swear. At last the pain surged too high and he fell back into the darkness where, if the pain was not gone, at least it was further away.

Psyché. He clung to the name, to the image of the tired, worried face that hovered in the fog, gentle hands pressing something cool and refreshing to his face, his throat, his shoulders. There had been something he wanted to tell her…

Another worried voice—Huntercombe. He tried to sit up, but something held him down. 'Stay down, Will.'

Psyché. Where was she? Had they shot her?

'She's safe, Will. See? Here she is.'

'I'm fine, Will.' That tender, worried voice held him securely.

There were bricks weighing on his eyes, *in* his eyes, but he forced them open. And she was there.

Keep her safe.

'I promise I'll keep her safe for you, Will. Rest now.'

Relieved, he let the weight of those bricks slide him back down into the fog.

When he surfaced again the weights were gone as well as the damn snakes. His side hurt as though a thousand devils had scorched it and he ached in every part of him, but his head was clear. Well, clearish. It felt as if his brain were stuffed with damp wool.

What had happened? Had he been ill?

A fire flickered in the grate and a branch of candles stood on a table by the bed. But these things were peripheral because Psyché was there. And he was in her bed again.

She sat in an old leather chair, sound asleep. A book lay open in her lap and her fingers entwined with his… What had happened?

'Stay with me, Will!'

Memory trickled back. Kit! They'd been the decoys and someone had fired. One of the Runners? That didn't seem quite right, for some reason. But he had a vague memory of Huntercombe saying Kit was safe and here was Psyché. Right here beside his bed.

Huntercombe? Wasn't he in Cornwall? Had he dreamt that the Marquess was here?

He stared at their linked hands. His pale, hers soft, bronze silk, long-fingered and elegant, yet he knew their strength now. More memory surfaced. Psyché pressing his own cravat to the wound in his side, caring for him, dressing the wound, dosing him with medicine—and reading to him.

He focused on her sleeping face. Shadows beneath her eyes spoke of how tired she must be to sleep so deeply in a chair. A soft sigh escaped her slightly parted lips. Lush, generous lips. The feel and the taste of them under his came back in the sweetest rush. He thought he could lie there watching her for ever, grateful to be alive.

However much the afterlife might have to recommend it, there was a great deal he yet wished to do in this life. He gazed at those lips, remembering something he definitely wanted to do…

Later.

It was later now and if he could only sit up he'd do it…but there was something else he absolutely had to do first… He shifted uncomfortably as his body made its needs known.

Carefully, not wishing to disturb Psyché, he attempted to sit up… A ripe curse escaped his control and his fingers inadvertently tightened as fire exploded through him.

'Will!' She was on her feet and leaning over him in an instant. 'You need to stay put.'

'I need to—' He choked that back. 'I need to get up.'

She frowned, setting her hand to his brow. 'Thank God the fever's broken. Why do you want—?'

'The chamber pot.'

'Oh. There's a commode in the corner.' She bent and slipped her arm behind him. He bit down on the curse this time, but realised to his complete disgust that, cursing or not, he couldn't have sat up without her help. Even with her help his head spun.

'Gently, then.' Her voice was very close and he realised his head was on her shoulder, that he was breathing hard.

Just from sitting up?

After a moment, she said, 'Now, if we swing your legs over the side—'

He'd never considered himself unduly modest, but God help him, he was stark naked under here. He clutched at the sheet as he found himself sitting on the side of the bed. The sheet didn't cover a great deal, but at least the essentials were hidden. And half his torso was bandaged anyway.

He sat there for a moment, sweating merely from the effort of sitting up. With help. And staying there—with help—while his head continued to spin. He shut his eyes and discovered that a room could still spin even so. How the hell was he going to reach the commode?

After a moment the spinning eased and he cracked his eyes open. When the room stayed completely still, he opened them fully.

'That's better.'

How the devil did she know?

'Yes.' He hoped. He wasn't sure what would happen when he stood up.

'Good. Stay there and—'

'Sweetheart—' Oh, God! How had *that* slipped out? 'I really need—'

'I'll fetch it.'

He stayed mercifully upright unsupported as she hurried across to the commode and considered it an achievement. Psyché brought the chamber pot back and handed it to him.

Was he supposed to sit here and—his mind blanked at the notion. *In front of her?*

'Ah, could you perhaps go into the other room?'

'Lord Huntercombe is asleep in there.' But she turned her back and walked over to the fireplace.

Another hazy memory floated up—Huntercombe's calm voice as the surgeon dug around in his side.

'Huntercombe *is* here? I thought I'd dreamt that.'

'No. Do you need help with that?'

'Ah, no. No, thank you.'

Conscious of burning cheeks that had nothing to do with fever, Will relieved himself as discreetly as possible. Damn it, never before had he realised how noisy a chap's stream could be against porcelain. Finally done, he sat there wondering what the hell he was supposed to do with it.

Psyché, apparently quite unembarrassed, solved that. She

came back, took the pot and replaced it in the commode. 'Let's get you tucked up again. If you need to swear, swear.'

He managed to grit his teeth and not swear, but that reminded him— 'Was the doctor here again?'

She swallowed. 'Yes. He debrided the wound.'

He hoped that excused the swearing he vaguely remembered.

'Am I allowed something to eat?'

Her smile leapt. 'You're hungry?'

Starving. 'Yes.'

'There's chicken broth keeping warm.' She hurried over to the fire.

He blanched. 'Ham and eggs?' he suggested.

Already pouring broth, she gave him a look that shot that hope down instantly. 'Broth.' Her tone of voice trampled the already dead hope into the dust. She walked over, set the broth down on the table and helped him back against the pillows. 'If this stays down, you may progress to calves' foot jelly tomorrow.'

'I can't wait,' he lied.

After the broth, which she spooned into him, his eyelids were weighted again.

Somehow she knew it and, after a very token protest, he found himself lying down again and tucked up.

He shut his eyes and drifted, listening to the soft, comforting sounds as she put things to rights. The mists cleared a little as a hand slipped into his, slender fingers sliding into place.

Nice. More than nice. Not quite how he'd envisaged being in bed with her...

Soft lips brushed across his. 'We'll do better next time, then.'

Chapter Twelve

'You are very much improved, Mr Barclay.' The doctor straightened from re-bandaging Will's wound. 'I hope I don't need to tell you that you've been damned lucky.'

'No, sir.' Will reached for his nightshirt and eased it over his head, wriggling it into place with care. He hoped like hell this was the last time he'd be poked and prodded.

'Can I get dressed now?'

Blake snorted. 'I said *improved*, boy. Not *fully recovered*. You should stay in bed a little longer. You don't want to tear that open.'

'Can I return home at least?' He'd been in Psyché's bed—sadly, by himself—for five days.

'There's no need for that.'

Psyché stood in the doorway holding a tray with a coffee pot and two cups. She had released her hair from the braids and the luxuriant curls were caught up loosely behind her head with a scarf of crimson silk.

'The deuce there isn't.' Will sat up a little straighter, ignoring the dull ache in his side. 'You're sleeping on the sofa, for God's sake!'

'That doesn't matter.'

'Yes, it does!'

Dr Blake shrugged into his coat. 'Hmm. If his lordship

sends a carriage, and you remain in bed at Moresby House for a few more days, I dare say you can be moved.'

He nodded to Will. 'Let me know. I can call on you there as easily.'

Will hid his reaction. 'Thank you, sir.' Huntercombe would be no more likely than Psyché to allow him out of bed against Blake's orders. And apparently he hadn't been poked and prodded for the last time.

Blake bowed to Psyché. 'Your servant, Miss Abeni. I'll see myself out and avail myself of a cup of your very excellent coffee downstairs. Good day!'

Will was left facing Psyché.

She fiddled with her skirts. 'I'm sorry it's so dull here and not at all what you're used to, but—'

'No.' Damn it. Now he felt guilty that she could possibly think her home, her very bed, inadequate to his finicky needs. And he liked this room. It was comfortable, soothing with the delicate watercolour paintings on the wall, plain furnishings and pretty, feminine oddments scattered about. 'It's not that at all. You've been more than kind and—'

'He would have shot me.'

'What? The Runner?' He stared at her, confused. 'I'm surprised one fired at all—if they thought you were Kit—'

'It wasn't a Runner,' she said. 'I thought you knew— remembered—it was Carshalton. He fired at me deliberately, thinking I was Kit.'

Memory flooded back.

'You stupid little bitch, Catherine! Stop or I'll shoot you myself!'

'It was nothing.' Oh, God! The last thing he wanted was her gratitude, for her to feel any obligation. 'He might have hit either of us.'

She reached out and took his hand. 'It wasn't noth- ing. And he couldn't have hit *me* because you deliberately dropped back to shield me.' Her smile trembled, doing strange things to his insides. 'Knowing that you would have done the same for Kit, or any other friend, only makes you more special.'

The blush, curse it, burned hotter than the fever. She was making him out to be some sort of hero. What kind of man let a woman take the risk she had taken? He should have tied her up and left her safely in Selbourne's shop when he'd seen that damned white velvet cloak!

But he couldn't say any of that because her eyes were wet, her mouth trembling and—

'Especially when it was my fault,' she whispered.

Her fault? It was that bastard Carshalton's fault. First, for being the sort of father who made a medieval baron look tender-hearted, second, for being the sort of fool to loose off a pistol without being sure of his shot and, third, for being the sort of bastard who would deliberately shoot at any fleeing woman, let alone his own daughter. And...

'It was my fault,' he said. 'I should never have allowed you to come at all, let alone in that blasted cloak.'

Some of the tears turned to smoke as her eyes narrowed. *'Allowed?'*

He winced.

'Just how did you propose to stop me?'

'I have no idea,' he admitted. 'Your logic was unarguable. That doesn't mean I have to like it. Or that I don't want to—' He broke off. She didn't need to hear that he wanted *her*. Or that he wanted above all to protect her. Even from himself.

'What do you want?'

He wanted...he wanted... He shifted uncomfortably as his want manifested itself in a very physical way.

'Are your pillows uncomfortable? Here. Let me.' Psyché leaned forward, bending over him to adjust the pillows at his back. And her mouth, that gorgeous, lush, warm mouth, was closer than temptation and a wish.

He braced himself carefully with one hand, reached up with the other and clasped it on the tender skin of her nape under the riot of spiralling curls. 'The thing is,' he said, 'this is not how I ever envisaged being in your bed.'

Wide brown eyes stared into his. 'It's not?'

'No.' He was aware of tension in her, of the wash of her breath, coffee, spices and sugar, along with sweet woman and a faint whiff of coconut. He wanted the kiss. Wanted it more than his own next breath. But he wanted this moment, too. This moment, caught out of time, before *now* could become…and perhaps *she* didn't want it, would protest…

But instead his name was breathed out on the softest of sighs and a smile trembled there on her lips. For him. There were the things he needed to tell her and it was important, but surely that could wait. Just for a moment, just for now…

He took the kiss and now *became*.

She had wanted the kiss. Wanted to know again the touch, the taste and texture of his mouth. It was everything, and more, than she remembered. Gentle, curious. A delight that promised enchantment. His lips were warm, firm and supple, moving tenderly against her own. Then the press of his tongue seeking, questioning. She answered, parting her lips in acceptance and invitation, falling deeper, deeper into the spell…

'Perhaps,' he murmured against her mouth, 'you might consider sharing the bed with me?'

A throat cleared in a sort of *Here we are* kind of way.

They sprang apart and Psyché was conscious of burning cheeks as she faced a shocked, middle-aged lady in the doorway, Huntercombe at her back.

'*Mother?*' Will sounded as though he'd swallowed his

pillow. 'What—how did you get here? What *brings* you here?'

Mrs Barclay approached the bed. 'A carriage. His lordship informed me that you were here when I arrived at Moresby House.'

'Ah, I had a little mishap.'

Despite her scorching cheeks, Psyché had to choke back a laugh.

Mrs Barclay narrowed her eyes. 'A bullet wound is a *little mishap*?'

This time Psyché didn't manage to control the laugh.

The lady fixed her with an icy stare. 'I am afraid I do *not* consider anything about this situation to be funny, young woman!'

Psyché shook her head. 'Nor I, Mrs Barclay. Merely Will's staggering talent for understatement.' She stood up. This changed everything.

Smiling at Huntercombe, she said, 'Dr Blake has just left. He says that it will be safe to move Mr Barclay now, as long as he remains in bed in Grosvenor Square.'

'But—'

Will's mother cut him off. 'It will be very much more convenient for me to nurse him there.'

She missed him.

She, who had guarded her privacy and her heart for so many years and never permitted a man to remain for the night, found herself turning to speak to a man who wasn't there. Her bed was lonely, even with the weight of Fiddle behind her legs every night. She had enjoyed coming up from the shop in the afternoon and sharing a pot of coffee with him along with the day's gossip.

She walked into the shop after church on Sunday morning a week after Will had left and Caleb looked up from his books. He'd taken to spending Sunday mornings in the shop reading and studying. 'You got a visitor, Miss Psyché.'

Her heart skittered. 'I do?'

He nodded. 'Mr Will's mother, I think. She came in his lordship's carriage. I thought you'd want me to take her up-stairs. She's been up there an hour or more.'

Despite the stab of disappointment, she smiled reassuringly. 'Exactly right. Thank you, Caleb.'

'I offered to make her coffee or a pot of tea, but she said as how she'd wait.'

She smiled. 'Very well. Are you going out now?'

He hesitated. 'You don't need me for anything?'

Exasperated, she made a shooing motion. 'Caleb! It's Sunday. For heaven's sake, go out and meet your friends. Have a little fun.'

He grinned and snatched up his cap. 'Thanks. I'll bring back some jellied eels if I see any.'

She laughed. 'Yes, please.' He liked to bring back a little something to share for supper on Sundays. She'd learned not to protest. 'You've got your key?' She opened the door for him.

'Aye.' He stopped in the doorway, jerking his thumb up-wards. 'Got her maid with her, she does.'

Psyché gave him a quizzical look. 'Well, of course. No lady goes anywhere without her maid or a footman. You know that.'

He shrugged. 'Yeah. But…she's like us. Thought I'd mention it.'

'I see.' She gave his shoulder a light pat. 'Thank you. Off with you now.'

Psyché stripped off her gloves as she walked into her apartment. 'Good day, Mrs Barclay. I am sorry to have kept you waiting.'

Placing the book she had been reading on the wine table,

Mrs Barclay rose from the sofa and nodded stiffly. 'Not at all. Your servant assured me you would not mind if I waited up here.' She turned to the Black maid, sitting quietly by the wall. 'Wait downstairs now, if you please.'

Psyché caught the maid's eye as she went past. 'I have left a pot of tea and some small cakes on the main shop counter. Please, make yourself comfortable.'

She smiled at Mrs Barclay. 'Tea? Or coffee, ma'am? Do be seated.'

'Thank you.' The lady sat. 'Tea would be pleasant. You did not need to trouble yourself for the girl.'

Psyché swung the kettle over the fire. 'It was no trouble.' She busied herself with the tea tray. 'I hope Will goes on well?'

'Very well, thank you. My son appears to hold you in high regard, Miss Abeni.'

She steadied the cup she'd nearly upset and gave herself a moment. 'Does he?' She glanced at her guest, who was watching her uneasily. 'I can return the compliment. He saved my life. And quite apart from that, Mr Barclay is a gentleman any woman must esteem.' Even if he did make her insides wobble like a blancmange.

She gestured to the book. 'I am glad you found a book to interest you while you waited.'

Mrs Barclay picked it up. 'Ah, yes. An interesting tale. I note that the author, a Mr Equiano, has inscribed it to you on the occasion of your sixteenth birthday. He is a connection of yours, perhaps?'

Of all the books Mrs Barclay might have chosen, she had selected *The Interesting Narrative of the Life of Olaudah Equiano*, an African captured and sold into slavery as a child, just as Mam had been.

Psyché raised her brows. 'Mr Equiano was a friend of my great-uncle, Lord Staverton. They had a number of interests in common. Sadly, he died not long after giving me his book.'

'One wonders, of course, how much credence to place in such a tale.'

Psyché clenched her fists in her skirts. 'I believe his story to be credible in every particular. It echoes much of my own mother's story of capture and enslavement. Perhaps you might care to ask Lord Huntercombe. I believe he read the early drafts.'

Mrs Barclay's lips thinned. 'His lordship, for all his undoubted excellences and many kindnesses to my son, is known for his very liberal views, of course.'

Views, Psyché was coming to suspect, that Mrs Barclay did not share. She waited for the kettle, poured boiling water into the teapot, readied the tray and took it over to the table. 'Milk? Sugar? A biscuit, perhaps?'

'A soupçon of each, if you please. No biscuit.'

Psyché handed her the cup. 'I hope it is to your liking.'

Mrs Barclay sipped. 'Thank you. Quite acceptable.' She set the cup down. 'You are very confident in yourself, are you not?'

Psyché sat down with her own tea. 'Should I not be? This is my home, situated above my business. I belong here. Why ever should I feel uncomfortable?'

'You have done very well for yourself.' Mrs Barclay glanced about the apartment. 'Very well, indeed. But I'm sure a little extra will not go astray.'

She drew a careful breath. 'Extra?'

Mrs Barclay picked up her reticule. 'I am returning home tomorrow. I should wish to make you some recompense for your service to my son.'

Psyché placed her teacup on the table with great control. 'There is no need, ma'am. Friendship counts no cost and requires no *recompense*.' Try as she might, she could not quite keep the edge out of her voice.

'This *offends* you?'

Her anger kicked the good manners Aunt Grace had instilled into the middle of next week.

'Yes, it does. There is no question of *service* between Mr Barclay and myself.'

'I see.' Mrs Barclay set the reticule down with a surprisingly heavy thud. 'You consider yourself quite the fine lady, do you not?'

Psyché laughed. 'If I were that deluded, I should still be living under my great-uncle's roof. Instead I chose to make a life for myself, using what talents I have. I consider myself an independent woman.'

'I wonder, then, that you do not remove yourself to a clime more suited to you.'

'More suited to me?'

'Yes. I found Jamaica intolerably hot, of course, but surely it would be more pleasing to you?'

The familiar apartment rocked a little around her.

'You lived in Jamaica?'

Mrs Barclay rose. 'For a time. We came home twenty years ago after my dear husband died. I must not keep you from your affairs, Miss Winthrop. I came only to make that compensation you have found so offensive, but that I, as a mother, felt the need to offer.'

Psyché stood up. 'If you feel the need to make such a gesture, ma'am, ask Lord Huntercombe to give the money to the London Committee to use in their work towards the abolition of the slave trade. That will be perfectly acceptable to me.'

Mrs Barclay's jaw sagged a little. 'I'll do that, then.'

Psyché, having seen her visitor off, walked back upstairs, her world still reeling.

He hadn't told her. Hadn't seen fit to tell her that little snippet about his background.

Chapter Thirteen

To Will's disgust, Huntercombe was very nearly as bad as his mother in his insistence on keeping him housebound.

'I promised your mother, Will. I'm supposed to keep you out of further trouble.'

To which end the wretched man had gone out and purchased half a dozen books from Hatchard's for him.

The worst of that was he simply couldn't argue. Because, without the Marquess saying as much, Will knew that Huntercombe blamed himself.

At least he'd won a concession that he might convalesce—Mrs Bentham's choice of word—in the library. Having won that battle, he submitted to being installed by the library fire to read. He didn't have a great deal of choice when every member of staff, right down to the bootboy, would rat him out to their master in a heartbeat for any rebellion.

Even though he was permitted to come downstairs, between the doctor and Huntercombe he remained confined to the house even after his mother left. He'd sent Psyché a note to let her know that his mother had gone, hoping that she would visit, but a polite little note had come back to say that she was pleased to hear he was improving. After that, nothing.

There had been little from Selbourne either. He understood that. The last thing any of them wanted was to give away any hint as to Kit's whereabouts. Kit's twenty-first birthday was still some weeks away. Until she was legally out of Carshalton's control, they could not risk him getting wind of her.

Will smiled. Kit, it seemed, had asked Selbourne via Psyché if she could learn to run the bookshop. Selbourne had leapt on the idea and enlisted Huntercombe's help in drawing up a trust to ensure that when finally Kit took over the business her father could not touch it, nor even, if she ever chose to marry, her husband.

Will set the documents on Huntercombe's desk. In his seven years as the Marquess's secretary, he'd looked over any number of legal documents and this was the tightest he'd ever seen. There was no loophole for even a mouse to squeeze through. Kit's name and Selbourne's, along with specifics of the property and business involved, had been left out. Blanks had been left so those details could be filled in later. They were taking no chance of word leaking out.

'You're certain there's no way around this?' Huntercombe was checking the second copy of the trust document, comparing it, Will noticed, to another document that he'd pulled out of his desk drawer.

The lawyer, Clinton, shook his head. 'None. However, if I may say so, my lord—' he scowled and pursed his lips '—I must say that to confer on any lady such a degree of control and independence, is *most* unwise.'

'Do you think so?' Huntercombe glanced over his reading spectacles.

The lawyer squirmed at the mild tone and Will suppressed a snort of laughter. Huntercombe was at his most lethal when he spoke like that.

'Yes, my lord.' Clinton looked at the Marquess earnestly. 'A female's delicate brain is unfit for such matters. Her natural female sensibilities must revolt at such things. And this!' He gestured to the papers. 'Even her husband would have no control!'

Will cleared his throat. 'I think that was the idea, Clinton.'

'It was.' Huntercombe removed his glasses. 'So a husband cannot circumvent it?'

Clinton shook his head. 'No, my lord.' Utter disapproval edged his assurance.

Huntercombe glanced at Will. 'Barclay?'

Will blinked. 'It looks unassailable, sir. I've never seen anything so stringent.'

Huntercombe smiled grimly. 'I have.' His glance flickered, for the merest instant, to the second document before him and Will understood.

The second document must also be a property trust drawn up to protect a woman running a business. This was how Huntercombe had known exactly what instructions to give and what questions to ask. Clinton was right; a woman being given the degree of control and independence this document would ensure was highly unusual. Will could think of only one other woman he knew to be the beneficiary of such a trust—Psyché.

He's one of her trustees, boy. Didn't you know?

The Marquess smiled. 'Excellent, then. Well done, Clinton. Thank you.'

Clinton inclined his head stiffly. 'I am glad to have been of service, my lord.'

After he'd seen the lawyer out, Huntercombe returned to the library. He let out a breath. 'Lock them up, Will. I'll show them to Selbourne tonight.'

Will cleared his throat. 'With respect, sir—'

'That sounds ominous,' observed Huntercombe.

'I will be coming with you.'

'If you have a rest this afternoon without arguing.'

'Sir, I don't argue—'

'The devil you don't.' Huntercombe seemed to be finding something highly amusing. 'But you may come on those terms.'

'Agreed.' He was pleased that he managed *not* to grind his teeth.

Huntercombe grinned openly and passed a letter over the desk. 'This was delivered yesterday while you were resting.'

Will read the letter from Selbourne—a brief missive inviting Huntercombe, *and Mr Barclay*, to supper the following evening.

He looked up at Huntercombe. 'I've been bilked,' he said drily.

Huntercombe nodded cheerfully. 'Always read the terms and conditions, Will.'

'Thank you. I'll remember that.'

Huntercombe's shoulders shook. 'In the meantime, I'm returning to Cornwall tomorrow.'

Will, putting his notes together, blinked. 'Do you wish me to go with you?'

Huntercombe leaned back in his chair. 'If you wish, but I'm only going to escort Lady Huntercombe and the children back to London.' He fiddled with his pen. 'I thought, if you were prepared to remain in London, that you could keep an eye on things.'

'Do you think Carshalton or Winthrop will cause trouble?'

Huntercombe nodded. 'Kit is safe enough in Cornwall under Cambourne's protection, but they are still watching The Phoenix. All my residences have been under watch. Bow Street, right up to and including Sir Richard Ford, is not very happy with me.'

Shock slammed into him. 'You said nothing of this, sir!'

'No. I chose not to worry you.'

'My lord—' Will barely retained control '—that was not your decision to make!'

'Will—'

'What about Psyché?' He still woke sweating from dreams in which *she* had been shot. Dreams in which her blood poured over his hands and into the gutter without ceasing. Dreams in which he wept over her body… He shoved those thoughts away. They were bad enough in the middle of the night. 'Have they dared to—?'

'Staverton forced Winthrop to back off.' Huntercombe's face was grim. 'She is perfectly safe.'

'Even so, I should have been informed.' He forced himself to speak calmly. This was Huntercombe. A man to whom he owed everything, not least affection and respect.

Huntercombe sighed. 'My apologies, Will.'

Will blinked. 'What? You don't have to—'

Huntercombe smiled. 'Yes, I do. You acted for me—'

'I acted for myself!'

'I understand that. But nevertheless, you responded initially on my behalf. No one, least of all myself, would have blamed you if you had awaited instructions.' Huntercombe paused. 'You never did tell me why you returned to London early.'

'No. I didn't.' And he didn't want to. Not after that last row with his mother and Rob.

Huntercombe cleared his throat. 'I see.'

Will suspected that he probably did.

'The point is that you acted.' The older man's fists clenched. 'I'm not sure I could have handled the business as well.'

'Well, of course—'

'There's no *of course* about it, Will.' Huntercombe's mouth flattened. 'My involvement would have brought them down on The Phoenix like an avalanche. You were far more effective. Speaking of which—' He frowned.

'Sir?'

'I had a letter from Foxworthy the other day.' Huntercombe pulled out a letter and passed it to him. 'He's ill.'

'I'm sorry to hear that, sir.' Foxworthy was Huntercombe's London agent, hardworking and intelligent.

'I went to see him and, after speaking to him and his wife, I've told him to take at least a month's leave. I thought you might act in his stead.'

'I'll remain in London then.' He could barely keep his voice steady. He wanted the chance to see Psyché again, when he was neither caught up in Kit's flight, nor recovering from a bullet wound. And the thought that Psyché might be in any sort of danger resulting from Kit's escape shook him to the core.

Huntercombe frowned. 'You wish to remain in London, don't you?'

'Yes.'

'Should I ask why?'

Will swallowed. 'I would have to ask you to mind your own business.' He fully intended to call on Psyché the moment his time was his own. If she didn't want him, well, he hoped he was gentleman enough to accept her decision, but he needed to know.

Huntercombe nodded slowly. 'I can't blame you. And—' he let out a frustrated breath '—she would say exactly the same.' His mouth twitched. 'Both of you too polite to tell me to go to Hades!'

Selbourne greeted them downstairs.

'Come up! Come up!' He scanned Will. 'The stairs will not be too much, Barclay?'

Will groaned. 'Not you, too, sir? Huntercombe is quite as bad as my mother!'

Huntercombe snorted. 'He's not a co-operative patient, Ignatius.'

'I was very co-operative,' Will argued. 'I took all my medicine, stayed in bed and tried not to upset my mother.'

'Yes. I heard about that.' Selbourne followed them up the stairs. 'We've another guest tonight.'

'Oh?'

'You'll see.'

Selbourne ushered them into a spacious, book-lined room upstairs. A table by the window overlooking the street was set for four and from a chair by the fire rose…

'Psyché.'

Every fibre in Will's body leapt at the sight of her. Completely disregarding the others, he went forward, hands outstretched.

She hesitated, and his heart stilled, but she laid her hands in his. 'You're better. I… I'm glad.'

The quiet reserve in her voice, in her bearing, shocked him.

Psyché had given some thought to declining the invitation to supper. Supper in Selbourne's rooms above the shop was always delightful. Good company, excellent if simple food, and a very fine claret. Knowing Will would be there shook her to the core, but refusing an invitation from Ignatius without reason was impossible. She couldn't do it. So she told herself that she was an adult, that she was perfectly capable of sitting across a table from Will Barclay without her heart skipping beats and her memory proving inconveniently acute.

Even the growing puppy, play wrestling by the fire with Ignatius's tabby cat, failed to distract her from that kiss they'd shared… The kiss Will had initiated and she had accepted. The kiss *they* had wanted. His fingers warm on the nape of her neck, drawing her down, inviting her in. And his mouth, so gentle and curious. In that moment they had been united.

She believed with everything she was that they had wanted the same thing—each other. How could she want a man who had not told her the truth? That his family had owned slaves. Her stomach churned. For all she knew his family could still have interests in Jamaica.

Her gaze drifted to Will, watching as the cat, tired of the pup's antics, delivered a cuff and arched her back with a hiss. The pup subsided, curled up and went to sleep.

'Where *did* you get that dog, Ignatius?' Huntercombe sipped his wine. 'You've always preferred cats.'

'An unexpected Christmas present.' Ignatius eyed the pup with resignation. 'One I couldn't refuse. But Kit likes dogs and since it's clearly first cousin to a bear I thought it might be useful.'

Huntercombe laughed. 'True.' He smiled at Psyché. 'Do you think of getting another dog?'

She did sometimes. She missed Nyx by the fire, at her heels. But how could she give a dog enough exercise? 'Not yet.'

He smiled, and patted her hand. 'Let me know when you are ready. I'll give you a pup.'

Psyché's heart melted for this kindly man who had so willingly seconded her uncle and aunt in giving her a new life. 'Thank you.'

'I'm sorry to break up the evening, Ignatius.' Huntercombe finished his wine at the end of the meal and set the glass down. 'But I am leaving for Cornwall in the morning, so I had better be on my way.'

Psyché took a controlled breath. If Huntercombe was leaving tomorrow, he might not return for a month or two. And Will would go with him. Perhaps it was for the best. Time and distance might dull what had flared between them, or at least what had flared in her. But she needed to speak with him, ask him why he'd never told her.

Selbourne rose. 'You have my thanks again—all of you.' The old man's smile encompassed the three of them.

Will glanced at Huntercombe. 'Shall I fetch the carriage, sir?'

'Thank you, Will.' Huntercombe turned to Ignatius. 'Cambourne will escort Kit to London after her birthday. I'll get word to you after I've spoken to Cambourne.'

Psyché took a steadying breath and reminded herself that an independent woman made her own decisions. If she didn't act now, he would be gone.

'Perhaps, Will, you might walk me across the road on your way to the Lion?'

He bowed. 'Of course.'

The picture of decorum, they walked downstairs together, through the shadows of the bookshop, to the front door.

'We need to talk, Psyché.'

The quiet voice sliced at her.

'Do we?'

'Yes. Even…even if you no longer want me as your lover, there are things I need to tell you, that I should have confessed to you long since.' He reached past her to open the door and cold air swirled in to twist around her with the surge of pain.

'That you'd lived in Jamaica? Owned slaves? Your mother mentioned it in passing.'

She made to step past him—the hand on her wrist, the merest touch, checked her. 'My *mother*?'

'She called on me.'

He cursed under his breath. 'I'm sorry.' He took her hand between both of his. She did not pull it back, but she forced her hand to lie passive in his.

'Why did you not tell me?' she asked. 'Did you think you could *not* tell me? That it wouldn't matter?'

He let out another frustrated curse. 'It looks like that,

I know. And believe me, it wasn't something I wanted to have to tell you.' He caught her other hand, raised them both between them. 'As it turned out, events moved rather too fast. I really wasn't intending to get shot that night.'

'You were going to tell me *then*?'

'Afterwards, yes,' he said. 'I thought we might return to your apartment, and I could tell you. Before that, well, there was Kit and we were busy planning her escape.'

She bit her lip. 'And then you were shot. But you *had* decided to tell me?'

He frowned. 'No. That sounds as though it were something I might have decided *not* to tell you. That was never a possibility. From the moment—' He broke off, cleared his throat.

'From the moment?' she prompted.

'From the moment I knew that I wanted you, that *we* wanted each other,' he said, 'I was always going to tell you. *Before* we became lovers. I'm sorry.'

The street was quiet save for the lively scrape of a fiddle in the Red Lion. Light spilled from a few windows and the lantern Psyché carried gave a little more.

'You were going to tell me.' She believed that. 'What have you to be sorry for?'

'My past. If you find it unforgivable—'

'You were a child. I don't blame you for that. And if you've been working for Huntercombe all these years something changed for you.'

He let out a breath. 'I heard Clarkson speak when I was up at Oxford. Thomas Clarkson, the Abolitionist.'

'I've met him.'

'Then you'll understand that he forced me to think, to question the whole basis of my family's wealth.' A short, harsh laugh broke from him. 'They were horrified when I came down for the summer. Every effort was made to return me to my senses.'

'I can imagine.'

'Psyché, if you no longer want me—'

'I *do* want you.' More than she could possibly say, more than she would have believed she could want any man a month ago. And now he was leaving London. Perhaps for months. 'Will you write to me from Cornwall?'

Her breath caught as his free arm came around her and she found herself a great deal closer to the warmth and temptation of his body than she had intended.

For an instant time hovered in the eternity of *maybe*, but then he seemed to recollect himself and eased back, breaking the spell.

'I'm not going to Cornwall.'

'Not going to Cornwall?' Her pulse beat wildly, insanely.

'I'm remaining in London to see to some business for Huntercombe.'

They stepped off the pavement. He'd be in Grosvenor Square, but—

'With your…permission, I thought to take a room at the Lion. For…er…appearances' sake.'

Her pulse was now a dancing, lilting rhythm that sang and fizzed all through her. 'A room at the Lion.' God help her, she was doing a passable imitation of a parrot!

'I can stable a horse there and I believe they offer a good laundry service.' He sounded utterly reasonable.

'Convenient.' Wonderful. She'd found an original word and they were on the other side of the street without, she'd swear, her feet touching the ground once.

'I thought so,' he said, still with that maddening, *wicked* gravity in his voice. 'I have your permission, then? I may come to you?' Only the tautness of his arm under her hand betrayed the tension in him.

Her permission. Instead of simply taking the room and presenting her with a *fait accompli*, he was asking if she wanted that. If she would welcome him into her bed, rather than assuming she would fall at his feet in gratitude.

She strove to match his seeming calm. An almost impossible task when her feet danced an inch above the ground and her pulse bubbled like champagne. 'On one condition.'

'Name it.'

'That after your business for the day is done, you don't spend *too* much time in your room at the Lion.'

There was a short silence. '*That's* your only condition?'

It surprised her, too. They had reached the front door of The Phoenix. She unlocked the door and stared at the key before holding it out to him.

'You'll need this. I've a spare, so you can let yourself in after—'

She stopped at his startled expression. Oh, God! She'd been too bold. 'I'm sorry. I thought… I thought you meant to stay tonight.'

His silence was damning. She'd shocked him. Perhaps even disgusted him with her eagerness and—

He took the key and his swift, urgent kiss, the arms that closed hard around her, banished all thought of having shocked and disgusted him. 'Sweetheart,' he murmured at last against her temple, 'I wasn't expecting the keys to the kingdom.'

She took a shaken breath. She hadn't been expecting to hand them over.

Will strode down to the Red Lion, passing a small, black carriage whose driver was huddled into his coat and muffler. A wonder the poor devil hadn't sought shelter for himself and his horses at the Red Lion, even if the horses were rugged up. He dismissed it from his mind as he turned into the yard.

Huntercombe's coachman stuck his head out of a stall. 'Hitch 'em up, Mr Will?'

'Yes. He's ready, Masters.' Will thought, for all of five seconds, about simply leaving a message for Huntercombe with the coachman…he couldn't do it. Simply couldn't do it.

'I'll walk back, and let his lordship know you're coming.'

'Aye, Mr Will.' Masters removed a rug. 'Won't be long.'

After checking the kitchen fire, Psyché hurried up the stairs to the apartment, fizzing with nerves she had never known before. Somehow, although there had been other men in her life, this was different. She *wanted* more. More from herself, more from him. She'd given him a *key*.

What was she *thinking*?

An affair. It could be no more than that. A very special affair, perhaps, but no more. She had decided years ago that marriage was a risk she dared not take. Not when marriage put every scrap of power into a husband's hands. Even though her inheritance had been tied up six ways from Sunday as Uncle Theo had once expressed it, she shuddered at the thought of submitting to the power of any man.

She reached the small landing and pushed the door open. Her dreams of marriage had died when she was seventeen.

Besides, Will was white. He might be fond of her, might care for her, he might even think he loved her. But he would never wish to marry her. So they were both safe from—

She nearly dropped the lantern as a figure arose from one of the fireside chairs.

Huntercombe was browsing among the books in the shop with Selbourne when Will tapped on the door. His lordship looked up and smiled, tucking a book under his arm. He said something to Selbourne, who nodded as they walked to the door.

'Thank you for a pleasant evening, Ignatius.' Huntercombe shook the older man's hand. 'Will, you might be so kind as to arrange payment for this volume since you are remaining in London.'

'Certainly, sir.' Will smothered a laugh. Huntercombe rarely escaped a bookshop unscathed. 'Goodnight, Mr Selbourne. Thank you for supper.'

Selbourne snorted, holding out a hand for Will to shake. 'Thank *you*. It's good to see you recovered. Come by again. You'll always be welcome.'

Huntercombe adjusted his muffler. 'Don't stand in the cold, Ignatius. The carriage will be along very shortly.'

Selbourne gripped his hand. 'Thank you again, Hunt. I can never repay—'

'Don't be a damned fool. Go inside before you catch your death and I have to explain *that* to everyone.'

Selbourne complied, closing the door behind them.

Will cleared his throat. 'Ah, sir. There's something I must tell you.'

'You're not coming home tonight, are you, Will?'

'I'm not—' He stared. For pity's sake—was the man a mind reader? And was he about to have a glove slapped in his face?

But Huntercombe's expression did not suggest anger or sorrow. Rather, he looked worried…

'Sir?'

'Hunt.'

'What?'

Huntercombe sighed. 'You've been my secretary for seven years, Will. You know me as well as any man alive. I certainly consider you my friend, despite nearly twenty years between us. It's Hunt.'

Will was speechless for a moment. 'I… I'm not sure I can do that.' Cambourne had said very much the same thing, but Huntercombe? That was different. He realised with a shock that he thought of Huntercombe more as a father than anything else.

'You'll get used to it,' Huntercombe said drily. He sighed. 'I certainly do not have any right to interfere with your private life, Will. Nor hers, but when I see Psyché, before I see an intelligent, beautiful woman, I see a little girl many thought Staverton ought to have quietly sent back to Jamaica.' He was silent for a moment. 'I see a vulnerable child for whom Staverton enlisted my protection should she ever need it and he was not there to give it. However, Psyché has made it very clear that she wishes to chart her own course. While there are certainly instances where I would step in to protect her whether she liked it or not, this is not one of them.'

'You do not think that I am taking advantage of her?'

Huntercombe laughed. 'She is more than capable of sending you to the rightabout should you attempt it. Besides, I know you rather better than that, Will. Your mother, though—'

'My mother has nothing to say to this.'

'On the contrary. She had a great deal to say.'

After a moment during which Will absorbed the fact that his mother had apparently confronted Huntercombe over Psyché, he said, 'I beg your pardon, sir. I hope—'

'She wished me to use my influence with you.'

'But—'

'I'm afraid I told her that the only influence I had ever exerted over you was to encourage you to think for yourself. Ah. Here comes the carriage.' Huntercombe held out his hand. 'Goodnight, Will. I will be back in London in about a month.'

Chapter Fourteen

'Who—Lucius? What are you doing here? And how did you get in?'

Psyché's heart hammered. She had locked, bolted and barred the back door before leaving for supper, and the front door… Yes, she'd had to unlock it—

'I borrowed Staverton's key, of course.' He shrugged. 'How should I have known when you might be home? I was hardly going to wait in the street!'

His arrogance took her breath away. 'Give it to me.'

He looked down his nose at her. 'Give you what?'

'*My key.* You have no right to it.'

He took it from his pocket and dropped it on the table. 'There.'

She stalked over and took it. Not that it mattered now. She would have to change the locks… Then it hit her. Fear knotted in her belly, chilled her. 'Uncle Theo—is something wrong with him?'

Lucius looked surprised. 'No. Not as far as I know. Why should there be?'

Relief edged her rising suspicion. 'Because I can't think of a single reason he would have let you "borrow" my key. Which means you took it without his permission.' The smirk on his face told her she was right.

'So, Lucius, why are you here?' She kept her gaze on his face, saw the flare of outrage at her familiarity wipe away the smirk.

She had hoped he did not know where she lived. But if he'd seen the Runners' report… Her skin crawled. This man who would have forced Kit into marriage was the same man who would have condemned *her* to a living death.

He shifted. 'This business the other week—Carshalton mistaking you for his daughter.' He manufactured a concerned expression. 'Surely it's only natural I should wish to assure myself you were not harmed.'

She considered telling him he'd left it a little late for plausibility, but decided to play the game out. 'I was not harmed at all. Rather Mr Barclay was wounded.' That much he would already know.

'Quite so, quite so. Most unfortunate. Huntercombe's secretary, I believe.' Lucius paced a little, glancing about him with a little sneer. 'Not quite what you're used to after Highwood House, is it? And not even a maid to lend you countenance.'

'I'm not lonely.' She drifted, seemingly aimless, but got the sofa between them. 'What did you wish to speak about?'

His mouth hardened. 'This business of Carshalton's daughter—Catherine.'

'Is that her name?' If she could get him talking, he might reveal something.

'Yes. You must know that I am very distressed at her disappearance.'

'Oh?'

He seemed not to know quite what to do with that. 'You did not know that I was—*am*—betrothed to Miss Carshalton?'

'I had heard that,' she admitted.

He nodded. 'Yes. A nice thing when one's bride vanishes! If she cannot be recovered soon, her reputation will be in tatters!'

'That would be very dreadful for you,' Psyché said mildly.

'Exactly. She must be found. The thing is, we know that Selbourne arranged her abduction—'

'I thought she ran away?'

'No such thing!' He looked outraged. 'She had no reason to run away. She was about to make a very fine match, much to her benefit.'

'But why would Mr Selbourne abduct her?' Psyché allowed shock to creep into her voice. 'I thought he was fond of her? I mean, if she were about to marry so happily?'

Lucius gave her a condescending glance. 'Selbourne's vaunted affection is no deeper than his desire to get his hands on a portion of Carshalton's fortune.'

'Fancy that.' Psyché heard a faint thump as the bar on the front door dropped into place.

'I do not know what you may have been told, but it is most important that Catherine is found as soon as possible. Carshalton is offering a reward for information.'

'A reward.' So that was it. A bribe. 'How interesting. Perhaps Carshalton should have mentioned that before shooting poor Mr Barclay.'

Lucius scowled. 'Your "*poor Mr Barclay*" is a scoundrel who has misled you very seriously. The involvement of Huntercombe in this shocking business—'

'You aren't suggesting *he* wants to marry Miss Carshalton?' Psyché asked. 'He's already married, you know. Besides, abducting heiresses doesn't seem at all the sort of thing he would do.' She kept her voice calm, but every instinct screamed a warning.

'Huntercombe has some baseless grudge against Carshalton,' Lucius said. 'He has hit upon this way of revenging himself by abducting Catherine to help his old colleague Selbourne and ensuring that her reputation is besmirched. The involvement of his secretary confirms it. Owing to your limited understanding of the habits of good society, you have been very foolish, Psyché, but if you co-operate—'

'Permit me to sum up, Lucius.' Psyché spoke clearly, praying Will would hear her and realise she was not alone. Her singing master would have been proud of the projection she achieved. 'You believe that Lord Huntercombe arranged the abduction of Miss Carshalton for Mr Selbourne with the assistance of his secretary, Mr Barclay. And that *I* assisted them?'

His right hand moved towards his coat pocket and Psyché stilled utterly.

'No doubt they duped you with some tale or other, but if you won't—'

Will had heard enough.

'It must have been quite a tale, Winthrop.' He stalked into the apartment, his hand on his sword. 'Perhaps you would care to explain your presence?'

Winthrop stared. 'Who the devil are you, sir? And how dare you simply walk in here as if—'

'As if he were invited?' Psyché's voice put sugar to the blush. 'As opposed to having stolen a key from Staverton House?'

Cold anger smoked through Will's veins. 'He did *what*?'

'Who *is* this?' Winthrop demanded.

Will turned to him slowly. 'Will Barclay.' He firmed his grip on the sword. 'I believe you were saying something about my involvement in abducting a young lady?'

Winthrop scowled. 'Listen, Barclay. You've made a

grave mistake becoming involved in this. Whatever grudge Huntercombe thinks he has against Carshalton—'

'Grudge,' Will repeated the word thoughtfully. 'Yes. I suppose a man could be construed as having a *grudge* if someone attempted to have his ten-year-old stepson killed. Very petty indeed. But I believe it is time for you to be leaving.'

He glanced at Psyché. 'I'll see your visitor out, shall I?'

'*We* will see him out.' The edge on her voice suggested that any request for her to remain safely upstairs would not be appreciated. He merely nodded and gestured for Winthrop to precede him.

'After you, Winthrop. Psyché, will you bring the lantern?'

For one blazing instant he thought Winthrop would do something stupid, but the fellow turned on his heel and stalked out.

Psyché, lantern in hand, was beside him in a heartbeat. 'Watch him,' she murmured. 'Right pocket. A pistol, I think.'

Will's veins iced. What if he'd been delayed, or hadn't been returning? What if—? He thrust the distraction of *what ifs* aside. He nodded and followed Winthrop down the stairs, careful to stay back far enough so he could watch the man's hands.

But Winthrop made no move to try for the pistol if indeed he had one. They reached the front door and Psyché set the lantern down and unlocked the door.

'Elaborate precautions for a second-rate shop,' Winthrop sneered.

Psyché's smile flashed. 'For the second-rate intruders, Lucius. Goodnight.'

He strode through the door, glanced down the street and raised one hand. The small black carriage Will had noticed earlier started forward, but Winthrop turned back.

'Tell me, Barclay—I was acquainted with a George Barclay years ago. Older than myself. He's been dead these twenty years. A connection of yours by any chance?'

The carriage had nearly reached them and Will's skin prickled. 'Very likely you refer to my father.'

As the carriage drew up, he caught Psyché's arm, dragged her back into the shop and slammed the door. He turned the key immediately.

'Will—?'

Will shook his head, gestured for her to step back and shot the bolts. Psyché, ignoring his wordless instruction, cracked open a small, sliding port he'd never noticed in the wall beside the door.

Together they listened, scarcely breathing, on either side of the opening.

The carriage rumbled to a halt.

'Sir? Thought you said—'

'Shut up!'

'But where's—?'

'One more word and you're dismissed!'

'Yes, sir.'

The carriage door opened and closed. With a rumble of wheels and a clatter of hooves it rolled off down the street.

'Damn,' Psyché muttered. 'We might have learnt something. Probably he could see the light through the peep.' She closed it.

'We did learn something,' Will said grimly. 'He wasn't expected to be alone.' He forced himself to stay calm. 'He was after you. And when you declined to co-operate he was prepared to take you by force.'

She caught her breath. 'To force me to tell them where Kit is? He offered a bribe, but—'

'I doubt he meant to pay up. But if he could get you outside…' Will let out a very careful breath. 'Now he knows

I'm here for the night.' He gave her a level glance. 'We'd better make it clear that I'm here indefinitely.'

Psyché opened her mouth and closed it. There were some arguments you couldn't win and she'd tilted at enough windmills in her life to recognise one when she saw it. Instead, she lifted the bar.

'I was intending to be a little more discreet than that.'

'Yes.' He helped her set the heavy bar. 'So was I. But your safety trumps discretion.'

The laugh that escaped felt wild, uncontrolled. She bore down. 'Are you staying to make love with me, or to protect me?'

He hesitated and she felt as though something in her was waiting, desperate for the answer.

'Are you accepting me as your lover?'

'Can you accept that I will be *your* lover, not your mistress?' She would never take a man who saw her as anything less than his equal.

His smile shook her to the core. 'I really can't afford a mistress as such, you know. But, yes. So my protection goes without saying, sweetheart.'

Her breath suddenly ragged at the heat in his eyes, she held out her hand. 'Come then.'

There were no more words as she led him back up the stairs and into the apartment, just the lantern and the shadows that shifted around them in gentle benediction. She took a moment to tend the fire, banking it for the night.

When she rose to douse the lamp he was watching her, fiercely intent. 'No lamp?'

She touched a taper to the fire. 'This will be enough.'

The lit taper danced and trembled in her hand as she brought it into the bedroom. She did not often light the bedroom fire, but tonight was for warmth and joy, light and truth. It was the work of a moment to touch the taper to the kindling, add coals as it caught.

Light flared, surrounding them, infusing them as she straightened and lifted her hand to touch his cheek, trace the slightly scratchy line of his jaw with her fingertips. He stood utterly still as she traced the edge of his lower lip, felt the warmth, the heat rising between them.

'Psyché,' he whispered.

It was statement and question all in one and her name had never sounded so sweet. As though the man who spoke tasted it on his tongue like the richest chocolate.

'Yes.' Such a simple word to encompass so much. She wanted it to mean everything between them. Consent, reassurance, joy and desire. She rose on her toes, slipped her arms around his neck and touched her mouth to his.

The very air fizzed about them as slowly, slowly they deepened the kiss. She neither knew nor cared who was kissing, or who was kissed. They kissed each other as though they had been starved and this was a feast set before them. Trembling fingers found knots—her fichu, his cravat—and buttons, laces—his waistcoat and shirt, her bodice. Searching hands found bare flesh and fire-lit shadow played and gleamed on fair skin and bronze. A meeting, a melding, more than mere bodies wanting.

This was more. Something altogether deeper and more urgent. She had known pleasure, had given herself before with affection and desire. But this... Her head spun and her heart, her foolish heart, whirled after it.

Will's mouth on hers, his taste—the man himself, spiced with wine and coffee—on her tongue. His hands, sure and gentle on her body. The drawstring of her chemise gave way at a tug and his forehead rested on hers, his unsteady breathing an echo of her own as he lightly traced the upper curve of one breast through the linen.

'Love?'

Oh, yes. She wanted that. Wanted to know fully the delight of his hands on her breasts. But when he bared her, what would he see? Want slid in hot ripples under her skin. Burning, demanding. She wanted everything. All the more since he took nothing of her for granted. Could he accept all of her? She could only know by risking.

'Yes. Yes, please.'

Another tug and the chemise fell open, baring her. She heard the sharp intake of his breath and then his caressing fingers made the linen free of one shoulder. He bent to her, kissed the strong curve. Her own hands shook as she returned the favour, eased his shirt tails from his breeches and helped him to pull it over his head, baring him to the waist.

Her eyes devoured him, and she leaned forward, pressed her mouth to the hollow at the base of his throat, dabbing at the slight saltiness with her tongue.

A rough groan broke from him and his mouth captured hers. A taking this time, a demand, fierce and hot, that she answered with everything in her. Clothes were cast aside, falling unheeded until only his breeches and boots, and her chemise remained between them. And then his hands slid over her hips, were at the hem of her chemise. And stilled.

Against her lips, the sweetest murmur—'You permit?'

Permit? Her throat tight with unshed tears, she eased back, set her own hands to the garment and lifted it slowly over her head. For an instant, before his wondering gaze, she held it to her breasts, then opened her fingers and let it fall. Let him see.

Chapter Fifteen

Will's mouth dried. For a moment he saw only *her*, the lovely wholeness of her. She stood before him, all gleaming, mysterious shadows in the firelight. Tall, slender, her tight curls, freed from all constraint, tumbled about her shoulders.

Shyness assailed him. What an oaf he must seem to her, this goddess revealed to his clumsy, mortal gaze. And there was the ugly scar now beneath his ribs, jagged and purple.

But then he saw and his own scar was as nothing. There, just below her right shoulder where her breast began its lovely rise—obscenity had been scorched into her living flesh in the shape of a *W*. For a moment he could not breathe as pain, shame, grief and rage all warred within him.

'I'm sorry.' Useless, inadequate words. Both for what had been done to her and to express his own guilt and shame.

'No, Will,' she whispered. '*You* did not do it, you were not responsible.'

Wasn't he?

'We all did it.'

A child. She had been a *child* when her—

'He was your—'

'He was my *master*, Will,' she said. 'He sired me, but he

was not my father. Not then. Not ever really, but certainly not then. Neither in my thoughts nor his.'

She came to him, raised her mouth to his in a gentle kiss. 'Don't put this between us, Will. Don't give them that.'

He answered her kiss. How could he not? And felt her fingers trace the bullet's searing path.

'Will.' The softest murmur. 'My Will. My warrior.'

Oh, God, he was nothing of the sort. He was—

She reached for the falls of his breeches.

He swallowed, as lust, desire, need and want stormed through him as the first button gave.

'Psyché. Love.' He had to fight just to breathe, had to remind himself to think.

'Hmm?'

Another button fell, on the opposite side to the first. God, he loved a methodical woman. What was left of his mind threatened to combust spontaneously. He caught her wrist, drew her fingers away from the third button—right beneath the first.

'Love, if you keep doing that, there's every chance I won't even get my boots off.' And while the heated, uncivilised, unregenerate part of him suggested that the boots weren't actually in the way, the remaining chivalrous, albeit feeble, corner of his brain thought they really ought to go.

The husky chuckle that escaped her did nothing to cool him, merely nudged the chivalrous, thinking part of him firmly aside.

'My apologies. It's been a while.'

His struggling brain reasserted itself marginally.

'Then you've...you aren't...'

He sounded like a halfwit and that was being generous. She drew back a little and he could have kicked his own sorry behind. Except his boots—hell! He was still wearing them!—were stuck in the quagmire he'd created.

'A virgin?' Her voice was even, uninflected, telling him precisely nothing.

Yes. That.

He nodded.

'N-no.' Only the slight hesitation betrayed her discomfort. 'Should I be?'

Should she? Should *he*?

'I'm not,' he admitted. 'Why should you be?'

That husky laugh again and her shoulders shook with it. And not just her shoulders.

'Because society invents all sorts of contradictory rules for women that never apply to men. Do you mind?'

'That I'm not a virgin?' He smiled at her. 'Not if you don't.'

Her smile bloomed. 'Not in the least. Shall I help you with your boots?' A wicked edge honed the smile. 'Or... not?'

'Not?' His mind went in at least three directions, all of them ungentlemanly.

'Mmm.' She almost herded him to the bed. 'Excellent choice.'

He was, he realised on a shock of delight, as the backs of his thighs hit the bed, being seduced. Or ravished.

He rather thought it was the latter.

But a man had his pride, damn it. He drew her down with him and rolled to bring her under him. And saw white-hot stars that sliced through him like the pistol ball all over again.

He swore, as sweat that had nothing to do with desire broke out all over him.

She half came up on one elbow. 'Will?'

'It's nothing.' Damned if he'd—

'Let's try this.' She sat up, shadows and firelight sliding on lithe curves, the dark mass of curls tumbling around her shoulders. One gentle hand pressed him back, the other stroked the length of his aching cock with wicked knowledge.

'I don't think he minds at all,' she murmured.

Will choked out a laugh. 'I can attest. Perhaps you'd like my boots?'

There was a sultry chuckle as she straddled him. 'Maybe next time.'

The thought that there could be a next time sang through him, but he put it aside. *Now* was what he had. *Now* was important. *Now* was beautiful and vibrant. He set his hands to her hips and drew her down against him. Not that she needed guidance, but he needed to touch, to feel, needed to show her how much he wanted her.

She used her body, sliding over his with that lush, wet heat until his control quaked, pleasuring him and herself until he could take no more.

With a groan he reached between them, positioned himself at the tight, wet entrance. A gasp broke from her and she eased down a little way as he stroked and teased the sensitive nub of her sex, his other hand at her breasts. And he watched, spellbound, as she held there, kneeling above him, rocking, teasing them both with the promise of more, until with a growl of need Will grasped her hips and brought her down firmly, sheathing himself to the hilt. Her head fell back, her mouth open on a silent cry.

Pleasure, hot and deep, speared her as his body slid within hers. Her eyes closed at the nigh unbearable pressure of this first possession. His of her, and hers of him. And his hands—oh, God, his hands! One at her sex, sure and knowing, the other at her breasts a tender delight. She held still for a moment, to feel, to absorb it all. He filled her so completely, in ways she had never known, the earthy, physical pleasure soaking into her heart and soul. Changing them, changing *her*. Then, as his hands shifted back to her hips and thighs, she opened her eyes to look down.

The contrast, his pale, strong hands against her dark flesh, stirred her. Kneading, loving—so beautiful. Dark and light fitting together to make a lovely wholeness. She tried to rock, but he held her down now and moved under her, driving deep, so deep. And she was close, burning on the edge, desperate to go over. But he held her there in that blazing need, his eyes fierce on hers, hands locked on her hips and his shaft hard inside her.

One hand slid from her hip, through the wet curls to find her. He stroked and she gasped and rocked, frantic for more. He pressed, her head fell back on a wild cry as the world convulsed inside her, and she tumbled, sobbing from the cliff, everything that she was, or could be, burning.

She collapsed on to him as the shocks rolled through her and he groaned in pleasure, his mouth as hot and demanding as the rhythm of his thrusts. He rolled them and she was beneath him, his weight and heat covering her as he drove deep, again and again, until with a strangled curse, he pulled free and spent himself beside her.

She knew an instant's regret mingled with tenderness that he had retained enough sanity to do his best to avoid that complication.

Her head nestled on Will's shoulder, Psyché listened to his breathing as his big, gentle hand stroked her back. Beneath her cheek his heart beat steady and true. She thought that her own heart might never regain its true rhythm and pace. She wasn't sure she knew what that was any more.

What had she done?

She'd never done *this* before. Never lain fully relaxed and warm, entangled with a lover in the aftermath. Her first brief experiences at eighteen had been with one of her uncle's under-gardeners. She had chosen Jesse very deliberately because he was like her—the child of a slave woman and a planter.

Uncle Theo had given Jesse a position and his freedom after his erstwhile owner, who was also his sire, had attempted to ship him back to Jamaica for sale. Psyché had given him her virginity one balmy summer's evening after Hetty's wedding.

Secrecy had been imperative for Jesse's sake no less than her own. She had liked him, respected him, and she had certainly not wanted him to risk his livelihood for her.

She had taken another lover here in Soho, but it occurred to her now that she had never even considered giving Hugo a key, nor had he ever stayed the night. It had simply been sex, friendly and enjoyable. But he had found her brand disturbing and when they drifted apart she had accepted it with equanimity. Hugo had also been a little shocked and hurt when he realised that she was taking precautions to avoid pregnancy. He had insisted that *of course* he would do the right thing if she became pregnant. He had not liked that she preferred to rely on herself.

A couple of other men had courted her with an eye to marriage and she had blocked them at once. She had The Phoenix and her freedom. And although The Phoenix remained hers if she married because Uncle Theo had seen to that in the trust that protected her, she remained uneasy about the power a man had in marriage.

Recently she had avoided the complication of men. Partly because she was unwilling to lead a man on, hoping for more than she would give. And partly because *she* had wanted more, only she had had no idea what that more might be, or how she might have it safely.

She had a dreadful suspicion that she now knew exactly what that *more* was. But how could she have known? This terrifying intimacy of lying safe and sated in a man's arms was completely new and she doubted that it would have felt so disconcertingly right with either Jesse or Hugo. They had been good men—kind, honest, affectionate even. But—

Neither of them had been Will.

And Will was safe. He would never want marriage, so her freedom, her independence would never be required of her. They could have a long-term affair without risk on either side.

But as that large, warm hand stroked, now circling her bottom, she wished for a world where there were no restrictions, no risks and no fear. She did not want to be other than she was. That would be to wish away Mam, or Uncle Theo, and she could not wish away love. So she snuggled closer to what she had. He had seen her brand and grieved. He hated that it had been done to her, but he had not been embarrassed as Hugo had been.

Will's arms tightened and a kiss brushed against her temple.

'Maybe you should have worn my boots,' he said thoughtfully.

Laughter shook her from her introspection. 'What?' She lifted her head and wanted to fall into those smiling eyes and stay there.

'Well, you rode me so beautifully.'

'Did I?'

'Mmm.'

There was a speculative glint in his eye and the world flipped over.

Or she did. Utterly breathless, she found herself laughing up at him and the glint in his eye had gone from speculation to satisfaction.

'However...' he stole a kiss '...that will have to wait.'

His weight—hard, male and so satisfying on her—stole her breath.

'Wait?' Why not right now?

'Mmm.' Another kiss, deep and hungry. 'Because this

time—' his body, fully recovered, confirmed that *this time* was indeed right now '—this time, *I* am going to ride *you*.'

'Oh.' His wound. She should say something to—no. He was an adult.

She trailed her fingers along his flank. 'Do you ride well, sir?'

His eyes darkened. 'You'll have to tell me.'

He rode extremely well. So well that she had no breath left to tell him anything. Instead, she fell asleep in his arms, only waking when he rose to put more coals on the fire. She lay quietly, watching him crouch there in the firelight. He came back to the bed through the shadows and slipped in.

Perhaps he wouldn't want to hold her again, perhaps he would roll over and—

He gathered her in so gently that if she'd been asleep she would not have woken. She lifted her head and placed a kiss on his jaw.

'Love?'

Yes, oh, yes. God help her, but she did. Her throat ached and she dared not speak, so simply kissed him again. He turned his head to capture her mouth and drew her deep. Long, tender kisses that promised everything. They made love again, slowly and quietly, and Psyché knew she was irretrievably lost. Nothing could ever be the same after this. After him. And she admitted in the silence of her heart as she drifted towards sleep that, if knowing her fate she could have avoided it, she would still have chosen the same path.

Will discovered that Psyché, a working shopkeeper, rose hours before the winter sun. By the time he dragged his clothes on in some sort of order, including his boots, she was downstairs cooking breakfast. He knew that because the aroma of eggs and coffee wafted up the stairs as he jogged down.

She was just removing the eggs.

'I did enough for you as well. And...coffee.'

She sounded oddly uncertain. He kissed her. 'Thank you.'

'Do you mind eating at the counter? I haven't set out tables yet.' Still that odd reticence. Was she regretting taking him as her lover?

'The counter is fine.' He sat on one of the tall stools across from her. The eggs and coffee were more than fine. Best to ask. If she'd rather step back— 'Psyché—'

'I've never cooked breakfast for anyone before.'

He sipped his coffee, looking at what she'd said from several angles. The view from all those vantage points was as fine as the coffee and eggs.

'I've never stayed for breakfast before. Or had a key.'

Her breath jerked in. 'No?'

'No. It's nice.' He put his coffee down and reached across the counter. She set her hand in his and their fingers twined, a perfect fit.

Something else niggled, though. 'There is one thing, sweetheart?'

'Yes?'

He cleared his throat, shifted on the stool. 'You might... that is, I didn't...er...finish inside you, but you might still, you know—'

'Get pregnant?'

He was *not* a green schoolboy to feel this awkward at a little plain speaking. 'Yes. That. I could use a cundum if you—'

She smiled at him over the rim of her coffee cup. 'Queen Anne's lace.'

For a moment he thought she was talking about Queen Anne's sartorial choices. 'You mean the plant?'

'Chewing the seeds avoids that complication.'

He stared. 'I didn't know that.'

She chuckled. 'You're not a woman.'

Chapter Sixteen

My dear Will

I hope this letter finds you as it leaves me and mine—in very good health and spirits. You will doubtless be pleased to know that upon examination the Donne edition is as claimed.

My lady and the children will accompany me as far as Isleworth, therefore the journey may not be accomplished quite as swiftly were it otherwise.

I will divide my time between Isleworth and Grosvenor Square. Would you be so kind as to advise Bentham and the staff at Moresby House of this?

I have received your letters regarding the business you have undertaken for me in London. I am your very grateful servant. Please set all in train as you have suggested.

I will spend a day or two at Isleworth before coming into town and will write from there so that you may make arrangements to move back to Moresby House.

Lady Huntercombe sends her best wishes, as do Harry and Georgie. Georgie wishes me to tell you

*that her backgammon is much improved and she
looks forward to a game with you.*
Huntercombe

Will read the letter again. It had been written nearly a
week ago, so by now the Marquess was well on his way to
London. Never before had he viewed a return to work with
such impending gloom.

For the past four weeks, despite his room at the Red
Lion, he had to all intents and purposes been living with
Psyché. And to his confusion and beguilement it was no
longer an affair as he recognised the phenomenon.

Will had conducted affairs before. It had been staggering to his younger self how many women were prepared
to indulge in a discreet liaison with him. He'd been far too
diffident even to think about it until several ranking ladies
had dropped unmistakable hints. At first he'd ignored such
invitations, but eventually he'd been attracted enough to
one to accept her invitation. He was no prude, but he tried
to be discriminating and he was careful to use precautions.

Most of his affairs had been convenient dalliances at
country house parties he had attended with Huntercombe.
Widows, or matrons with complaisant husbands, wanting
only a pleasurable interlude. He'd always *liked* his part-
ners—he'd never understood why anyone wanted to be intimate with someone they didn't actually like—but never
before had he deliberately fixed on a particular woman he
wanted above all others to be his lover.

At country houses a gentleman visited the lady's room
under cover of night and discreetly slipped away before the
servants were about. The name of the game was discretion. Never before had he engaged in a relationship where
he was all but living with his lover. And day by day he felt
that relationship, and his feelings, deepen.

He had always made certain to protect the reputation of

any woman he was involved with. But with Psyché? It was not so much the social demand for discretion, as a fierce determination to protect her. And that warred with a growing joy that made it so much harder to hide his feelings. Feelings that shocked him. In the past he had accepted without a qualm that his lover would enjoy other affairs after they parted. He hadn't minded in the least. He had never been possessive about a woman.

Now he could no longer imagine wanting any other woman and the idea of Psyché taking another lover lodged in his gut like a lump of frozen lead.

The morning after their first night together he had taken a cab to Grosvenor Square, packed up enough of his belongings and the papers he needed for the work Huntercombe had left him, and ridden back to Soho. He'd booked a room at the Red Lion for the sake of appearances, but he hadn't spent a single night there.

He breakfasted there occasionally, or took supper there before slipping back to The Phoenix to spend the evening and night with Psyché. During the day he went about his work, calling on Huntercombe's London tenants, and making lists of properties requiring repair or modification, leases needing to be updated and properties needing to be re-let.

If he got back before The Phoenix closed he might work in his room at the Lion. More often he slipped into The Phoenix through the back to work upstairs. Every so often he worked quietly at a table in the shop itself, enjoying the rush and bustle. Oddly enough, for a man who had always treasured the peace of his employer's various libraries or his own office, the noise did not bother him in the slightest.

The noise was outweighed by the joy of being near Psyché, of simply watching her, admiring her efficiency as she worked, the cheerful way she managed her staff, the calm dignity of her interactions with the gentlemen who frequented the shop.

But it was the evenings he liked best. Not merely the taking each other to bed, but the quiet companionship as he wrote up his notes and she updated her account books. Or if they had no work they might simply read. He was happy, he realised. Happy in a way he had never known before.

Not that he had been *un*happy. He had always been happy, content with his life. He found his position challenging and fulfilling. But this, this relationship, was more. More than he had expected, or even thought possible. Because without ever suspecting the danger he courted, he had fallen head over heels in love.

Always he had thought of love as something sweet and tender, moderated by reason. Sweetness and tenderness were certainly involved. But it was also a fierce burning in his soul that scoffed at reason and refused to acknowledge its claims.

Now the clock ticked loudly. Huntercombe's return to London would end this time out of time. In returning to Mayfair in preparation for the Parliamentary sitting, Will would not only be busy during the day, but there would be evening engagements he was expected to attend. He often went out of town to deliver particularly private or sensitive messages.

Where would that leave this relationship? There would be odd evenings here and there. Perhaps one a week. That would have been more than sufficient for an ordinary affair. But this was Psyché. He didn't want to be sneaking into her bed once a week and leaving before dawn. Everything in him revolted at the thought of treating her like a whore. As if all they had between them was sex.

The obvious thing to do, dictated by reason, would be to bring the relationship to a close. Perfectly natural when it was no longer convenient for either of them…only his heart lurched at the word *convenient*. Psyché was not *convenient*. She was a very great deal more than that. In fact, she was damnably *in*convenient. It would have been convenient if he only wanted sex or if he had possessed the sense to fall in love with a woman he could—

And there it was. The word he had been circling around. The word he had scarcely dared to acknowledge.

Marriage.

He wanted to marry her.

And he had the distinct impression that marriage had not as much as approached the outer boundaries of Psyché's mind, let alone crossed it. Not only that—if he married Psyché his own world would turn upside down.

The firelight touched Will's face with flickering shadows, playing across every familiar angle and plane. Something was bothering him. In the past weeks she had come to know not only his face and body, but his every mood. The slight frown of concentration as he worked at his writing slope on the dining table, the slow smile that lit his eyes when he looked up at her. A smile that could turn her heart upside down and inside out.

Not that he had brooded like this before. That was the thing. He'd come home—and that she thought of his arrival each evening as *coming home* terrified her—frustrated on occasion if his day had not been entirely successful, but never moody. Always before he'd talked about whatever was bothering him: a hitch in negotiations, a stubborn tenant or a problem for which he couldn't see an immediate solution. Sometimes, by talking about it, the solution had come to him. But tonight he kept reading and re-reading that letter from Huntercombe as if it contained bad news. News he didn't wish to share with her.

Huntercombe's seal was as well-known to her as her Uncle Theo's. Surely a letter from him couldn't contain bad news? Unless…she swallowed…the Marquess knew about *this*. Since Will had stayed that first night, obviously Huntercombe knew about their affair. But what if he knew his secretary was practically living with her and disapproved? She doubted he would disapprove on Will's behalf, but he considered her, in a way, under his protection. Could he be angry with Will for—as he might see it—taking advantage of her? If that was so, she would have to put it right somehow. But how, if she wasn't sure what was troubling Will?

She could ask him what was wrong, but hesitated to cross the invisible boundary set by his silence.

Affairs were not meant to include asking your lover what bothered him. Only this arrangement did not feel like an affair any longer, if indeed it ever had. Affairs did not usually include your lover living with you. And, despite that room at the Red Lion, that was exactly what Will was doing. His linens were in one of her drawers, his shaving kit in another. A pair of boots stood in the closet. He had a hairbrush and toothbrush here.

Even that might not have mattered if his things did not look as if they had always been here. As if they belonged. And if she had not wanted so very much for them to stay here.

That had not been part of their agreement. Except she had given him a key…

'What's worrying you, sweetheart?'

The gentle concern in his voice tore at her self-control. She blinked and found his worried gaze on her. He had folded the letter, set it aside.

Honesty. She'd never liked playing games. '*I* was worrying about whatever is worrying *you* in Huntercombe's letter.'

'Oh.'

'I recognised his seal.'

He nodded slowly. 'He's on his way to London.'

So that was it. He was worrying about telling her that their affair would have to end. The least she could do was make it easy for him. But despite having known that this couldn't last, that he would have to return to his world, the pain of knowing it was over was shocking.

'I see.' She managed a smile. 'You'll be returning to Grosvenor Square—'

'Yes. But—'

'We knew you would have to go back.' She galloped into speech, desperate to make it easier for him. Easier for her. Because if she didn't say *something*, she would say what must not be said. 'You can still visit. Stay here if Huntercombe is out of London for a few days and doesn't—'

'Psyché. That's not—'

'No.' Her resolve shook. 'Don't—'

'I'm in love with you, Psyché.'

Shock reared up at the simple, steady declaration. Joy and terror warred. And she knew, deeply, just how much she loved him. How could she not? From the very first he had *seen* her, truly seen her, as she was. He saw her humanity *and* the colour of her skin. Many of Uncle Theo's circle had seen her humanity, but failed to see that it was not despite her skin colour.

'Such a clever child! You would hardly credit that she's Black.' Or even: *'What a shame she is Black!'*

How often had she heard that as a child? As a young girl? People who, rather than seeing and *accepting* her colour, simply pretended that it wasn't there? But Will had never done that. He found her beautiful and clever *as she was*. He didn't need to pretend that she was a miscoloured white person—to him, she simply *was*.

But even if he did love her… 'You don't have to say that.'

'Don't I?' Those raised eyebrows and the wry smile turned her heart inside out. 'Psyché, love, I'm thirty-two, not twenty. Nor am I entirely inexperienced. I've known lust, infatuation, before.' He reached out, took her hand. 'And while I'd have to admit that lust is definitely an element here, it's not only that. It's love. And love needs to be spoken.' His mouth twisted. 'Unless you cannot return my affection?'

It would be wiser to say she wasn't in love. So much safer to lie and to let him go.

She drew breath, searched for the words, reached for the lie.

The words refused to be spoken. They refused even to form in her mind. Not for the man who saw all of her.

'I…you don't understand.'

For an instant his fingers tightened, then, very deliberately he released her hand. 'Then will you explain?'

That smile, the one that had stolen her heart, crept into his eyes, edged with sadness. 'I might not like it if you don't love me, but it's scarcely incomprehensible.'

Oh, yes, it would be. She couldn't understand why she hadn't realised from the very beginning the danger Will posed to her peace of mind, to the safe, contented course she had charted. And he was not demanding an explanation as if he were owed one, as if he had offered something priceless and couldn't accept that she might not want what he wanted. He was simply trying to understand her. That made it even harder to deny him.

'I do love you, Will.' She could give him that. 'We can continue our affair. Nothing has to change.'

'Is that what you wish? That nothing should change?'

She had to be honest with him. 'That is all it can be. I fancied myself in love once. When I was young.' She had wanted everything. Marriage, children. She had longed for it with all her heart and soul, believing herself loved in return.

She had been shatteringly, heartbreakingly wrong.

'And you are so dreadfully aged now.'

The dry tone made her laugh despite the ache of memory. 'I was seventeen.' And now she knew beyond all doubt that what she had felt for Charles had not been love. It had been calf love. Immature and fleeting.

He nodded. 'You were very young.'

'Not so young that I didn't understand why he decided in the end against marrying me.'

Will's gaze hardened. *'"Decided in the end"?'*

Beyond Charles, only Huntercombe had any inkling of what had happened that night out at Hampstead. She had never spoken of it, not even to Uncle Theo or Aunt Grace. Certainly not to Hetty. She had persuaded herself that to do so would be a betrayal driven by spite and jealousy.

Nor had she dwelt on that evening in years, yet the fragrance of roses, hothouse lilies and candlewax came back so clearly…and the young girl in a dusky rose-pink gown floating down the stairs of Highwood House to her very first formal dinner and party… If she made Will see that girl, would he understand?

Chapter Seventeen

Highwood House—midsummer 1797

At seventeen Psyché knew herself to be safe and valued. She managed the stillroom for Aunt Grace, helped with the household accounts and oversaw the menus. She had acted as her uncle's amanuensis and secretary for the past two years since he had left public life, and he vowed she was the best he'd ever had.

But far and away the best thing in her life, that made her heart sing for very fullness, was that she was loved. She was loved for who and what she was.

And tonight, for the very first time, she was to eat in company with guests at a formal dinner. Not even Lucius had been able to move Uncle Theo on that point. Hetty, now eighteen, had been fully out in society this past year, but Uncle Theo and Aunt Grace had dissuaded Psyché from making her come out.

'Not everyone would accept you, child.'

Uncle Theo had never attempted to sugar-coat society's attitude. She knew that the majority would snub her and worse should she make a formal come out. It might ruin Hetty's chances of a respectable marriage. She could not do that to the cousin she loved like a sister.

So when there was company, more often than not, she dined on a tray in the library and joined the family and guests in the drawing room after dinner. There, she understood, people might avoid her or not, as they wished. She had no desire to foist herself upon anyone who thought her somehow *less* because she was Black.

She neither put herself forward nor cowered in the corner on these occasions. She handed the tea and coffee around with Hetty, spoke if she were spoken to and did a great deal of embroidery.

She *hated* embroidery, but did it well on principle—just to show that she *could*.

If Hetty were asked to sing, she accompanied her on the pianoforte, and every so often someone, usually the Marquess of Huntercombe, would ask her to play something on her own account. She had learnt to let any surprise—*'Oh! She's actually quite talented! Who would have thought?'*—roll straight off her back. She had learnt to ignore the disapproving murmurs, the discomfort crawling on her skin as she entered a room in which she was the only non-white person apart from a footman or two.

But tonight she was dressing for *dinner*. Granted, she was to sit between Lord Huntercombe and Mr Fox, both of whom had known her since she was a little girl and accepted her place in Uncle Theo's family as a matter of course. Already her stomach was knotting itself into tangles.

Lucius was furious and had tried only half an hour ago to persuade Uncle Theo to change his mind. She'd heard the argument echoing from Uncle Theo's dressing room, even if Sarah, helping her dress, had not given her a full account gleaned from Uncle Theo's valet.

'Stormed out, he did, so Marney said.' Sarah twitched the overskirt into place as she wound up. 'You'll be careful tonight, Miss Psyché, won't you?'

'Of course, Sarah.' She reached up and patted the kindly hand on her shoulder.

She was always careful. She had been determined upon that from childhood. She must be extra careful and extra good, work extra hard at her lessons to make it quite clear to anyone outside the family that she wasn't a *mistake*. No one should have an excuse to call her *Staverton's Folly*. She didn't think Uncle Theo realised that she knew about that, but she was determined *never* to give anyone the least justification for questioning his judgement. She cultivated the quiet dignity practised by Aunt Grace—although, not her aunt's occasional acerbic remarks. In Lady Staverton, or even Miss Hetty Winthrop, that would be accounted wit. In herself it would be unbecoming, uppish and *'only to be expected, my dear'*.

Having always to be *extra* was exhausting.

'You're sure you want to go down, miss?' Sarah's worried frown in the mirror touched her to the core, even as it exasperated her. 'I'm sure his lordship would—'

'He would. But I want to go down.' Psyché smiled reassuringly, ignoring the icy knots in her belly. 'Especially tonight. Hetty has been away for the whole Season. And Uncle Theo wants me there.' Not for worlds would she disappoint him. Now that Hetty was established, surely people would not turn on her because she had a Black cousin. They would see that she was quite an ordinary young lady.

Hetty had been the toast of London this past spring and, while she had written daily, Psyché had missed her bitterly. With the Season over Hetty was back at Highwood House for this midsummer dinner, brimming over with excitement and something she refused to talk about. A secret, she insisted. And, much to Psyché's surprise, had not divulged it. But there was another reason she wanted to go down tonight…

Psyché had her own secret. For it was not only Hetty who

had returned to Highwood after a long absence... Psyché's breath caught and her heart beat faster at the thoughts she scarcely dared permit... Last year, well, of course she had been far too young, a child at only sixteen. She saw that now. But now she was turned seventeen, *perfectly* marriageable, and tonight everyone would see that she was worthy; accomplished and pretty. It would be like the fairy tales Aunt Grace had read to her as a child. There was to be music, dancing and *everything*. Her whole life was downstairs, ready for her to arrive and get on with it.

'Well, if you're sure, miss.'

'Quite sure.' She turned and pirouetted in the mirror. 'Thank you, Sarah. You've made me look so nice.'

'Done that for yourself, Miss Psyché.' Sarah shook her head. 'That Mr Lucius, though. You be careful, that's all.'

'I will.' Impulsively she hugged the maid. 'You've always been my friend. Thank you. I'm going to see if Hetty's ready.'

Sarah gave a snort. 'Not likely. Still worried about her choice of gown when I passed. In case it clashed with the flowers.'

Psyché blinked. 'She's wearing white. How can that possibly clash with anything?'

Sarah grinned. 'There's a question for the ages, dearie. Off you go!'

Psyché's feet danced in their silken slippers as she hurried along the upper corridor to the main stairs. Hetty was not quite ready. Her maid was putting the finishing touches to her golden curls. She looked, Psyché thought, like a fairy princess tonight. Her blue eyes sparkled with the secret she still wouldn't tell.

'You'll know tonight, dearest, but Uncle Theo made me promise not to say anything.'

Psyché would not have pressed the point anyway. Any

promise should be kept, but promises to Uncle Theo and Aunt Grace should be respected without sulking or temptation. Besides, surprises were fun and she might have one of her own.

She skipped down the first flight, her heart bubbling over, because tonight she would see Charles again.

Charles—but she must remember to call him Lord Harbury—had been her friend from the very first. He had spent part of each summer here at Highwood right through her girlhood. He'd taught her to play cricket, or at least to bowl. How else might he practise his batting? And he had once punched George Mainwaring for calling her a dirty—well, she wasn't going to think about George this evening, let alone what he had called her.

Charles had punched him on the nose for it and told Uncle Theo, who had ensured George was not invited again. That was three years ago when she was fourteen—still a little girl really. Charles had been eighteen, about to go up to Oxford.

She had not seen him again until last summer when she had been nearly, but not quite, grown up. Now everything was different. Charles had inherited and she *was* grown up. Most importantly he had reached his majority.

Last summer, on the evening before he left to visit his mama, Charles had walked with her in the gardens after dinner. He had talked a great deal about Oxford and the larks he and his friends got up to and how he'd be finished in a year, and he'd be twenty-one and could do whatever he pleased.

She'd thought that doing whatever you pleased must be rather nice. It wasn't something that fell to the lot of young ladies…

And then he'd said, *'I'll be back next summer. And you'll be here, won't you, Psyché?'*

Well, of course she'd be here. Where else would she—

And he'd kissed her.

Kissed her.

It had been the most shocking and wonderful thing imaginable—that Charles Harbury, heir to a barony, should have kissed *her*, Psyché Winthrop.

'Darling Psyché.' The muffled words had tickled against her ear. *'You'll wait for me. Promise you'll wait for me.'*

She would have promised him anything at that point.

'I'll be twenty-one by then. My own master.'

He'd kissed her again, one fumbling clumsy hand clutching at her breast... *'Psyché, let me—'*

His mouth had become hot, hungry and not very pleasant.

'Charles!' She had jerked free.

For a single shocked instant she'd thought he'd grab her, pull her back...

He hadn't. *'Psyché, little love—you know I'd never hurt you.'*

'Of course not. But we can't...' Her cheeks had burned. Unlike Hetty, she did know how babies came about. *'Uncle Theo would not like it—'*

He had turned away. *'You're right. But you'll wait for me?'* He'd swung back and given her that dazzling smile. *'And you're careful with other fellows, I hope!'*

'Yes, of course.'

'You're a good little thing.'

She'd frowned at that. She was not a 'thing', good or otherwise, but he'd meant it kindly.

Schooling herself to descend the last flight sedately, she relived those stolen moments, hugging them to herself. She knew from listening to Hetty and Aunt Grace that gentlemen did not kiss young ladies much less take other liberties unless they had serious intentions. So that meant...

She was practically *betrothed*.

Psyché reached the entrance hall as Viscount and Viscountess Lindfield were admitted. She knew they were close friends of Lucius, and dropped a polite curtsy. Lord Lindfield's brows shot up. Lady Lindfield drew an audible breath, her mouth pinching. Then, without a single word or even a nod of acknowledgement, although Psyché had several times been in company with them after dinner, they turned away towards the drawing room.

She took a trembling breath.

You knew what it would be like. Even if Uncle Theo hadn't warned you. You knew.

But knowing was not the same as feeling the snub, the disgust, hitting your body like a stone from a slingshot. If she turned around now, went back upstairs, no one would know…except the dining table was laid with the expectation of her presence. And the Lindfields had seen her. If she turned tail now, they had won and the story would spread in sneers and sniggers. By letter, over cups of tea, in the clubs over bottles of brandy.

Lucius would be delighted. And Uncle Theo would be a laughing stock.

She took a steadier breath. This was her home.

You can do this. Otherwise, you may as well hide in the attics for the rest of your life.

Psyché slipped into the drawing room to find Uncle Theo and Aunt Grace mingling with the company. A quick sideways glance showed her the Lindfields sequestered with Lucius.

But one person drew and held her gaze, allowing her to quell the squirming of discomfort as most of the company turned to stare at her.

Tall, his fair curls gleaming with pomade, his evening clothes immaculate and a diamond dancing in the froth of lace at his throat, Charles was a young girl's dream come true. His hand rested lightly on Uncle Theo's arm in a gesture of affection.

All at once he turned, smiling, and saw her and her heart jolted as his smile grew.

'Why! 'Tis little Psyché, all grown up at last!'

He came to her, hands held out. And Psyché, her heart tripping, fluttering—doing anything but what a well-regulated young lady's heart was supposed to do—placed her hands in his.

'I am not quite forgotten then, little friend?' His voice was caressing, like his thumbs on the back of her gloved hands.

'Oh, no, Char—Lord Harbury.'

'Well, well.' He tucked her hand into his elbow and drew her into the company, murmuring, 'Soon we shall see a great deal more of one another,' and cheerfully presented her to various persons, including several who looked less than pleased about it. Inwardly she squirmed, but kept a polite smile in place and curtsied gracefully. She must show herself as worthy of him in every way.

But she saw those who removed themselves discreetly from Charles's path, edging around behind them. Chills flickered over her skin despite the warmth of the summer evening. Couldn't he *see*? Didn't he realise that by forcing her on people he was actually making things worse? She wanted to jerk her hand from his arm and stop this foolishness, but it was impossible. To do so would draw even more unwanted attention to herself.

'You remember my mama, dear Psyché?'

She swallowed. He had that back to front. One presented the lower ranking person to the higher. Nevertheless, she dropped a curtsy and murmured a polite greeting at the stiff nod of acknowledgment.

Psyché remembered Lady Harbury all too well. Lady

Harbury, she knew, disapproved of her. Something she had not permitted to intrude on her idyllic dreams in the past year. Now, faced with a frozen block of disdain, she wondered—what *would* Lady Harbury say when confronted with Charles's choice? And people like the Lindfields—what would *they* say?

Aunt Grace appeared at her side, a welcome diversion. 'Dear Psyché, come and say good evening to Lord Huntercombe.' She favoured Lady Harbury with her most charming smile. 'You will forgive me for stealing her away. The Marquess is a great admirer of my niece's musical talent. He is hoping she will indulge us with a little music later.'

Psyché took her place at the dinner table between Mr Fox and Lord Huntercombe and found herself seated opposite Charles, with Hetty at his side. Hetty was in high spirits, delicately flushed and laughing. On her other side, Mr Sidney appeared captivated, paying her extravagant compliments and vowing that he must die of a broken heart should she not grant him a dance later.

Was Mr Sidney Hetty's secret? Were they about to announce a betrothal? Was that why Lucius was here, seated to the right of Aunt Grace, and why Uncle Theo had insisted on her own presence at dinner? Oh, how lovely! And if Charles were to declare himself as well, then...

'May I prevail upon you, Miss Psyché, to play that Scarlatti sonata for me later?'

Lord Huntercombe's quiet voice drew her out of a daydream in which Lady Harbury had been miraculously won over and she and Hetty planned a double wedding. 'I would be honoured, my lord.'

Charles sent her a wink across the table and she felt her cheeks heat. He glanced at Huntercombe and rolled his eyes. Her lips parted a little in shock. Why—that was *rude*! Confused, she looked away, back to the kindly Marquess, and discussed music with him for the remainder of the course.

At the very end of the course Uncle Theo rose and tapped his wine glass. 'Dear friends.' There was a flurry of movement as the footmen filled up glasses. 'I am sure many of you have guessed our happy news this evening.' He paused to dab his handkerchief to his eyes. 'I am touched and honoured to have you all in my home on this occasion. You know my great-niece, Miss Henrietta Winthrop—she has been raised here by Lady Staverton and myself as if she were our own daughter.' He smiled down the table at Hetty, who was staring at her lap, cheeks ablaze. 'But of course, she has a papa and I shall defer to him in making this happy announcement.'

He sat and Lucius rose, clearing his throat. 'It is with great pride and pleasure that I make public the betrothal between my dearest Henrietta and Lord Harbury.'

He continued speaking, but Psyché was only vaguely aware of it as a sort of faint buzzing. From a distance she noted that one of the footmen had filled her glass with lemonade. Habit and good manners had her standing with the rest of the company for the toast:

'Miss Winthrop and Harbury!'

Beneath the ensuing hubbub as everyone sat down, Huntercombe spoke softly. 'Keep your chin up and smile. You don't want anyone to know. Least of all Harbury.'

That bracing advice got her through until the ladies withdrew to the Orangery. She might then have laid claim to a headache and slipped away, but Hetty, all aglow, caught her hand.

'Oh, Psyché! Is it not wonderful? I am to be married!'

Yes. Quite wonderful.

In the face of such joy how could she say she had a sick headache? She stiffened her spine and handed the teacups around for Aunt Grace. Hetty was far too busy fielding good wishes for her forthcoming connubial bliss to hand tea around herself.

Lady Harbury and Lady Lindfield were seated together gushing over the *'charming couple'* and how nice it was see such an *'eminently suitable match'*.

'But dear Charles has always been very ready to be advised on such important decisions.' Lady Harbury accepted her tea without as much as glancing at Psyché, let alone offering a smile, or word of thanks.

'I know Lucius is delighted, not least with the prospect of Henrietta being removed from certain *radical notions*.' And Lady Lindfield allowed her gaze to slide over Psyché as she took her cup. Psyché kept her face expressionless. With a choice between being thought stupid and insensible, or dropping the cup in Lady Lindfield's silken lap and embarrassing Aunt Grace and Uncle Theo, she chose self-discipline.

To her relief, the gentlemen did not tarry over their port, but arrived in a flurry of talk and backslapping, Charles in their midst, allowing her to retire into the background.

Psyché gave her wilting spine a stiff talking to and avoided Charles's gaze. Humiliation slithered around in her belly in an oily tangle. She had been close, so close to confiding her dreams to Hetty. What if she had told Hetty about those kisses last summer? That she believed Charles loved her and that she hoped they would soon be betrothed?

Chills skittered through her as she picked up her embroidery bag and deliberately chose a small single chair so that no one might sit beside her. She watched Hetty, the absolute centre of attention, lovely and glowing with triumphant joy. Shame flooded her. She *loved* Hetty. How could she begrudge her this?

But always, always they had promised each other that when they were married there would be long visits. Naturally, being the elder, Hetty would marry first.

'And then I shall present you to all the nicest, wealthiest men, Psyché darling! Just see if I don't!'

She saw now how useless it would be for Hetty to attempt such a thing, if Aunt Grace would even permit it… if she even wanted it for herself. There would be endless evenings like this one, knowing herself to be an outsider, an oddity, an exotic creature from afar to be viewed with wide eyes and caution like the beasts at the Royal Exchange.

'Oh!' Hetty fanned herself. ''Tis so hot in here! Dearest Aunt, please may we stroll in the garden before the dancing?'

Aunt Grace frowned, but Uncle Theo patted her hand, chuckling. 'A short stroll for the young people will do no harm.' He signalled to the footmen who moved to open the doors to the terrace.

Psyché sat quietly as the other younger guests strolled out. Hetty glanced across with her hand resting lightly on Charles's arm.

'Do you not come with us, Psyché?'

She managed a smile. 'No. I shall remain here in case I am needed.'

'As you are.' Lord Huntercombe smiled at her. 'That is, if I am to be indulged with Scarlatti.'

She smiled back, unspeakably grateful. 'Of course, my lord.

Chapter Eighteen

She played Scarlatti and Mozart to a ripple of applause and surprised murmurs.

'So clever, some of them...'

'Quite extraordinary what a good account she gives of herself. You would hardly credit her unfortunate origins, were they not so apparent...'

Her skin prickled. They made it sound as if a Black woman playing the piano well was next thing to a divine miracle. And they seemed also to believe that she was deaf, both physically and mentally. Or perhaps her feelings were not considered quite so human as her musicianship. The anger and resentment burned.

'Thank you very much, my dear.' Lord Huntercombe, who had turned her pages, offered his hand as she rose from the piano bench. 'Your music always gives me great pleasure.' Quite as if her playing was simply the playing of an ordinarily talented young lady who took the time to practise, rather than something to be marvelled over as if a monkey had rattled off Mozart's 'Rondo alla Turca'.

'Thank you, sir.'

The revellers in the garden returned as the small orchestra tuned up, with Hetty and Charles in the rear of the group, flushed and laughing.

'Quite brazen, the way she thrusts herself forward. Poor Staverton, to be so sadly taken in!'

Psyché flinched at Lady Harbury's soft voice directly behind her, the blade delivered straight between her shoulder blades. She moved blindly towards Aunt Grace, wanting only to escape.

Aunt Grace was frowning at Hetty. 'My dear, where is your shawl?'

Hetty's lips parted in surprise. 'Oh, goodness! I must have left it under the loggia. We...we were sitting there, and it must have slipped off. Lord Harbury, would you—?'

'I'll fetch it.' Psyché clutched her own shawl closer. 'Which bench, Hetty?'

'Oh, thank you, dearest.' Hetty smiled at her. 'The one closest to the lily pond.'

Aunt Grace frowned. 'Psyché, dear, one of the footmen—'

'I should like to go, Aunt. Just a little fresh air.'

Aunt Grace smiled. 'Very well. But straight back, my dear.'

'Yes, Aunt.'

'And I shall hope you have a dance for an old friend!' Charles's caressing smile nearly choked her.

Psyché slipped out past the returning stragglers. She'd return the shawl and ask Aunt Grace's permission to retire for the night. There were limits to her self-control, and if Charles asked her to dance she could not refuse.

The moon hung low, bright and joyous in a sky quivering with stars. She wished it were cloudy, pouring with rain to match the weeping of her heart. But, no, she scolded herself. That was selfish. People did fall in and out of love and Hetty was so happy. She should be happy for her. Above all, Hetty must never suspect the dreams she had cherished.

She stepped into the shadows of the loggia and waited

for her eyes to adjust. Sure enough there was the shawl on the bench closest to the pond, in the deepest shadows. Had Charles grabbed Hetty's breast here in the shadows—would Hetty have allowed it because they were betrothed now? And what if *she* had not known enough to stop Charles last summer?

She sat down with the shawl a silken tumble in her lap. Just a moment to steady her thoughts, her resolve. Maybe she could see out the evening rather than returning to her room like a little girl. She wanted to draw the shadows around her, to hide while she gathered her courage.

The music floated across the lawns and she imagined the dancers forming their prescribed patterns. Where did she fit into society's patterns? For the first time she wondered if, as an adult, she could fit into the world she had been raised in. How had she deluded herself into believing that Charles, heir to a barony, could seriously wish to marry her? Or even if he did, that society would accept the match? A match that would break the pattern.

She should go back, not sit here being melancholy on the evening of Hetty's joy.

'Aha! Were you waiting for me?'

Charles's smiling voice made her jump up, clutching the silken shawl in front of her. 'No. Of course not!' Had she been? Oh, God, she hoped not.

He strolled towards her, confident as ever. 'Dear little Psyché—' That caressing tone seemed sticky now, the delicious thrill of last year gone. Had she been deaf to the condescension before?

She rose and edged past him towards the light. 'Excuse me. Aunt Grace will worry.'

'Will you not stay a moment?'

A year ago she would have stayed for ever. But now for ever yawned between them.

He continued, 'Who knew a woman could keep a secret so well?' He gave that boyish laugh that had always enchanted her. It had become tinny. 'I made sure Henrietta would tell you.'

'Tell me?'

'Yes.' He held out a hand. 'I could see it was a shock to you.'

Damn. She kept her fingers tightly laced.

'She promised Uncle Theo,' she countered. 'We were taught to keep promises.' But she gathered her courage. 'Why, Charles?' she demanded. 'Last year you *asked* me to wait for you.'

'Ah.' His smile was charming. 'I should not have done so, but I was carried away by my sensibilities. But surely *you* knew, even if I did not, romantic boy that I was, that it was all quite impossible.'

Why should she at sixteen, have known what he, at twenty, had not? Why should *she* be responsible for educating his romantic sensibilities? The same way *she* had been the one to halt things last year?

She was wiser now, but she was damned if she would be the one to say it. *He* should say it.

'Why impossible, Charles?'

He blinked. *'Why?'*

Anger surfaced, subsuming the hurt. He even sounded shocked.

'Yes. Why?' She kept her chin up. 'Is there some law that prevents such a marriage?'

'My darling Psyché—'

'I am *not* your darling.'

He looked as startled as if Nyx had bitten him. Then that momentary bewilderment vanished, replaced by a gentle patronage. 'I had hoped not to have to say such a thing to you, but in short, Psyché, your breeding precludes marriage to any gentleman.' He sighed. 'Marriage must always be a matter of breeding and fortune allied. Yes, you have a respectable fortune, but that and affection alone are not enough for marriage between us.'

Affection? Had he ever felt true affection for her?

'And if my fortune were greater?' she demanded. 'Could my illegitimacy be brushed away then?'

'Your illegitimacy? Perhaps. But—' He tugged at his cravat. 'You are making this deucedly awkward!'

She waited. Why should she be expected to make it easy for him?

'Damn it! I cannot marry a…a *mulatto.* I did my very best tonight to show you how society must see such a match!'

He had done that on purpose? Paraded her around as though he considered her no more than a tame beast on a leash? Deliberately exposing her to ridicule?

She kept her head high. 'Mulatta. I believe marrying a man would indeed be impossible for you.'

'What?'

'I'm female. Mulatta.'

He scowled. 'You know what I mean!'

'Now, yes. But not last summer. You asked me to wait.'

'Oh, Psyché!' His caressing tone churned her stomach anew. 'That *was* badly done of me. I admit it without reservation. But all does not have to be at an end between us.'

She tried, and failed abysmally, to make sense of that. 'What are you saying?'

He smiled. 'Henrietta wishes you to stay with us after we marry. And, of course, she will need…a companion. You would not be expected to go into society. No need to fear a repeat of tonight.' His voice took on a tone of reproof. 'It was unkind in Staverton to hide the truth from you so well.'

He was criticising Uncle Theo? For protecting her? And he thought she wanted to be a *companion* in his household?

'We will be very discreet. No one will know.'

Know what?

'It will be our secret,' he went on, his voice as tender as a girl could wish. 'We can still be together as we dreamed.'

A few short hours ago she had thought herself quite grown up. *Now* she was grown up.

'I could be your mistress?' Somehow she kept her voice even.

He smiled. 'Yes, you can still belong to me.'

Belong. The very word stained the air. Unable to help herself, she clenched her fist over the place, hidden by her deliberately modest gown, where hot iron had burned into her. *Belong.* Like a favourite bitch or mare. As Mam had *belonged* to the father.

'What about Hetty?' Did he think Hetty so stupid that she would not notice?

He dismissed that with a shrug. 'What concern should it be of hers?' He strolled towards her. 'As my wife she must do as she is bid. Never fear, my sweet. She won't be able to send you away.'

It sickened her that he considered a potential mistress a chattel. That he could also think of his wife as a creature who must do his bidding, even if that was to turn a blind eye to his affair with her cousin, enraged her.

She stood quite still, let him get close. His cologne was overpowering as he took her in his arms. 'Dearest Psyché, I knew you would—'

She slammed her knee upwards, exactly as the still-room maid had described. And even Molly's descrip-tion—*'Dropped him cold, it did'*—did not do justice to the wheezing gurgle as Charles collapsed at her feet.

'No,' she said clearly. 'I won't.' And she walked back to the house.

Psyché lay in her bed, staring up at the ceiling. The girl who had floated down the stairs a few hours ago would have cried. But that girl was gone and in her place was the girl who had walked back to the house alone, handed Hetty her shawl, danced with her great-uncle and a few other old friends, and remained to smile and pretend she was over-joyed. This new Psyché had known only cold satisfaction when a very pale Charles finally reappeared, moving as though he'd been kicked by a horse.

She knew now that words were cheap. Cheap and eas-ily spoken. Charles had taught her that and something else that chilled her heart.

In marriage a woman had no say, no right to protest should her lord and *master* take a mistress. She must obey: it was in the marriage vows. She could even, according to law, be physically chastised, beaten, to ensure her submis-sion. A married woman could own nothing: all was her husband's, even her body. She had *known* all that, but she had never really thought about it. Believing in love, she had never considered that for a woman the terms of the mar-riage contract put her completely in her husband's power.

Now, with Nyx's comforting weight on her feet, she understood. Marriage, for any woman and especially for her, was potentially a gilded trap that men baited with lies about love.

Not *all* men. And not all marriages. Not even most mar-riages. She knew that. She had only to look at Uncle Theo and Aunt Grace. Or Lord Huntercombe. His wife had died several years ago and still he grieved for her.

But how could you know that you were making the right choice? A safe choice.

She had a respectable fortune. But what man of whom Uncle Theo would approve would look past her illegitimacy and her skin colour to really *see* her? How could she be sure it was not merely her fortune that made her acceptable? And how could she ever be sure that a husband would not

come to resent her and everything she was? If that should
happen, she would have no protection.

You can't know.

Will only realised his hands had knotted into fists when
she laid a gentle hand on one. He drew a breath, turned his
hand under hers and held it as much to steady himself as
anything else. 'And Staverton let that...that bounder marry
your cousin?' He wanted to hit something, pound something—or rather *someone*—to a bloody pulp. Charles, Lord
Harbury, to be exact.

Psyché shrugged. 'I never told him about it. How could
I? And it was not his decision. Lucius is Hetty's father. *He*
was delighted with the marriage.' She went on painfully.
'I thought about telling Hetty, but—'

'Would she have believed you?'

Her smile was bitter. 'She was in love. What do you
think *I* would say to someone who came to me and told
me something like that about *you*?'

He managed a smile. 'I'd like to hope that if it was someone you knew loved you and cared for your interests, like
Staverton, Selbourne or Huntercombe, that you would pay
them heed.'

She laughed. 'Perhaps. I'm not eighteen, though, nor was
I ever quite as sheltered as Hetty. I told myself it could do no
good. Charles can be very convincing. He would have told
her I had read too much into a little flirtation. Or that *I* had
offered myself.' She met his gaze. 'At the time I thought she
would have wanted to believe him. Besides, Lucius wanted
the connection. He would not have brooked opposition and
I doubted Hetty would have had the backbone to defy him.'

He thought about that. 'All probably true.'

'But I was a coward, too.'

'What?'

'Apart from the rest, I feared exposing myself to humiliation. I didn't want Uncle Theo and Aunt Grace to know that my folly made it possible for Charles to make me that offer.'

'*You* made it possible? You think you invited that insult? Because you trusted the bastard when he asked you to wait for him?' He felt sick at the narrow escape she'd had—Harbury must have truly feared Staverton's reaction. Otherwise he might well have asked a trusting young girl for a great deal more. Or simply taken it.

'Both times I was alone with him in the garden at night.' Her tone was level. 'Many would have said I invited it.'

He hated that hypocrisy. That a woman must always be guarded and protected because if she were not a man could consider it an invitation to help himself. It shouldn't be like that. 'Your uncle's garden and Harbury was a trusted visitor. I don't think we have to make his argument for him. He's a wart.'

'That was the point when I started to think about ways of making my own way in the world rather than relying on any man to give my life purpose. And I told Uncle Theo I wanted to use *Abeni*—my mother's name for me—as part of my surname.'

'All that?'

She chuckled. 'Not quite immediately. But I started to think perhaps no one would want to marry *me*—'

'Sweetheart—'

'In distinction to my fortune.'

I don't want your damned fortune! For a shattering instant he thought he'd actually spoken aloud.

'Then Aunt Grace died a year after Hetty married. That changed everything.' She bit her lip. 'I knew that I couldn't stay for ever.'

Will waited. It was not for him to ask. If she wished to tell him…

'For ever could only be until Lucius inherited the title,'

she said quietly. 'Once that happened I would have been out on my ear anyway. I preferred to leave well prepared, at a time of my choosing.'

'But you were provided for.'

Her smile was slightly cynical. 'Very well provided for. Uncle Theo persuaded my father to leave me the bulk of his fortune and he set up a trust to ensure that it remained mine no matter what.'

So he'd been right—Huntercombe had modelled the trust to protect Kit on the trust that protected Psyché's fortune.

He remembered something else, too. Something Psyché had once said…

Once a woman is married, she no longer owns her own body, let alone anything else. She has no rights beyond what her husband chooses to grant her.'

'But by then you had decided against marriage, had you not?'

'Not exactly. I knew I couldn't be part of the world Uncle Theo and Aunt Grace raised me for, so I needed to make something else.' She wrinkled her nose. 'I'm really not suited to sitting about in ladylike seclusion watching the world happen. I wanted to be *in* the world.'

'And marriage would preclude that?'

'How many men want a wife who is running her own business?'

Not many. But— 'You might find one who didn't mind.'

She shook her head. 'He might *say* he didn't. But if he changed his mind, he would have every legal right to order me to stay at home and employ a manager.'

He wanted to argue, to reassure her that not *all* marriages were like that. That if a man truly loved her, he would accept her as she was. Not try to circumscribe her independence in any way, let alone with physical force. He wanted to reassure her that *he* would never…

'Love does not have to mean marriage, Will. Any more than a marriage must include love.'

'And trust?'

From the sharp intake of breath he knew that had gone home.

After a moment she spoke. 'It's not about trusting you.'

'Isn't it?'

'No. It's about trusting my own judgement.' She sat, pleating creases into her skirts. 'Hetty fell in love,' she said at last. 'As children we were as close as sisters. I attended her wedding, but I sat very discreetly at the back. Hetty cried when she told me, but insisted that it was just for the wedding so Charles's mother should not be upset.'

She swallowed. 'She is barely permitted to see me. *He* controls that because he has the legal right to do so. He has the right to chastise her, physically, to ensure her obedience and submission. Hetty can do very little about it—we see each other if we meet at Uncle Theo's house, and...' a wry smile flickered '...she writes me a letter whenever she visits him, which he sends over to me.'

'And you send one back to him for her?'

'Of course.' Again that faint smile. 'I doubt it would ever occur to Charles that Hetty might defy him in this way.'

'He's an idiot, then.'

'Yes. And that's the man I fancied myself in love with.'

He nodded slowly. 'You've said it yourself, love.'

'Said what?'

'Fancied yourself in love.' He smiled. 'You were very young. Don't you think you might make a better choice now?'

Later, after they had made love with a fierce, unspoken desperation, he lay sleepless in the bittersweet joy of holding her in his arms and knowing that, despite the precautions she took, the precautions *he* took, there was one risk that would eventually catch up with them that he was not prepared to take.

What if they made a child?

A child would change everything. He couldn't allow a child to face a censorious world without the protection of his name. Perhaps it might be different if he were sufficiently wealthy, or had a great title. But he was plain Will Barclay and a child born out of wedlock would suffer that stigma. And so would the woman sleeping in his arms.

As if his troubled mind had breached her dreams, she stirred, crying out.

'Mam! Mam! No!'

'Shhh.' He drew her closer as he always did when she dreamed of her mother. 'It's all right, love. Just a dream.'

'Don't! It was my fault! Don't hurt her!'

Tears poured down her face, and she fought, crying out, struggling. *'Mam! Please. Let her go! I didn't mean it. I'll do it. Anything. Don't hurt her!'*

He held her close, pressing kisses to her wet cheeks, murmuring nonsense, anything. Gradually she stopped struggling. And that was worse. Because she lay limp and broken, weeping her heart out in a dream that he knew was deeper than any nightmare.

A nightmare could be banished with the dawn. Memory crouched in the heart and soul, waiting for another chance to strike.

Chapter Nineteen

Two nights later a groom brought a note from Hunter-combe to say that he had reached Grosvenor Square and would expect Will in a day or so.

Will re-read the note. It had been addressed to him at the Red Lion. There was nothing to suggest that the Marquess knew exactly where his secretary was...except *'in a day or so'*.

He would not have written that unless he knew. There had been other notes from Huntercombe over the years asking Will to re-join him *'at your earliest convenience'*. Easy enough for him to know. A single letter from Ignatius would have contained the information.

He folded the note, slipped it into his pocket and turned back to Psyché.

'Huntercombe is in London. I'll need to return to May-fair.'

Was that pain in her eyes? And was he wrong to hope she felt it?

'At once? Now?'

He swallowed. 'In the morning.'

She felt Will leave the bed very early, carefully disentangling himself. She, who liked her own space and privacy, had become used not only to sharing her bed, but sleeping in a man's arms. Even if she tried to keep to her side of the bed, by morning she was back in Will's arms. She felt tired as she sat up, her eyes gritty as if she hadn't slept well. And her stomach was knotted, as it was sometimes if…if she'd had a bad dream.

Had she? She usually woke from them, crying and disoriented, and she hadn't woken like that recently. Or had she?

'Did I disturb you last night?' The question was out before she'd even thought about it.

He looked over, his head on one side. 'You had a nightmare. Don't you remember?'

She forced her restless hands to be still in her lap. She didn't need to remember the dream—the reality was all too close. 'Not really. Has…has it happened before?'

Slowly he nodded. 'Yes.'

'I'm sorry.'

His mouth flattened. 'Don't be. Should I have woken you? You always settle without my doing so, but—'

'No. That's all right.'

'But this morning you remember it.'

She shook her head. 'No. But…usually I wake up. So I know what I was dreaming and—'

'About your mother.'

Words, thought, froze into unspeakable grief.

'You cried out for her,' he said simply.

He came back to the bed in his breeches, shirtsleeves and boots, and sat down. When his hand closed over hers, she realised that she was shaking. 'Sweetheart, if she is still in Jamaica—'

'She is dead.' Her throat closed on a choking lump.

He let out an audible breath. 'I'm sorry.' Then he leaned forward and pressed a kiss to her forehead.

'Did you think I would have left her in *hell*?' The words

burst from her as if something inside had broken, releasing them.

'Not willingly, no, but—'

'I killed her. My stupidity *killed her*.' She flung back the covers, snatched up her robe and flung it around her. 'I should get dressed myself. There's…there's a lot to do.' God only knew what it was, but she'd find something. She had to. Otherwise she would spend the entire day grieving over what she wanted, but could never have.

She whisked herself behind the screen. 'I'll be down shortly. Ask Caleb to get the kitchen fire going.'

'Very well.'

She heard his footsteps receding, heard the door to the landing open and shut. Part of her shook with relief, but the rest of her curled up in a tight little ball inside to weep.

Since Will's watch announced it to be some fifteen minutes shy of five o'clock in the morning, he refrained from rousing Caleb and dealt with the fire himself. A month of watching Psyché each morning and he felt reasonably confident in grinding the coffee, sugar and spices ready for her to brew. He also sliced ham, but felt far less confident about cooking eggs so left them alone.

She appeared downstairs a few minutes later, bright, cheerful and completely unconvincing. Her gown of deep red wool was one he particularly liked on her, but this morning it struck the wrong note. Under her chatter—when was she ever chatty?—lurked a resounding chord of pain. A warning even: *Don't touch!*

When was it right to disregard such a warning sign? Reluctantly he accepted that in this case, perhaps never. He wanted to comfort her, grieve with her—for surely she was still grieving—and reassure her. Yet he could force nothing on her. Certainly not for his own peace of mind.

Caleb came out to join them, his eyes sleepy. That was

something else that had changed—the boy now lived at the shop, using the sleeping closet by the back door. He never intruded, but Will had taken to reading with him after the evening meal, helping him study.

Psyché poured the boy a cup of coffee and pushed her ham and eggs towards him. 'You have this. I'm not hungry.'

Caleb frowned. 'I was going to eat down at the Lion like usual.'

'Eat here.'

He smiled. 'Thanks, miss.'

The boy polished off the food and carried his plate to the sink. 'I'll wash up when I've set the tables and chairs out.'

'Thank you, Caleb.'

Will reached across the counter for Psyché's hand. 'Sweetheart, I don't know when I'll be able to visit, but—'

'It's all right, Will. I understand.'

He drew a frustrated breath. 'No. I don't think you do. In fact, I'm damned if *I* understand. But this isn't how I want to treat you—sneaking off from here as if you're something to hide, something I'm ashamed of.' He rose.

'Will—'

Leaning across the counter, he kissed her. Hard.

'I love you. That's all. Think about that.'

She stared, dark eyes wide and shocked.

'Just that. Promise me?'

'I—all right.'

'Good.' He kissed her again. Gentler this time, lingering. Not caring in the least that Caleb was right there in the shop making a deliberate clatter with the tables and chairs.

In the following three days Will flung himself into his work. Huntercombe was busy preparing for the Parliamentary session, as well as reviewing the work Will had done for him in the past few weeks. There were letters to be drafted, written and sent. A meeting for one of his Parliamentary committees to arrange and minute. And all the time Will was conscious that, much as he loved his work, he had lost something vital.

On the fourth morning after his return to Grosvenor Square, Will had sorted the correspondence by the time Huntercombe appeared in the library, accompanied by his spaniel, Fergus. His lordship's personal correspondence lay in a neat pile on his desk, a letter from Lady Huntercombe on top, and Will was reading the rest and making notes.

Fergus trotted straight over to greet him, his tail a flurry of pleasure, then went across to the fire and made himself comfortable.

Will smiled at Huntercombe. 'Good morning, sir.'

'Good morning, Will.'

Huntercombe had said nothing about Psyché beyond asking how she went on. He'd also asked after Selbourne. No change in his demeanour, no hint of disappointment or disapproval suggested that he was aware that his secretary had been openly living with a woman—it was only when he understood that Huntercombe would not raise the subject that Will realised how much he had dreaded it. He should have known better. Only once in the seven years of his employment had Huntercombe said anything about a woman Will was interested in. And that had been to warn him that the lady was less than discreet and her husband far less than complaisant. No judgement, not even of the indiscreet lady. Just a friendly word of advice. Will put it out of his mind to focus on a letter from one of Huntercombe's London tenants. He scribbled notes, and a couple of possible solutions to the problem outlined, and went on to the next letter.

A peculiar noise from Huntercombe made him glance over.

Reading spectacles perched on his nose, the Marquess

was staring at Lady Huntercombe's letter as if it had bitten him.

Will frowned. If he needed to know he'd be told, but the Marquess looked up, met Will's gaze and, to Will's disbelief, turned crimson.

'Ah, a letter from Isleworth.'

'Yes, sir.' He hesitated to ask, but Huntercombe looked dazed. 'There's nothing wrong with one of the children, I hope?' If Lady Huntercombe was writing letters, it was reasonable to assume there was nothing too much wrong with her.

'No, no. Nothing like that. Nothing wrong at all.' Huntercombe cleared his throat. 'Er, just some news. Yes, news. Private news.'

'Of course, sir.' Slightly startled at this uncharacteristic lapse into babbling, Will went back to his own task. But his mind slid elsewhere. Huntercombe's remarriage late last year had been contracted as a marriage of convenience to provide an heir. Will had realised fast enough that both Huntercombe and his Marchioness felt a great deal more for each other than mere convenience and Lady Huntercombe's two children from her previous marriage thought their 'Uncle Hunt' to be positively top of the trees. They were all happy, but there was that need for an heir...and since when did the man ever babble?

Will glanced at Huntercombe again, just as Huntercombe shot him a surreptitious look. The Marquess was still red, which to Will's mind suggested... No. He wasn't even going to think it—

'The Sight, allied with discretion.' Huntercombe shook his head. 'Say it, Will.'

Will gulped. 'Congratulations?'

Huntercombe laughed a little wildly. 'It might be a trifle early for that, but thank you. Lady Huntercombe has reason to believe we are expecting an addition to the family later in the year.' He smiled over his reading spectacles at Will. 'One day I hope I'll be congratulating you.'

'I don't think…ah, that is, thank you, sir.'

His own cheeks burning, Will dived straight back into Huntercombe's business correspondence. Psyché was utterly sure of the efficacy of Queen Anne's Lace, but what if she were wrong? What if—?

'Will? Will!'

Belatedly he realised that Huntercombe had been speaking to him. 'I'm sorry, sir. You said something.'

Huntercombe gave him an amused look. 'Several somethings. Is there anything in your pile I should look at?'

'There's a letter from Bickby. He wishes to make some alterations to the buildings to expand his business.' He passed the letter and his notes across.

Huntercombe went through them. 'Good ideas, Will,' he said at last. 'I suggest that you—'

There was a knock on the door.

'Come.'

Mark, the African footman, came in. 'A visitor for Mr Will, my lord.'

Will stiffened. 'For me?'

Mark came over to him and held out a salver bearing a single visiting card.

Will took the card. 'Thank you.' He glanced at it and his stomach lurched. 'Mark, please inform Mr Long that I am—'

'Mark—' Huntercombe's voice betrayed nothing. 'Show Mr Long in here. And add an extra cup to our morning coffee tray, if you would be so good.'

Mark bowed. 'Yes, my lord.'

'Sir—' Will floundered for words as the door closed behind the footman. 'I—he should not have called like this!'

Huntercombe leaned back in his chair. 'He is your godfather, Will, and your mother may have mentioned your injury to him.'

'I know you do not like each other—'

'That's an understatement, but—' Huntercombe gave him a quizzical smile '—I can probably receive him without succumbing to the temptation of tipping him a leveller.'

'I know *that*, sir!'

Huntercombe snorted. 'I'm glad you're confident. Frankly I'm stunned that he has brought himself to step across my unhallowed threshold.'

The door opened again. 'Mr Long,' Mark announced.

Huntercombe rose, and inclined his head. 'Long. How do you do?'

'My lord.' Edward Long executed a dignified bow. 'I beg your indulgence for the intrusion. I had a most worrying note from William's mother. My cousin, you know.'

Huntercombe's smile was his most reserved and formal one. 'Of course, Long. You need not apologise.' He began to gather up his papers.

Long's hooded gaze slid to Will, who rose to his feet. 'I am glad to see you recovered, my boy.'

Did Long have any idea how much he *loathed* being called, 'my boy'?

'I am very well now, sir.' If he ignored the occasional twinges in his side. 'My mother should not have bothered you. I was well on the way to recovery before she went home.'

Long smiled. 'Of course, but mothers, you know. And naturally I wished to assure myself of your recovery. You are hard at work, I see.'

'I'm trying not to overwork him, Long.'

Huntercombe's tone held a world of dry amusement.

'Of course not, Huntercombe.' Long glanced around the room. 'I see you still have your spaniel.'

'Naturally.' Huntercombe clicked his fingers at Fergus,

who immediately went to him. 'I find him excellent company. And most discerning.'

Will nearly choked. Fergus, who greeted most visitors with enthusiasm, had not bothered to do more than raise his head from his paws for Long.

Long's mouth thinned. 'No doubt.'

Polite conversation ensued: the weather—so nice that spring had finally arrived; the probability of rain being thoroughly explored; good wishes extended on the recent marriage of Long's daughter; a passing mention of the Parliamentary session in which any mention of politics was conspicuous by its absence. Not by so much as a word did either man betray their mutual dislike.

Huntercombe finally said. 'Long, perhaps you will excuse me? I am leaving town this afternoon, so I must alert my valet, and before I leave I had best take my dog for a walk.'

Will stared. After Lady Huntercombe's letter it was hardly a surprise that the Marquess was leaving London, but... 'Sir, I will be packed as soon as may be.'

Huntercombe shook his head. 'No need. You are on leave. At least, you are after you have seen Bickby. Either solution is more than acceptable to me. He may make his choice or negotiate a variation with you.'

Will blinked. 'What if you don't like our variation?'

Huntercombe smiled. 'Apparently I've more confidence in your abilities than you do yourself. I trust your judgement without reserve, Will.'

'Very well, sir. Please give my best to Harry and Georgie, and say...' he grinned '...all that is *proper* to Lady Huntercombe.'

Huntercombe's eyes twinkled faintly. 'Of course, Will. I shall use my best judgement.'

Will choked back a laugh. '*Au revoir*, sir.'

'And to you.' Huntercombe turned to Long. 'Good day to

you, Long. I hope you will not scold Will too harshly over his injury. While I quite understand Mrs Barclay's concern, and, of course, your own, I consider Will's act in shielding a young lady from harm to be admirable.'

He strolled from the room, Fergus at his heels.

The door had barely closed when it opened again. Huntercombe stuck his head in. 'Here is Mark with the coffee, gentlemen.'

The footman came in, bearing a tray laden with coffee and biscuits.

'I'll be gone for a week, Will. And I neglected to say that you may remain here or come and go as you please. With my blessing.' And the door shut.

Mark set the tray down on the desk as usual and turned to Will. 'Should you prefer it on the tea table by the fire, Mr Will, sir?'

'Thank you, Mark.'

The tea table was duly moved and the tray set upon it. Mark placed two chairs and bowed as Will and Long seated themselves.

'Thank you, Mark. That will be all.'

The footman smiled, and bowed again.

Long drew a deep breath as the door closed. 'Huntercombe's confidence in you is most flattering, my dear Will. But I was always sure you would do well.'

'He has been very good to me, sir.'

Long sighed. 'I do not doubt it. Even though I must deplore his stand in certain areas.'

Will inclined his head, reaching for control. 'His lordship makes no secret of his opinion on the rightness of Mr Wilberforce's Abolition Bill. Coffee, sir?'

'Thank you.' The words sounded as though they'd been ground with a load of sand.

Will poured the coffee. 'Sugar?'

Long raised his brows. 'Dutch East India sugar, I presume?'

Will clung to his temper. 'It is. And the coffee.' Long had considerable interests in Jamaica and slave-produced sugar and coffee.

Long took the offered cup. 'I should not have brought it up. Most improper in his own house. And yet it leads me into what I wished to say to you, Will. A delicate subject, one which your dear mother raised with some embarrassment.'

'My mother?'

Long smiled. 'I dare say it is nonsense, but she is most concerned for your safety.'

'As you may see, I am perfectly recovered,' Will said steadily. 'My injury—'

'And there is something very odd about *that* tale,' Long said. 'As I understand it, Carshalton is convinced of your complicity in the abduction of his daughter!'

Will took a fortifying sip of his coffee. 'Really? My understanding was that his daughter abducted herself to avoid an unwelcome marriage.'

That much was now common gossip, so safe enough to repeat.

'A disgraceful affair!' Long pronounced. 'A pretty pass we are come to when a young woman decides for herself whom she will or will not marry! I fear Selbourne will see a sad falling off in his business when it becomes generally known the part he has played. And as for Huntercombe—that he should have entangled *you* in such a tawdry scandal—'

'You're drinking his coffee, sir.' Will kept his voice mild. Just. 'And I make my own decisions about what I will, or will not be, involved in.'

Long set the cup and saucer down sharply. Words appeared to fail him and his lips set in a hard line. Then he recovered. 'But that is by the by. No, Will, your dear mother is far more concerned about your involvement with—' He cleared his throat, shifted uncomfortably. 'Staverton's... er...that is...the young person known as Miss Winthrop-Abeni.'

'My mother has no reason to concern herself.' Will set his coffee cup back in its saucer with extreme care.

'Of course not.' To his absolute horror, Long winked. 'Young men, eh? I did hint as much to dear Helena. Naturally I was reluctant to do so—ladies do not understand these things and God forbid that they should! She was much concerned that your interest in this, well, that your *interest* was far more serious.'

The very excellent coffee was bitter in Will's mouth as he saw himself clearly for the first time.

Long continued. 'I'm sure the cr—she is very *alluring*. They can be, you know, the women of her race. And she has, no doubt, traded upon that allure to her best advantage.' He smiled understandingly. 'In that she is no different from any white woman of a certain—'

'You misunderstand me, sir.' Will bit each word off with great precision. 'I meant that there was no need to be concerned that I might be harbouring dishonourable intentions towards Miss Winthrop-Abeni. Quite the opposite, in fact.'

He wanted to slam his fist in Long's face, but in a strange way hearing those foul assumptions and prejudices applied to Psyché, had been necessary. No less than the bullet, they had ripped a hole straight through him. He'd thought himself a good man, a just man, perhaps even a little bit of a hero in defying his family's views and espousing the cause of abolition.

He was no such thing.

Never before had the dreadful reality of the beliefs underpinning those proponents of slavery been driven home to him. For him it had been political, about lofty principles of justice. Never before had it been personal and about the day-to-day reality of facing people who thought you somewhere below the status of a favoured dog.

As it was for Psyché every day of her life.

Long stared at him, horror clear on his face. A shocked silence hung between them, in which the bridges Will had finally set alight burned and crumbled. After a moment he rose, his face sorrowful. 'Then we have reached a parting of the ways, Will. I am sorry for it, for I feel that I have failed your father very badly. Goodbye, my boy. I will continue to pray for you.'

Will gritted his teeth as he rose. 'I beg that you will not, sir. Such a plethora of contradictory prayers would confuse even the Almighty. Goodbye.'

He watched as Long walked from the room, his head and shoulders bowed. Relief and pain warred within him. Relief at the breaking of a weight of chains he had never quite realised and pain that he could not doubt Long's sincerity. The old man, for all his hideous views, had in truth always had what he perceived to be Will's best interests at heart and even now would forgive the prodigal and welcome him back with open arms. Yet he could feel no shame at having dealt such a painful blow.

Will sank back into his chair, staring at his godfather's barely touched coffee. Blindly, he reached out to pick up his own and drained it. He pulled out his watch. If he saw Bickby today, then tomorrow he could leave early on horseback. That would give him plenty of time to make the call he had to make and still reach Psyché by late afternoon.

Chapter Twenty

Will left Mayfair straight after breakfast, enough clothing in his saddle bags to last several days. He clattered out along the Edgware Road, climbing steadily out of the Thames Valley, eventually turning off on to Hampstead Heath itself. On the Heath and in the ditches daffodils trumpeted the arrival of spring in golden rivers and lakes. London was far behind and the higher Will rode up the Heath in the crisp, bright air, the deeper his stomach sank into his boots.

What was he thinking, calling on Viscount Staverton in this way? The man would kick him out with the proverbial flea in his ear for his presumption.

And thinking that was in itself presumptuous. Far more likely he'd be told Staverton was *not at home*. Which was a handy way of informing someone that he didn't even rate the flea.

Ahead of him, through the budding branches, the tender green haze of spring, he caught glimpses of the great house where Psyché had grown up. Highwood House perched in its park and gardens at the very top of the Heath, far above London and the village of Hampstead itself.

When he stopped to give Circe a breather from the steep climb, he looked back to see London below sprawled along the river. At this distance it looked serene, ineffable, all the smoke and grime, bustle and noise, muted by distance. Riding triumphant above it all, St Paul's great dome watched and guarded the city and her people. A city that teemed with life, humans of all races, creeds and colours. A city that over the past seven years had become his home and dear to him.

He understood that every change came at a cost. Accepting the post with Huntercombe and moving to London—and wherever else the Marquess happened to be—had meant moving away from his family and not only geographically. *This* change, this choice, would open a rift within his family that might never be bridged. In addition, he would need to find new employment that did not entail him spending so much time away from London.

Circe shifted restlessly and Will patted her. 'Very well. Can't have you getting cold.' He nudged her on with his heels and an encouraging word.

The young liveried footman looked uncertain. 'The master is not receiving visitors, Mr—what did you say your name was?'

'Barclay. William Barclay.' He stood on the doorstep, still holding Circe's reins. Only someone very close to the family would simply ride around to the stables.

The footman frowned. 'A moment, sir.'

He hurried off and returned shortly with another servant.

This second servant, an elderly man whose bearing and plain suit screamed gentleman's gentleman, approached followed by the younger man. 'Mr Barclay?'

'Yes.'

'Peter will take your horse around to the stables. If you would follow me, sir?'

He was led to the back of the house. The servant opened a door and ushered him in. 'If you would wait here, sir?'

It was a large library very different from the book-lined, somewhat untidy libraries in Huntercombe's various houses. Those were intimate with dark wood, bristling with books and papers.

This was full of light, a gilded poem in palest blue and shell pink, the barrel ceiling rioting with cupids and other mythological beings. Huntercombe's libraries were all about the books. This was about the room itself—a space designed and decorated to impress. Chilly, too, although a fire was lit. There was a painfully tidy desk and Will smiled, trying to imagine Huntercombe working in this room, although—he noted as he strolled along the shelves—there were some fine old editions and—

'Sir?'

He turned.

'The master will see you.'

He was shown to another door across the hall and ushered in.

'Mr Barclay, my lord.'

And now Will understood. The room across the hall was only to impress and overawe. *This* was where the real work was done.

It was much smaller and far warmer. Books, higgledy-piggledy, lined three walls completely and the desk held a scramble of papers and open books, as well as a battered-looking inkwell and pen stand.

Staverton—Will assumed it must be he—sat by the fire, his slippered feet propped on a footstool. There was a second chair and a tea table between them laden with books.

'Come in, Barclay. Marney!' This to the servant. 'Coffee, if you please. I dare say Mr Barclay needs something to warm him after riding all that way.'

The servant gave him a severe look. 'My lord. Please. The doctor insists that coffee is bad for your heart.'

'Oh, pish!' The old man waved that away. 'At my age

doctors' warnings are wasted breath. Bring the coffee and be blowed to all this mollycoddling!'

He beckoned Will forward. 'Sit down, lad. Sit down. Can't be peering up at you.'

Will sat. 'My lord, I realise my visit is unexpected and—'

A rusty chuckle escaped the old man. 'Not entirely. I was told to expect you by tomorrow, but—'

'You were?'

Staverton laughed again. 'Oh, yes. And I took leave to doubt it, I might as well admit!' He brooded for a moment, scowling into the fire. 'I should have just given him that tenner as it turns out.' He twinkled at Will. 'Still, I don't think he expected you to be here quite this soon. You've only missed him by an hour or so.'

'Missed who?'

But the question was rhetorical. Will knew who Staverton's other visitor had been.

'Hunt, of course. Called yesterday on his way to Isleworth.' Staverton snorted. 'First I knew that Hampstead was on the way to Isleworth from Mayfair. Anyway, he stayed to sup with me and set off after breakfast.' He smiled at Will. 'Always was a knowing one, that boy.'

Will had to agree, despite the jolt of hearing the Marquess described as a *boy*. How had Huntercombe known he'd call on Staverton before he'd known it himself?

Then he remembered… *'One day I hope I'll be congratulating you.'*

Huntercombe had known exactly what he was saying.

Staverton continued chatting generally until the door opened to admit Marney again.

The older man looked up, scowling. 'There'd better be two cups on that tray!'

'Yes, my lord.'

Marney set the tray on the tea table closest to Will who

pushed a couple of books aside to accommodate it. 'Thank you, sir. If I *could* prevail upon you to pour?'

'Oh, yes, yes. Dare say you think I'll drop my lady's Sèvres on the floor!'

'Yes, my lord. Her ladyship was very fond of this service.' Using his body to block Staverton's view, Marney placed a thin forefinger on one of the cups.

With a spurt of amused liking, Will saw that the cup was already half full of steaming water. He smiled at Marney. 'Of course. I shall take the greatest care.'

Marney winked and removed himself.

Will poured the coffee and handed Staverton the diluted brew.

The old man took one sip and grimaced. 'Wishy-washy stuff these days. Hardly worth drinking. Nothing *tastes* the same any more. The fact is, I'm dying, Barclay. But I look back on a happy life and I like to believe I've done some good. And there's one thing I did that was right and good when it might have been easier not to have done it.' He sipped the coffee again, apparently resigned to the taste. 'I think you must know what I'm talking about.'

Will took a deep breath. 'Yes, sir. Your great-niece.'

Staverton leaned forward. 'Have you come to ask my permission to pay your addresses, as Hunt said you would?'

Will was fiercely aware of the shrewd old eyes boring into him. 'Not quite, sir,' he admitted. 'Rather, I am asking your blessing.'

The old man sat back and stared at him silently, eyes narrowed. After a moment he tugged out a large, rose-embroidered handkerchief and blew his nose.

'Sir?'

'That's the right answer for Psyché.' Staverton gazed into the fire for a moment. 'She set her face against marriage seven years ago when Hetty married young Harbury.

'Said marriage gave all the power to the man, and she'd

have none of it.' He let out a breath. 'After my lady died, she begged me, rather than dowering her as I intended, to set her up in her own business. I didn't agree at first. Thought she'd got a bee in her bonnet and she'd see sense and change her mind.'

Staverton's laugh held a touch of bitterness. 'She'd seen sense better than I had. There were one or two men who would have taken her to wife, but they baulked when they realised her money was tied up tighter than usual.' He glanced at Will. 'That was to protect her as far as I was able. Finally I came to see that beyond that the best way to protect her was *not* to protect her in the usual sense, but accept that she had to manage for herself.'

He sighed. 'It's not what you want or expect for your daughter.'

It took a moment for that to sink in fully. 'Sir?'

Staverton looked straight at him and tears stood in the rheumy old eyes. 'Since I gave her her very first rose here in this house.' He wiped his eyes. 'Dashed fire's smoking. My blessing? You have it.'

Will nearly choked on his coffee. 'Just like that?'

Staverton laughed. 'Hunt vouched for you. What more could I ask for my girl?'

'I'm Edward Long's godson,' he confessed.

Staverton nodded. 'Hunt mentioned that. Well, you can't choose your relatives, although there might be one or two you don't acknowledge, and even your godparents are chosen for you.'

'But—'

'Hunt said Long called on you, and that he'd wager a pony the fellow would have queered his own pitch.'

'And that connection doesn't matter to you? Or that my family is—'

'If it doesn't matter to Psyché?' Staverton shrugged. 'No. You couldn't choose your godfather, but you've chosen Hunt as your mentor these seven years. I've been out of politics longer than that or I'd have met you long since. Perhaps you might pour me some more of that witch's brew Marney brought in?'

Will obliged, not having the heart to dilute the coffee quite as much.

Staverton sipped and still pulled a disgusted face. 'Anyway, you're here now. I know all about your prospects and it will suit Psyché down to the ground.'

He was glad someone knew about his prospects, because he was damned if he did.

'My prospects, yes.'

Staverton gave his wheezy chuckle. 'You'll do nicely for her.' He fiddled with the edge of his shawl. 'Something more, lad. You have my thanks. From what I'm told you saved Psyché's life.'

'It was nothing of the sort, sir!'

Staverton raised his bushy white brows. 'Put yourself between her and Carshalton's pistol getting the bastard's daughter clear, didn't you?'

'Huntercombe *told* you?'

A withering look. 'Where I'm going, lad, what I know that I shouldn't, isn't going to matter. Gave me a good laugh, always excepting that bullet—to hear about Carshalton being thwarted, not to mention Lucius bilked of a bride.'

His brows drew together. 'I remember Ignatius Selbourne's Kit. Poor little scrap of a thing she was when he took her in after her mother died.' His mouth hardened. 'Well, she's safe now. And you're going to make my girl happy.'

'If she will accept me.' He needed to be honest with the old man. 'She—marriage, as such, is still unwelcome to her.'

Staverton nodded slowly. 'I take your meaning. Most

men, Barclay, would consider that an advantage, especially in this case.'

Will gritted his teeth. 'For some it would be.'

'But not for you.' Staverton was silent for a few minutes, his head leaning back against the chair, his eyes closed. Will was wondering if he should summon Marney and leave, when the old man's eyes opened again.

'On my desk. A document.'

Will walked over to the desk. There were any number of documents, but he knew instantly which one Staverton meant. He stared at the sealed document with his name scrawled across it.

'The contents of that are included in my will,' Staverton said. 'But I had several copies of this drawn up, properly notarised, signed and witnessed. My lawyer has one and I gave Hunt one yesterday. There's a copy for Psyché herself. Didn't quite know why I had the fourth drawn up, but it must have been for you. Read it.'

Will broke the seal and complied. Then he stared at the old man, struggling to understand. 'But—'

'She's never been anything else in my mind, Barclay,' Staverton said softly. 'But this makes assurance doubly sure should anyone ever dare think otherwise. No need for you to tell her about this. I'll do it myself and make sure she understands why I've done it.'

'Have you sent for her, sir?'

Staverton nodded. 'My coach is going into London shortly. I've sent a rider with notes for Psyché and Hetty, asking them to come tomorrow. I'm glad I had the chance to meet you.' His eyes shut for a moment. Then he opened them and smiled. 'On my desk there—take the miniature.'

Will glanced over. 'There are several, sir.'

The old man laughed. 'Look closer, lad.'

She was younger. Sixteen perhaps. Glowing on ivory,

dark eyes alight with mischief as she held a little black spaniel on her lap.

'Take it, Will—I may call you that, I hope? Take it with my blessings, whatever compromise you come to with her.' He reached for the bell. 'I'll tell Marney you have it, but the gift is noted in the ledger of such bequests. As my executor, Hunt knows.'

Will's throat tightened, as he smiled back at the decent, kindly old man, who had taken in and loved a little girl most would have tolerated at best, or shipped straight back to hell.

'Thank you, sir.'

Staverton waved that away. 'Thank *you*, Will. I'm sorry I won't have the chance to know you better, but I'll go peacefully knowing you have her safe.'

Chapter Twenty-One

Will rode into the yard of the Red Lion as evening drew in. His heavy greatcoat held off the drizzle and cut the bite of the wind that whipped snarling around corners. The miniature was safely wrapped in several layers of cloth to protect it from harm. Ironic that, since he very much doubted that the original would ever consent to being cosseted and protected from all harm and, if he wanted her, he was going to have learn to accept that.

The upstairs windows of The Phoenix were dark and the shop was closed, but the shutters were still open and he could see the neatly stacked tables and chairs in the glow of lamplight from the scullery. Someone must be there. Caleb, perhaps, washing up.

Will rapped on the door instead of reaching for the bell. Time slowed as he waited. The church bell chimed six. He remembered distinctly that the clock in the stable yard had shown the last quarter-hour when he left.

Worry slid into his mind and he knocked again. He had no right to expect Psyché to be anywhere in particular, but it was rare for her to go out of an evening. And surely *someone* was there. She would never risk leaving a light burning. Except…light shone from Selbourne's apartment.

Could she have stepped across briefly, or would Selbourne know where she was?

As he was about to cross the street, movement caught his eye in the side of the bay window. His breath came out in a rush.

Psyché stood there, a deeper shadow in the darkness. She vanished and he waited.

There was a click and the door opened. She stood there in her plain woollen gown, the sleeves pushed back. 'Will.'

'Yes. May I come in? Is it too late?'

She shook her head. 'No. Come in.'

She locked the door, slipped the key in her pocket and stepped back. Will lifted the bar, but she shook her head. 'Caleb is out.'

She led the way back through the shop and pushed the curtain aside. 'Come through.'

The sink was half full of steaming, sudsy water. She picked up a saucer, washed it.

He frowned. 'Caleb usually does this.'

She set the saucer in a wooden rack. 'He's having a lesson with Ignatius. I wanted to be alone anyway.' She took a deep breath. 'You are very welcome to stay, but I'm going out to Hampstead first thing tomorrow morning. My...my great-uncle...he's—' She broke off, swallowed. 'He's sent for me. For Hetty. To say goodbye.'

Again that shuddering breath.

'I'm sorry.' If he confessed that he already knew this, she'd want to know why he'd called on Staverton. There were other things he needed to say first.

He gestured to the sink. 'Can I help?'

She stared and through the sadness he saw laughter rise up.

'Will, have you ever washed a dish in your life?' She picked up another saucer and washed it.

'It can't be that difficult,' he said defensively.

She handed him a cloth and the saucer. He blinked. What—?

'You rub the saucer dry with the cloth,' she said helpfully.

He knew that.

By the time he thought the saucer was dry enough she had ten more and several cups lined up on the draining board. They worked in silence for a few minutes, the cups and saucers gaining on him steadily.

Picking up a cup from the rack, he finally spoke. 'I had a visit from my godfather yesterday.'

She set another cup in the rack. 'Oh.'

He grimaced. 'You may have heard of him. Edward Long. He wrote—'

'*The History of Jamaica.*' She nodded slowly. '*He's* your godfather?'

'And a cousin of my mother's. He...was very good to us when we came home to England after my father died. I was eleven.'

She nodded. 'So was I when I left.' That beautiful, lush mouth trembled. 'My mother had...my mother was dead, but I did not expect the—my father to bring me to England.' She began to wipe the benches, using the cloth he had dried with. 'Certainly not as his daughter.'

'No. You wouldn't have expected that.' He finished the last cup. Planters raped slave women all the time. Any children they sired were also condemned to slavery. She had been branded.

'I expected to be sold.'

His stomach churned. He *knew* how the system worked, knew his own father had likely sired children, sold them as well as other children: it was a body blow to hear her say it.

'You were a *child.*'

Her laughter chilled him. 'Will, you *lived* there. I was a

commodity and he had a very good offer for me. His overseer wanted me.'

Will wasn't sure he was still breathing. She didn't mean
she'd been wanted as a kitchen maid, or a field hand, not
that either occupation would have protected her from rape
and she would still have been a slave…but, she'd been a
little girl. *Eleven.*

His overseer wanted me.

'Did he—?'

'No.' She turned away, but not before he saw her mouth
tremble.

'Psyché—'

A single, swift stride took him to her, but she flung up
one hand, stepped back.

His heart cracked.

'What did you tell Long about me?'

He fought to keep his voice steady. 'About you? Nothing. It was none of his business.' He took a deep breath,
knowing that if she refused he had to accept it. 'I simply assured him that my intentions towards you were honourable.'

Her eyes widened. 'You told him *what*? *Why*?'

'Why?' He reached for her hands and this time she allowed it. His heart began to beat normally again. 'Because
I can't continue to compromise with them. All these years
I told myself that it was only politics. That we could agree
to disagree, that family was more important than my political leanings.'

'They're your family. You love them.'

How often had he told himself that? 'Yes, they are my
family. But what about *your* family?'

She stared. '*My* family? Uncle Theo and Hetty?'

'No.' He gripped her hands. 'Your mother.'

'My *mother*?'

'What if she hadn't died? And your father had decided
to sell her? Or to sell you? Separately.'

Her hands trembled in his. 'If he had sold Mam?' She shook her head as if to clear it. 'That happens all the time, Will. It's not your—'

'And it *shouldn't* happen. None of it should happen. I finally understood that it's not about politics and some theoretical concept of justice. It's about people, families destroyed. How can I say that *my* family is important when I have no doubt that my father destroyed families exactly like yours? Like your mother's.

'What happened to her, Psyché?'

The question was so gentle, so natural, that it slid straight through her defences. She couldn't *not* answer. All these years and she had never spoken of that day. Not to anyone. Uncle Theo had asked very gently about her mother, but when she had shaken her head he'd dropped the subject. So perhaps she needed to speak at last.

She was *there* again, a little girl, sitting in the shade of the lignum vitae tree on a blanket to protect her pretty new gown. How odd that she had remembered that dress all these years. They'd both had new dresses, her and Mam. The father had given them the dresses only that day.

She'd never worn hers again.

The air was close and humid, the evening sea breeze not yet awake, and the little girl sat playing with a child's copper tea set, pouring tea for her doll, Amabel, her only playmate. Footfalls sounded and she looked up.

Flint, the father's overseer, stood over her. She looked down quickly. Flint looked at her as if... Her skin crawled even as she shut off her thoughts and became clammy as he remained towering over her.

'Is your master here, girl?'

Taken by surprise—he'd never spoken to her directly

before—she looked up at him and reminded herself to speak nicely. 'Good day, Flint. The father is in the house.'

His eyes narrowed, his mouth became a thin line and a metallic taste soured her mouth. Frantically she searched her mind. What had she said? What had she done?

'"Flint..."?' Low, cold.

And she knew. The way she'd spoken to him. As an equal. Not the way a—

'"The father"?'

'He...he is the father,' she whispered. Oh, God! She'd answered back. Been impertinent and—

'Winthrop is your master, you uppish little slut, and it's more than time you learned your place!'

She coiled herself to run, but her wrist was already crushed in his grip as he hauled her up and shook out the lash of his whip.

She wriggled and squirmed, but he held her effortlessly.

'I'll enjoy this.' His voice bit into her as she knew the whip would. 'And maybe later I'll teach you something else about your place. You're old enough, in my book.'

He raised the whip and she screamed, striking at him in terror. The blow missed, but he released her wrist, grabbed her even more painfully by the hair, and shook her like a terrier with a rat until she was dizzy, sick with the pain.

He finally let her fall limp and raised the whip again.

The blow never fell. A whirlwind hit him, shrieking in a polyglot of Akan, French, Portuguese and English, and sent him flying. The child looked up, dazed, and saw Mam in her pretty new gown, her eyes fierce as she stood over the fallen overseer, his whip in her hand.

'Leave her alone!'

She flung the whip away and spoke in Akan to the terrified child. 'Go, Abeni! Go to the house!'

But the child was frozen in terror as Flint got slowly to

his feet, wiped at the blood trickling down his cheek where Bess's nails had raked him.

'By God, you'll pay for this!'

He grabbed Mam's wrist, jerked her close and raised his fist.

'Let her go, Flint!'

Pounding footsteps came from the house—the father, breathless and red in the face.

'What the hell are you doing?'

He pulled Mam away, pushed her behind him, but Flint squared up.

'I'll tell you what I'm doing, Winthrop! I'm disciplining your slaves!' He pointed at the child. 'The whelp tried to hit me when I told her she was impudent—and your bitch came at me for correcting the uppish brat!'

The father paled. 'Bess? What—?'

'God damn it, Winthrop! You don't ask a slave its opinion! You don't ask for its side of the story!'

'Steady on, Flint. I'm sure—'

Flint stepped right up to him. 'Either deal with the slut properly yourself or I'll report it. You can dismiss me. I'll find another position easily enough.'

The father clenched his fists and there was a terrible silence in which the hot, humid air seemed to wrap about the child's throat.

No! He couldn't!

But the father turned to the small group of gathered slaves and beckoned. 'Jonah. Daniel. Take her.'

The two grooms moved forward and seized Mam, who went with them silently towards the stable...

'No!' The child ran after them, clutching at Mam, striking at Jonah and Daniel. They pushed her away, gently enough, and she tried again.

A large hand caught her shoulder, swung her around— the father.

'Please! Please! You can't—'

His fist felled her to the ground. 'Isaac! Confine her to her room.'

She was picked up, dazed from the blow, and slung over a powerful shoulder.

Flint exploded. 'Damn it, Winthrop! The brat's earned a flogging, too! Or make her watch if you won't flog her!'

'Her room, Isaac.'

And Isaac kept walking, ignoring the child's screams and the blows she landed on his back.

Will couldn't bear it any longer. He gathered her into his arms and held her. There was no comfort he could offer. What comfort could there be?

'Isaac locked me in.' Her voice shook. 'I would have climbed out, but the windows were barred. I'd never thought of that before. He left me there because they all had to go and watch.' She shuddered. 'I stood at the window and watched them all walk down to the stables. The whipping post was behind it. And…and I heard…'

That first scream, high and terrible, seemed to go on for ever. Again, and again, until the child's tears and sobs drowned out the dreadful sounds.

After a long time she heard slow footfalls out in the hallway, the scuffing sound of something being dragged. The lock clicked and Isaac and Jonah brought Mam in. She hung barely conscious between the two men, her mouth slack, and her gown hanging loose, exposing her breasts and the brand that marked her as a slave.

The child cringed back, horror a clawing thing in her belly.

They laid her face-down on the bed and the child saw why. The pretty new dress had been ripped open down the back, baring Mam's once gleaming skin.

No more.

Now it was flayed bloody and mangled. More meat than skin.

An agonised incoherence swallowed the child and she dropped, weeping, to her knees beside the bed.

'The master...he's sent for medicine and cloths,' Jonah said. 'Cynthia'll be up to help.'

The child found her voice. 'He...he let Flint do this? I'll... I'll kill him!'

A hard cuff to the side of her head knocked her sideways. She struggled up and found Jonah crouched beside her.

'You listen, girl.' His voice was hard. 'Talk like that gets you this.' He gestured to Mam, silent but for her ragged breathing.

'But—'

'You think she wants this for you?' His voice softened a little. 'Learn, girl. And keep your mouth shut.' A large hand rubbed her head where he'd cuffed her a moment before.

They turned to go, but at the door Isaac looked back. 'It weren't Flint did this. The master done it himself. Reckon if Flint had done it Bess'd be dead.'

'Mam *was* dead,' Psyché whispered. 'We just didn't know it yet. Infection took hold and the pain—'

He held her closer, grief for her closing his throat.

'Mam always said the father protected us, but in the end he didn't protect her. He probably couldn't.'

'Or thought he couldn't.' Useless rage burned through him.

Psyché shook her head. 'It amounts to the same thing. If Flint had reported what happened, Mam would have been hanged. And I would have been flogged. As it was—' he could feel the shudders tearing her apart 'the next day— that was when...'

She'd been dragged screaming to the blacksmith's forge and branded by her own father.

He could only hold her for long moments as she broke and wept in his arms.

Finally she spoke again. 'By flogging her himself and branding me I think he hoped to save us. Even if he'd thought of it, he wouldn't have been able to get us out before Flint reported the incident. It would have been seen as encouraging rebellion.'

He had no idea what to say. How many floggings had his own father ordered when they had lived in Jamaica? How many slave women had he violated? Did *he* have half-siblings there? Blood relatives condemned to hell? And his own guilt was his to bear. It could not be added to Psyché's burden of grief. Later, he would think what to do about that. Now he needed to tend to what was before him.

'But then he brought you to England.'

She nodded. 'I think… There was talk about what had happened. Open disapproval of the way I had been allowed to *get uppish*. He probably thought bringing me to England would solve the problem.'

'Whatever he thought, it brought you here in the end.' Will tightened his arms. 'And despite his intentions, Long's visit brought me here to you all the faster.'

She pulled away a little and looked up at him. 'What do you mean?'

'He made me see that I was trying to have my cake and eat it. And that it couldn't be done. Not honestly. If I continued trying to appease my family, then I was insulting you.'

'Will, you don't have to abandon your family to remain my—'

He feathered a kiss against her temple, found her mouth briefly. 'I'm not. I'm choosing myself and my beliefs. Which leaves me free to choose you. If you'll have me. My family will have to make their own choices.'

'*If I'll have you?* Will, if you are offering me—?'

'I'm not *offering* anything,' he said. 'I've nothing *to* offer. Rather, I'm *asking* you to marry me.' He reached for her hands. 'I know what you said the other night. You offered to be my lover. As my equal. And I do understand your reservations about marriage. I don't agree with all of them, but I understand your point.' He swallowed. 'If…if you would still rather not marry, we can agree to a compromise.'

'A compromise?'

'Yes.' Because sometimes it couldn't be all or nothing. Not when all for one meant the other lost everything important to her. 'We can continue as we are if that is that what you truly wish. But we have to make every effort not to have a child.'

He'd thought about this all the way back from Hampstead. 'I don't wish to coerce you into marriage, but I won't willingly bring a child into the world without the protection of my name. Nor would I wish to face my son or daughter one day and try to justify not marrying their mother. I do not say I like the way the world thinks about these matters, but a child would have to live in the world as it is. So we do whatever is necessary to avoid that. But—'

'But?'

'If we make a child, we marry.'

'And if I don't agree to this compromise?'

He could tell nothing from her tone. Calm. Neutral. 'Then we have to part.' He shoved his untidy hair back out of his face.

Her expression was inscrutable. 'But you would continue our affair with that caveat. Would you live here?'

'If you will permit it, yes.' How the hell he would find another position in those circumstances he had not the least notion. He thought Huntercombe would understand his problem, but if he were to live with Psyché whether married or not, his current employment would be untenable. He wanted to be *with* her.

'You'd help me run The Phoenix?'

He still couldn't read her. 'Only if you wanted that. I had thought to find another position that would not entail following my employer about the country or sponging off you.'

She let out a huff of breath. 'Damn it, Will. You're trying to ensure that *I* can have my cake and eat it!'

'Yes.'

And his heart cracked as a smile wobbled on to her lips. 'Sweetheart?'

'Perhaps I should bake a different cake, one we can share.'

'A different cake?'

'A wedding cake,' she said softly. 'Will you think me terribly flighty for changing my mind?'

'About marriage? No.'

'Not about marriage, per se,' she corrected. 'But about marrying *you*, yes.'

Joy welled up, flooded him. 'That's good enough for me.'

Chapter Twenty-Two

Every doubt had burned away in the blaze of his honesty. He had been prepared to give everything, compromise his own beliefs—everything except risk harm to an innocent baby. Even had she not already known the truth—that with Will she had found the impossible—that knowledge would have banished doubt. She could stand here in the place she had made for herself and know that he would share it with her in the truest sense of the word.

'Can you stay tonight?' she whispered. And remembered the note from Uncle Theo, and the one from Hetty. 'At least, I have to go out to—'

'Hampstead?' he said gently. 'I know.'

'How?'

His arms were a haven of warmth and comfort. 'I called on Staverton today.' He gave her a little shake. 'Did you think I would ask you to marry me without speaking to him? Asking his blessing?'

'Not his permission?'

'Certainly not.' Laughter shook him. 'I wouldn't have dared. But he gave his blessing, whatever we chose.'

Her breath caught. '*Whatever* we chose?'

His smile was tender. 'He understands you and he trusted me.'

Words were lost in a possession of mouths. Their kiss promised a lifetime of tonights and tomorrows, all the time in the world to love each other and meld their lives into an equality of joy. She pressed against him, wound her arms about him, loving the fit of their bodies and mouths that echoed and reflected the fit of mind and heart. It wouldn't be easy, their union, but it would be everything and more that she had ever wanted for herself, even when she had thought it impossible.

'Come upstairs,' she murmured against his mouth.

He broke the kiss, resting his forehead on hers. 'The doors. Caleb.'

For a moment she was confused. 'Oh. He has a key. He'll set the bolts and bar.'

Apparently that was all the invitation he needed.

'Right.'

He swung her up in his arms and headed for the stairs.

Together they tumbled on to the bed, tugging at clothes, his boots, her shoes. Caught between tears and laughter, Psyché rolled, blissfully naked, to rise up over him.

'My love.' Words she had never before given, never thought to give, and they were sweeter on her lips, in her heart than she could ever have imagined. They felt right, utterly right, spoken here in this place, to this man.

He reached up for her, drew her down against him, skin to skin, heart to heart. Love, desire, and pleasure shimmered between them. The faint tang of his shaving soap, the warm male scent of his body, enveloped her. The quickened rush of his breath, the slight scratch of his cheek on her breast and the fierce tug of delight as he drew the crest into the heat of his mouth. She cried out in the joy of this possession, arched up wildly. This, then, was everything. This was all. And yet, as he loved her and as she loved him, she understood that there would be more. That was the nature of everything. There was always more than you could ever imagine.

And there was more to give as she freed herself, sat up and leaned over him, tasting, teasing. Circling the flat nipple and knowing her power at the sharp intake of his breath. Tracing a path with her hand and feeling the strength in him tauten, muscles flickering, jumping under his skin as she went lower and her hand encircled the hard length of him.

Slowly she stroked, wondering at the silk-steel texture. Such power, yet so sensitive.

She bent to him, used her tongue, tasting him.

'*Psyché*. You...you don't have to—' He groaned.

She hesitated. She'd heard of this, but never before had she even wanted to...and perhaps he wouldn't want it. 'Would you rather I didn't?'

His eyes opened, blazing with heat. 'Do I *look* as though I've lost my mind?'

She blew gently, watched his eyes close in desperation. 'Do you want to?'

A choked laugh escaped. 'I've already lost my heart— why not my mind as well?'

She licked, savouring his shuddering breath. 'I promise to keep them safe for you.'

She took him into her mouth and he clung to control by a hair's breadth as she pleasured him with flagrant delight until he could take no more.

'*Enough.*' He freed himself gently, pulled her up his quaking body and rolled her beneath him. She opened to him and he entered slowly, loving her hot, wet welcome. Deep, so deep. Fathoms deep in joy, he fought for control, to remain still for a moment despite the silken shift of her body under his.

'Stay with me,' she murmured, her eyes hazed with passion. 'Everything. I want everything. I'm yours. Be mine.'

Everything. He lost the fight and began to move, deep

and sure. She moved with him, loving, giving, demanding, and he responded with everything he had, was and would be.

He felt her tense beneath him, heard the cry as she broke and shattered, clenching around him. With a groan he let go, spilling himself inside her for the first time, the fierce pleasure burning him to his soul.

Psyché lay limp and utterly content in his arms, her cheek resting on his chest. 'I can hear your heartbeat,' she murmured. And it was strong, steady…

His arms tightened and she felt his lips at her temple. 'It's yours. Along with the rest of me.'

She snuggled closer.

'Sweetheart?'

'Mmm?' Sleep drifted around her.

'Take Caleb with you tomorrow.'

She nudged sleep back. 'Take Caleb? Why?'

A large, gentle hand stroked her back, slid under the mad coils of her hair. 'I honestly couldn't say. But if your uncle dies—I don't trust Winthrop.'

'Caleb is just a boy. He's only sixteen.'

'He's loyal to you. Only to you.'

'And to you.'

She felt laughter shake him. 'Because of his loyalty to you. You'll take him?'

'It will make you happy?'

More laughter. 'No, love. You do that. But it will quiet my mind.'

'Very well.' Give and take. It was a small enough thing he'd asked for. Asked. He hadn't tried to dictate. And there was something she needed to ask.

'Will you write to your mother tomorrow? Please?'

He sighed. 'I'd rather do that after we're married.'

'Writing to her first is better.'

'Is it? I hope you aren't going to insist on having her blessing?'

She eased up and leaned her forearms on his chest. Her heart stumbled as he smiled up at her and she traced the scratchy line of his jaw with a fingertip, loving the quiet determination, the steady certainty in his eyes. 'No.'

'Good.' He reached up, sliding his fingers into her hair. 'I won't cede her that power.'

Trust Will to see to the heart of it. 'Tell her. Invite her to our wedding. Don't mention blessings. Let it be her choice.' She tickled the corner of his mouth. 'You never know, she might surprise you.'

He turned his head, captured the teasing finger and nipped it. 'We'll hope for that.'

Standing in the bay window of The Phoenix with Psyché the next morning, Will watched the street awaken in the growing light. Shopkeepers opened doors, setting out wares in the cold, bright air. Several lads hurried along, laughing and pushing at each other. The road was filling with traffic and noise.

Behind them, Sally bustled about supervising the other staff setting up chairs and tables. Caleb was helping, although his valise stood beside Psyché's at the door.

Psyché turned to him. 'Here's the coach.'

Will brushed a kiss across her lips. 'Godspeed. I have some business in the City for Huntercombe, then I'll ride out to Isleworth to inform him that he needs a new secretary. And before all that—' his mouth twisted '—I'll write to my mother.'

Her fingers entwined with his. 'And your brothers.'

He squeezed her fingers. 'Very well. They won't be happy, but I am.'

He opened the door for her, picked up her valise.

Staverton's coachman drew up, set the brake and doffed

his hat. 'Morning, Miss Psyché. Got her ladyship here. Bert! You right? Good lad.'

The footman was already down and taking Psyché's valise. He stowed it in the boot and the carriage door opened.

'Psyché!' The pretty golden-haired woman jumped down without the step. 'Oh, it's so good to see you!' She put a hand over her mouth. 'I shouldn't be glad, with poor Uncle Theo so unwell, but—' She broke off, seeing Will.

'Hetty, may I present Mr Barclay? Will? My cousin, Lady Harbury.'

'How do you do, Mr Barclay?' Lady Harbury held out her hand, her gracious smile laced with speculation.

'How do you do, Lady Harbury?' Will shook her hand and bore the inspection with equanimity.

'Hetty? Will and I are betrothed.'

If Will had ever entertained doubts that Psyché's cousin cared for her, the squeal of joy banished them.

'*Betrothed?* Oh, how wonderful! *When?*' She flung her arms around Psyché, hugging her fiercely.

Psyché's smile turned wicked. 'Last night.'

Lady Harbury smirked. 'I actually meant when is the wedding taking place, but never mind.' The glance she cast Will now had gone from speculative to positively assessing.

On the box, the coachman cleared his throat. 'Wishing you very happy, Miss Psyché.' He grinned at Will. 'Congratulations, sir. I'd heard the master expected something of the sort. He'll be right pleased.'

The footman let the step down and held the door open for Lady Harbury to get back in.

'You can tell me everything on the way, Psyché.' Lady Harbury stepped into the carriage.

Psyché beckoned Caleb forward. 'I'm bringing one of my servants, Hetty.' She smiled at Caleb. 'Would you rather ride outside or inside?'

Caleb cast a longing gaze at the horses, then up at the coachman. 'If it won't be a trouble—'

'None at all, lad.' The coachman shifted over slightly. 'Up you come.' He held out a hand for the boy.

Will took the satchel and passed it to the footman. 'I'll hand Miss Psyché in.'

'Yes, sir. Many congratulations, sir.'

'Thank you.'

He turned to Psyché. 'You'll take care?' he whispered.

'Of course, but—'

'I know.' He gripped her hands. 'I'm being foolish.'

She shook her head. 'You're being loving.' She sighed. 'You might not approve, but I have a pistol.'

He blinked. 'Loaded?'

'It's not very useful otherwise. It's in my muff. And, yes, I know how to use it.'

'You can't possibly think I would have queried that.'

She raised her brows. 'After you asked if it was loaded?'

Laughter shook him as he handed her in, put the step up. 'Put it down to shock.' He closed the door on her chuckle.

He watched the carriage rumble off down the street, then went back into The Phoenix.

'Coffee, Mr Will?' Sally gave him a friendly smile.

'Yes. A pot, please. I'll take it upstairs.'

He was going to need privacy as well as strong coffee to write those letters to his family.

'He makes you happy.'

Psyché smiled. 'I was already happy. But, he—' Oh, how to explain it? She'd always thought it was important to be happy independently of others, to be self-sufficient, not needy.

'Joy. He makes me joyful. He doesn't love me because I'm Black, or despite my being Black. He just sees *me*. Psyché.'

Hetty said nothing and Psyché reached for her hand. 'Hetty?'

The slim gloved hand turned under hers and linked fingers. 'I'm glad. So glad for you. I wish—' She broke off, turning away slightly to look out of the window, yet leaving their hands linked.

'You wish?'

Silence stretched between them.

Seven years ago she had held her tongue. 'Will you be allowed to come to our wedding?'

A tear fell. And another. 'I don't know.'

Her stomach churned. 'Never mind.'

Hetty faced her. 'Well, I *do* mind. We've acquiesced to his stupidity long enough. If...' Her face crumpled. 'If Uncle Theo dies, we won't even be able to write to each other.'

'I'm surprised he's permitted *this*.'

Hetty's smile threatened to turn over. 'Believe me, he wasn't happy. But Uncle Theo's summons trumped all. He won't risk my being disinherited.' Her hand went to her mouth. 'It's not that *I* care for that, but—'

'Don't be a ninny.' Psyché squeezed her hand. 'As if I'd think that.'

'Maybe he'll pull around and—'

'He's tired, Het. And he misses Aunt Grace so very much.'

And us.

Should she have stayed with him? But Uncle Theo had agreed in the end that it was best for her to forge a life independently on her own terms. He had understood.

'I thought that he'd come around eventually, you know.'

She blinked. 'What? Who?'

'Charles.' Hetty's fingers tightened on hers. 'I was so disappointed that you weren't there on Christmas Day. I... I was so angry with him.' She sounded as though she'd eaten gravel. 'He was frightfully condescending. Saying it showed *very proper feeling* on your part not to *intrude*.'

Psyché was unable to suppress her snort.

'Exactly. Anyway, Uncle Theo took me aside and said that was why you'd visited him on Christmas Eve instead—'

'Hetty—'

'They're wrong—Papa and Charles. And now with Uncle Theo dying—' Hetty's mouth flattened. 'I'll *never* see you, unless I defy him. And I'm going to!'

Psyché stared. Was this her gentle, conventional cousin?

'He has a mistress.' Hetty's voice rang bitter. 'He hasn't come to my bed since little Julia was born nearly eighteen months ago. He has an heir, two spares, and now a daughter. He says daughters are too expensive to dower to risk another.'

Psyché raised her brows. 'You might ask him if he's looked at the cost of kitting out a second son for the military.' That was Charles's family tradition. The third son was destined for the church, a much cheaper alternative. 'Or the cost of his mistress. Does he know that you know about her?'

Hetty nodded. 'When I asked why he did not come to me any longer, he said that I should be grateful not to have to bear children year after year. So I told him I knew.' She grimaced. 'He was simply furious and said that *proper women* did not know about such things, let alone speak of them.'

'Convenient for him.'

Hetty scowled. 'Isn't it just? Of *course* we know. But if we pretend we don't, then everyone can pretend to be happy. And Charles has been very clear that whatever *he* might do, sauce for the gander is not sauce for the goose. So if I were to have another child—' She broke off, flushing.

Psyché was silent for a moment. Uncle Theo had once said that while he accepted her need for a greater knowledge of certain subjects than most young ladies, Hetty did not require that knowledge. Or did she?

Once she had held her silence, believing that Hetty would be better off not knowing the truth about Charles. She had thought Hetty would neither want the knowledge, nor act on it. Now she thought that she should have spoken out—what Hetty did with the knowledge would have been up to her. Sometimes knowledge was your only protection.

'There are ways to avoid conception that don't—'

'Do you know if—?' Hetty stopped short, staring. 'That's what I was about to ask. Because it appears that very few high flyers of the *demi-monde* have babies.'

Chapter Twenty-Three

Hope Psyché hadn't realised she was nursing died as she saw the change in Uncle Theo since Christmas. Then, despite weariness and frailty, he had still been an imposing figure. Now he was propped up in bed on several pillows and swathed in shawls. Shrunken, fallen in on himself, the old energy sapped. Despite the fire the room held a waiting chill.

Hetty's soft gasp told her that her cousin saw what she saw: a man waiting to be called. At first she thought he slept, but when Marney stirred from the chair beside his master, Uncle Theo opened his eyes. A faint smile chased through the wrinkles.

'Here they are, Marney. Go away and have a nap. That's an order.'

'With respect, my lord—'

'Respect? That's a plumper! You've disobeyed orders for years.'

'Orders like that, my lord, yes.'

'Marney.' Hetty gripped the old servant's hands and touched cheek to his. 'Do, please, get some rest in the dressing room. I promise that Miss Psyché or I shall fetch you the moment he needs you.'

There was moisture in the old man's eyes, but he bowed.

'If it please you, my lady.' He disappeared into the dressing room.

Psyché moved to the bedside and bent to kiss him. 'There. That's how you should give orders, Uncle.'

He snorted. 'Pandering! I'll wager he would have backed off if *I'd* made to kiss his cheek!' He let out a contented sigh. 'But you're here now. Both my girls.'

Hetty smiled. 'Yes, and we have such news! Or Psyché does.'

'Is that so?' He reached out and took Psyché's hand. 'Going to make an honest man of Barclay, are you, girl?'

Laughter welled up through the grief. 'Yes. We are betrothed.'

He let out a sigh of contentment and smiled at Hetty as she brought a chair to sit opposite Psyché. 'That's it, then. All's well now.'

Late in the afternoon as the light faded and the old man dozed, the rumble of a carriage arriving came up to them.

'It's probably Papa,' Hetty said softly.

Psyché's stomach twisted as she remembered sitting across from Lucius at another deathbed in this house. She hoped it was anyone *but* Lucius.

Uncle Theo's eyes opened. 'Lucius, eh? Nothing to say to him.'

'Uncle,' Psyché chided him gently. 'He will wish to bid you *adieu*.'

The snort held a pale flicker of his old fire. 'It's too late in the day for pretty stories, girl.'

He drifted again. Psyché shared a rueful smile with Hetty and they slid back into companionable silence. Everything needful had been said without anything much being said at all. Sitting here with the old man who had joined their childhoods had set a final seal on the friendship and love that bound them as closely as sisters despite all differences.

The dressing room door opened to admit Marney.

He crossed to them and spoke softly to Hetty. 'Lord Harbury has arrived, my lady. He begs the favour of your company.'

Be careful what you wish for. How often had Aunt Grace said that? A pity she hadn't remembered before wishing for anyone but Lucius. Charles's presence was no better.

'Please inform his lordship that I must remain here,' Hetty said firmly.

Marney bowed and departed.

'That's telling him.' Uncle Theo did not open his eyes, but a wicked little smile teased about his mouth for a moment before it fell slack again.

Hetty shot a glance at Psyché. 'He'll be up in five minutes,' she muttered, 'worrying about it being too much for my—'

She broke off as the door opened and Charles walked in.

In the years since Psyché had seen Charles his golden boyish charm had tarnished to smug assurance. Not like Will's confidence, but a top-lofty air of certainty in his own superiority and importance.

His gaze fell on Psyché and she could have sworn his eyes narrowed. The impression was gone instantly as he looked at Hetty and the old practised smile curved his lips.

'My dear Henrietta.' He came to Hetty, took possession of her hands and raised them to his lips. 'I know you said I must not worry, but you should not be without family at this time.'

Psyché barely refrained from rolling her eyes. She was right *there*, for goodness sake. Was she invisible?

'I'm hardly without family with Psyché here, Charles.' Hetty pulled her hands free.

Charles continued. 'Oh, quite. But I cannot rid myself of the thought that this must be too much for—'

'My delicate sensibilities?'

'Your delicate sensibilities.'

Psyché bit back a laugh at Charles's startled expression. 'Do you have any, Hetty?' she asked.

'Course not.' Uncle Theo's eyes did open this time. 'Grace didn't either. Just something we gentlemen pretend ladies should have so we can trot 'em out every time a woman actually wants to *do* something.'

Charles didn't seem to know what to do with that observation. 'Ah, quite so, sir.'

Psyché reached out and patted Uncle Theo's hand. 'You're becoming very philosophical, Uncle. Good afternoon, Charles,' she added. 'You are well?'

'Yes, I thank you.' He affected an expression of sober reflection. 'But deeply saddened by this sad occasion.'

Again the old eyes opened. 'Sad occasions will do that. Sit down if you're staying, boy. Hetty, love, your hand.'

'Of course, Uncle.' She sat down, reaching for his hand. The frail old fingers closed over hers.

Charles affixed a tender smile to his face. 'I should not dream of intruding, sir. I shall simply bid you farewell and leave you in Henrietta's safe hands.'

Psyché let her narrowed eyes raise to his face and had the satisfaction of seeing him flinch before he turned away to the door.

Uncle Theo roused as soon as the door closed. 'Psyché, my writing slope, if you please.'

'Uncle, there's no need to distress—'

'Then bring the slope,' he said, with a very fair approximation of his old determination. 'And, Hetty, help me sit up.'

Exchanging glances, they did as they were bid.

'Here you are, Uncle.' Psyché set the battered old slope on his lap.

'Open it for me, my dear.'

She did so and he raised the leather-clad writing surface to reveal the space beneath. He drew out two folded and sealed documents, handing one to each of them. Psyché's fingers brushed his, felt the chill in them.

'All this is in my will,' he said. 'Signed and tied up so no one can block it, no matter how much they might wish. Go on,' he urged. 'Open them.'

Psyché forced her trembling hands to steadiness as she fought tears and broke the seal. In shaky writing there were listed several items of Aunt Grace's jewellery. But that was not what mattered.

To my great-niece, Psyché Winthrop-Abeni, natural daughter of my nephew, John Alexander Winthrop (deceased), and his mistress, Elizabeth Black (also deceased), I confirm her Freedom.

A breath shuddered in and out. She dragged in another. 'Uncle—'

'I know that's not something you needed to be told, my dearest,' he whispered. 'But in case anyone might ever think to challenge it.'

She swallowed hard and laced her fingers with his. She knew exactly what he'd feared for her. There were many instances of Black servants brought to England, believing themselves free there, only to be dragged to a ship, shackled and sent back to the auction block in Jamaica or America. He had done everything in his power to ensure her safety after his death.

'Thank you. For everything. For loving me.'

He smiled. 'That wasn't difficult.'

'And...' she bent forward to kiss his cheek '...even for protecting me.'

He gave a wheezy chuckle. 'I knew you never liked that I did that. In a better world it would not have been necessary.' His fingers tightened. 'I gave a copy of that to your Will. You've chosen well. You've always had my love, now take my blessing and think of me sometimes.'

On the other side of the bed Hetty sat, her own letter open in her hands, tears sliding down her cheeks. 'Uncle, you...you can't do this.'

'Already done, girl. Done, signed, witnessed.' His voice cracked, audibly weaker.

'But Papa—'

'Lucius will have plenty. It's yours.'

Hetty looked across at Psyché. 'Highwood. He's given me Highwood.'

'Tied up in a trust the devil himself won't break,' Staverton said. 'No one, not even Charles, can touch it or the income to maintain it.'

'Papa will kill me,' Hetty whispered.

'Won't help him.' His eyes were closed again. 'Just go to your daughter on the same terms, and after her, Psyché.'

'Thank you, Uncle,' she whispered.

He opened his eyes again and smiled at them. 'Swore I'd protect you, both of you, any way I could. It's done now.'

Despite the clock on the chimney piece, time seemed scarcely to stir in the quiet room, measured only by the flickering fire and Uncle Theo's increasingly laboured breaths as the evening wore on.

Psyché persuaded Hetty to nap for half an hour on the day bed.

'I'll wake you, I promise.'

She sat, holding Uncle Theo's hand, knowing that with every tired breath he slipped further away. Marney came in, crossing to the fire to put more wood on before coming to the bed. Midnight crept closer.

'Stay, Marney,' she whispered. 'He's going.'

The old man nodded. 'Yes. I think...let him go now, Miss Psyché.'

She stared up at him, saw the grief sliding down his cheeks. He'd known Uncle Theo far longer than she had. They were closer to friends than master and servant.

'Let him go?'

Marney smiled through his tears. 'You're holding him here, child. Let go.'

For a moment she didn't understand, then her gaze fell on their entwined fingers. She remembered the room in the inn where her father had joined their hands, then the day he'd taken her hand to lead her down to the library in this house. Her small brown hand safe in his large, pale clasp. It was reversed now. Her hand was the stronger, holding death itself at bay if Marney were to be believed.

'I don't want him to feel alone,' she whispered.

'He knows you're here,' the old valet said gently. 'He waited for you and Miss Hetty. Now it's time to release him.'

Tears blinded her as she slipped her fingers free and went to rouse Hetty.

Hetty blinked awake at once. 'Is he—?' She clutched Psyché's hand.

'Soon.'

They sat together, holding hands, Marney across from them, and waited.

The clock had slid over the edge of midnight into to-morrow when the old man's eyes opened again on a rattling breath.

He glanced at Marney. 'You were right about that damned horse.'

'I know, sir.'

He looked at Psyché and Hetty. 'My girls.' His gaze focused on Psyché. 'Don't...' Another rattling breath. 'Don't make the boy wait.'

A moment later he was gone.

'What now?' Hetty's fingers trembled in hers and her voice shook. 'What should we do, Psyché?'

She had no answer, but Marney spoke. 'Sleep.' He leaned over and closed the empty eyes. 'Your old rooms are prepared.' He looked at Hetty. 'I believe you will find his lordship waiting for you.'

'Oh.' Hetty let out a sigh. 'He'll insist on returning to London, I suppose.' She looked sadly at Psyché. 'I'd rather stay here with you.'

Psyché gave her a hug. 'I must go back as well.' She felt numb, frozen, as if everything had stopped. 'I'll come back for the funeral.'

Hetty grimaced. 'Charles will say it's unladylike, but—'

'Will you attend?'

Hetty's mouth firmed. 'Yes. Unless he actually locks me up, yes.'

Psyché woke to the sound of someone stirring up the fire and was surprised that she had slept at all. But the old, familiar room had closed about her like comforting arms. And Sarah, her first friend here, had been there to help her undress.

'Don't you be telling me you don't need help, Miss Psyché. Well do I know you can do for yourself. But there's times a body needs a little comfort.'

So she had yielded to the luxury of someone to fuss about her, ease the broad-toothed comb through her hair and wrap it in a length of silk to keep it from tangling.

Now she rolled over to discover Sarah mending the fire. 'Did you go to bed at all? What's the time?'

'Certainly I did, miss.' Sarah straightened. 'And it's nine o'clock.'

Psyché threw back the bedclothes and swung her legs out of bed. 'I didn't mean to sleep this late!'

Sarah sniffed. 'Not to be wondered at. Why, you weren't in bed till after one.' Her head tipped to one side. 'You all right, Miss Psyché?'

Psyché's eyes burned. 'No. But I will be. It's just...'

'Takes time, it does.' Sarah brought a robe over.

She shook her head. 'There's a black gown in my valise, Sarah. I'll dress now.'

Psyché went downstairs in the sober black gown. It was one she'd had for mourning Aunt Grace, kept tucked away in lavender in her old camphor wood chest. She crossed the hall and smiled at the black-clad footman.

'Good morning, Peter. Is breakfast ready?'

'Yes, miss.' He hurried to the parlour door to open it. 'Ah, his lordship is down already, miss.'

'Oh. Thank you.'

She passed into the sunny parlour and Charles looked up from his newspaper.

He rose. 'Good morning, Psyché.'

She blinked. After his studied effort last night to avoid speaking to her... 'Good morning, Charles.'

She went to the sideboard, helped herself to ham and made a pot of tea. About to carry them to the table, she found Charles at her elbow.

'Permit me to help you to eggs, dear cousin.'

'This is quite sufficient, thank you, Charles.' Her skin crawled at his nearness. 'Is Hetty coming down?'

'I fear my poor Henrietta has overtaxed herself,' Charles said seriously. 'I have persuaded her to remain in our room.'

She sat down at the table, well away from Charles's chair. 'I'll go up to her after I have eaten and—'

'She will be readying herself to leave.' Charles sipped his coffee. 'I must return to town. There is a great deal to be arranged.'

Psyché couldn't imagine what Charles might have to arrange. 'I see. Is Hetty going with you?'

He smiled. 'Of course. There is room for you, too. No need for two carriages travelling back to London.' The smile became indulgent. 'She will like to spend a little more time with you.'

Something about his smile gave her an itch between her shoulder blades. She shrugged it off. 'How kind.' She could easily slip down to the stables and order the carriage without him being any the wiser...or she could be there as a sort of buffer when Hetty informed Charles of her unexpected inheritance.

'Not at all.' He glanced about the parlour, scowling. 'I cannot think why the servants have not darkened the rooms yet! Poor Staverton lying dead and—'

'Uncle Theo gave orders otherwise,' Psyché said. He had done the same when Aunt Grace died. 'He always said he would rather keep the house in the light.'

His laugh was patronising. 'I dare say, but people will think it very odd. I gave orders last night that the windows should be covered. I expected to be obeyed!'

Anger slid through her. Did he know already that Hetty had inherited this house?

'Anyway, no doubt Lucius, or *Staverton* as we now must call him, will put all to rights when he arrives later today.'

'Of course.' She bit her tongue. He did *not* know. Very well. Instead of arranging to go back alone, she *would* go with them. It was the least she could do for Hetty.

Peter entered, carrying a covered dish. 'Miss Psyché, Cook sent up poached eggs—exactly as you like them.'

The grin on his face, even though she really didn't want eggs, spread a warm glow through her. 'Oh, Peter. How nice! Please thank Cook for me.' She blinked back tears as Peter set the plate with two perfectly poached eggs at her place. Her throat felt tight, but she asked, 'Has something been taken up to Lady Harbury?'

'No, miss. But I'll—'

'Her ladyship is *not* to be disturbed.' Charles laid his newspaper down sharply. 'She will ring if she requires anything. That will be all.'

Peter removed himself without so much as the flicker of an eyelid to betray his thoughts.

'Damned impudent fellow!' Charles glared at the door.

'He was responding to my query,' Psyché pointed out.

'Nonsense!'

'I asked if anything had been taken up. As I would have done for Aunt Grace when she was ill.' Annoyed, because Charles's arrogance could well cost Hetty a reliable servant, she added, 'Highwood was my home for a very long time. The servants are used to taking directions from me.' She had never been very comfortable issuing orders, but she could give directions.

For an instant she saw the outrage on Charles's face at her assumption of authority.

'Your pardon, cousin,' he said stiffly. 'I never realised that Staverton appointed you his housekeeper.'

'He didn't,' she said coldly. 'I'm sure you are aware that Mrs Titchmarsh is still here. But apart from acting as his amanuensis when Mr Smalley retired, I also filled Aunt Grace's role as chatelaine after her death.'

That had been possible because Uncle Theo had largely retired from public life. She had only needed to oversee the accounts, menus and ordering for the household, along with his correspondence and infrequent engagements.

'Something,' she added, anger bitter in her mouth, 'any unmarried daughter of the house would have done without being considered a servant.' Not that *she* had an issue with being a servant, but Charles had meant it as a set-down. Damned if she'd let him get away with that.

'Oh! Er...quite!' Charles fumbled with the coffee pot, pouring another cup and making great play adding cream and selecting the right lump of sugar.

She pushed a little harder. 'Has the Vicar been informed?'

Charles blinked. 'I'm sure Staverton will arrange all that. You must not worry yourself about such things. *I* know you mean well, but others would see it as most improper!'

Improper. From the man who had once offered to take her as his mistress with the betrothal ring scarcely upon her cousin's finger. More and more she regretted not speaking out seven years ago.

Psyché ate her eggs and ham in silence, then rose. 'You will excuse me, sir. I must see to my packing.'

'Of course.' He remained seated, sipping his coffee and reading the paper.

She waited a beat, until he looked up.

'Is there—? Oh.' He set the cup and paper down hurriedly and rose.

Eyes narrowed, Psyché raised her brows. 'What I find *most* improper, Charles?' She didn't wait for a response. 'Hypocrisy.'

His jaw dropped and she turned her back and walked from the room.

Chapter Twenty-Four

Upstairs, Sarah had beaten her to the packing.

'All done, Miss Psyché.' Sarah laid her nightgown, carefully folded, on top.

'You shouldn't have, Sarah. I could—'

'You could, miss.' Sarah fastened the first buckle. 'But there's something I wanted to ask you.'

'Yes?'

'Mr Marney says that the master has left the place to Miss Hetty—is that true?'

She released a breath. It was really not her place to tell the servants this, but if Marney knew... 'Yes.'

'Not to Mr Lucius?'

'No.'

'Well, that's something.' Sarah buckled the other strap. 'But I dare say Lord Harbury will be as bad ruling the roost. Don't suppose you'd have a place at that coffee house of yours?'

She considered. If she had children, she wouldn't want to spend her whole life in the shop. 'I might, but what happened?'

'Took Miss Hetty's tea up this morning. Like she requested on her way to bed. His lordship wouldn't even let me in the room! Said her ladyship hadn't rung, *he* hadn't rung and that was all about it if I valued my position!' She looked close to tears. 'So I don't know if I'd even have a position any longer if *he's* to be master.'

Psyché took a deep breath. 'I believe Miss Hetty's inheritance is very carefully tied up in trust. He probably can't dismiss you, but come to me if necessary. And anyone else. I'll help even if I can't employ everyone.'

Sarah smiled and wiped away a tear. 'That was the best day's mending I ever did.'

Psyché nodded. 'For me, too. Are you finished here? If so, could you send a message to Caleb, my servant? Ask him to be ready when Lord Harbury's coach is leaving. I'm going back with his lordship and Miss Hetty.'

Sarah looked dubious. 'Well, I will. I don't know that her ladyship will be ready, though. She's not rung yet to be dressed and I daren't ask after his lordship's carry-on.'

'Don't worry, Sarah.' She smiled reassuringly. 'I'm sure Miss Hetty will be down shortly.'

'I'll send Peter up for your valise.'

'Thank you.'

Psyché slipped on her pelisse and buttoned it. Picking up the muff, she felt its weight and remembered her pistol. She had unloaded it last night. It was dangerous to keep a pistol loaded for too long.

With a sigh, she took the pistol out and looked at it.

'Never travel alone without a loaded pistol.'

Uncle Theo had insisted on that when she went to live in Soho. He'd taught her to shoot himself and ensured that she was proficient. He'd made her load and reload this pistol over and over again. He'd taught her how to care for it.

'Not something I ever envisaged teaching you, but if you're going to do this, you must be able to protect yourself.'

She would not be precisely alone this morning, but…she hesitated. Did she want to depend on herself, or a man she knew to be a bully and very likely a coward?

Five minutes later she tucked the pistol, reloaded, back into the special pouch inside the muff and strolled downstairs.

Charles was already pacing back and forth, swathed in his greatcoat.

'There you are.'

She stopped. 'Where's Hetty?'

He waved that aside. 'She'll be down directly. I cannot think what is taking her so long.'

She frowned. 'I'll go up and see if she's all right. Perhaps—'

'No, no.' He hurried past her. 'I'll go. Wait in the carriage so we may leave the moment she is down. Most inconsiderate to keep me waiting like this!'

Psyché glared after him, but turned to smile at the waiting staff. They were all there down to the scullery maid, some already in black livery, and some in black armbands. She wondered if Charles had even noticed. Could he possibly understand that between Uncle Theo and his household there had been a very real affection and respect? She took her time, starting with the scullery maid and working her way up to the senior staff. Finally she turned to the housekeeper.

Mrs Titchmarsh's eyes were red-rimmed. 'We'll look forward to seeing you back here soon, Miss Psyché.' A wobbly smile came. 'And your young man.' Mrs Titchmarsh patted Psyché's arm. 'We know what's what when a fine young man comes calling on the master.' She blew her nose. 'Mr Marney said he went easier for having you and Miss Hetty by him and knowing you were happy.'

A choking lump rose in Psyché's throat, tears threatened. She gripped Mrs Titchmarsh's hands. 'I'll see you soon, Titchy.' The childhood name came unbidden. 'And you all know where to find me.'

'That we do.'

'Cousin!' Charles's annoyed voice accompanied his hurrying footsteps. 'Why are you not yet in the carriage? Her ladyship will be down directly. We'll be late if we do not hurry!'

She leashed her temper. 'I was making my farewells, cousin.' Picking up her valise, she walked out on to the porch and saw Caleb.

He was seated on the bench beside the door, but rose and whipped off his cap.

'Miss Psyché.'

'Good morning, Caleb. We're leaving now.'

He grimaced. 'As to that, miss. That Mr Bragg—' he jerked his thumb at the carriage '—he says he won't take my sort up on the box.'

'Is that so?' She turned to Charles. 'It appears that I will be remaining.'

'Remaining? Certainly not!'

'Your coachman declines to take Caleb up, and there's no room inside, so—'

'Caleb?' He saw the boy and frowned. 'Oh. Well, I'm sure the boy can make his own way to—'

'No.' She didn't bother mincing words. 'I'm not leaving him to walk home.'

Charles scowled. He strode to the carriage and spoke to the coachman in an angry undertone.

'Miss Psyché—' Caleb touched her arm lightly. 'You're sure this is a good idea? Mr Winthrop is here. He arrived early, before the sun was up, and he's still hanging around the stables. Seems funny to me. Nobs like him, they don't spend time in the stables.'

She patted his arm. 'He's probably avoiding me.'

Charles walked back. 'A misunderstanding. Bragg thought the boy was cadging a lift.'

'I explained,' Caleb muttered. 'And so did Bert.'

Psyché silenced him with a quick shake of her head. 'Up you go, Caleb.'

The boy clambered up nimbly and Bragg scowled.

'Now, cousin.' Charles gestured her into the carriage ahead of him.

She hesitated. 'Hetty?'

He gave a long-suffering sigh. 'She's coming. Do get in and I'll hurry her along. Again.'

Psyché stepped into the carriage and Charles stepped in after her closing the door.

'What? You said—'

He banged on the roof. 'Drive on!'

The carriage lurched forward, throwing her into a seat. Her skin prickled and fear tasted sharply metallic in her mouth as she felt the increasing speed of the carriage.

'Cousin! Charles, what are you—?'

'We're going to London, my dear. Henrietta will follow along at some point.'

She lunged for the opposite door, but the handle was gone. Every nerve screaming, she faced Charles.

He smiled. 'No, *cousin*. You won't get out that way.'

Caleb grabbed for a handhold as the coachman whipped up the horses. 'What? Isn't her ladyship coming?'

'Mind yer own bleedin' business.'

Nearly at the great wrought-iron gates, Caleb tried again. 'We're leaving her behind?'

This time the coachman, negotiating the gates with the horses in a canter, ignored him.

Fifty yards on, the coachman eased the horses, pulling them up.

'Are we going back?' A man stepped from behind a tree and shock jolted through Caleb. 'That's that Mr Winthrop! What's he—?'

'Shut up if yeh know what's good for yeh.'

Winthrop got into the carriage.

Caleb's mind leapt to one appalling and terrifying conclusion as Bragg whipped up the horses. Sweat broke out all over him and he took a shuddering breath. If he was wrong, he'd say sorry later, explain himself. He reckoned Miss Psyché would understand. Because if he was right… Well, he'd never forgive himself, let alone face Mr Barclay and say he'd just sat there.

He gathered himself as the horses broke into a canter and jumped.

'Oy!'

Caleb landed slack-kneed and rolled into the ditch full of icy water and daffodils. Without a backward glance he scrambled up and sprinted for the gates.

'My lord!'

Psyché heard the coachman's yell as Lucius seated himself.

'The boy! He jumped!'

'Forget him!' Lucius shouted. 'Drive on! Fast!'

The coach lurched forward and Psyché realised that the coachman had sprung the horses.

Lucius smiled in satisfaction. 'About time we dealt with you.'

Fear licked through her. Caleb was safe, and he'd raise the alarm, but— 'What have you done with Hetty, Charles?'

He looked affronted. 'Done? Nothing, of course! Merely ensured that she obeys me and doesn't interfere.'

'Interfere with what precisely?' She kept her voice calm as she slid her hand deeper inside the muff.

Lucius smirked. 'Your protection died with Theo. I'm finally going to be rid of you. Selling off part of my inheritance, if you like. We're taking you to the West India Dock where Carshalton has a ship waiting bound for Freetown.' He watched her and smiled. 'You've heard of Bunce

Island? That's where you're going, bitch. Where my fool of an uncle should have sent you at the start.'

'I don't think so.' Braced in the corner against the swaying and jolting, Psyché withdrew her right hand from the muff.

Charles's eyes went wide. 'That's...that's a *pistol*!'

She barely flicked him a glance. 'Well spotted, Charles. *Don't move, Lucius!*'

Lucius froze, his hand hovering by his pocket.

'Any closer to that pocket, Lucius, I'll shoot you and be done with it,' she said. 'At this range I won't miss. Put both hands on your head, fingers linked.'

He complied, a snarl of fury on his face. 'You've got one shot,' he said. 'You think Harbury can't overpower you after you've shot me?'

She shrugged. 'He can try.'

She removed her left hand from the muff and Lucius swore.

Charles shrank back in his corner. *'What?'*

'That's a knife, Charles,' she said in helpful tones. She kept her eyes on Lucius.

'She won't shoot, Harbury,' he said, easing along the seat.

She cocked the pistol and he froze again. 'Why not, Lucius?'

He laughed. 'You think you'd get away with self-defence? For shooting a peer of the realm?'

She shook her head. 'No. Chances are I'd hang. But think, Lucius. A hanging coupled with the knowledge that I sent you to hell first? Or Bunce Island?' She levelled the pistol at his chest. 'It's not even a choice.'

He stared at her and she saw the moment he understood his miscalculation.

'You see, I *do* know about Bunce Island.' Even though Mam had refused to speak of it, there had been whispers from the other slaves. Her gorge rose, but she spoke coldly. 'I know about the sorting yards, the room where the women and girls are herded to be raped. Where they're branded. And the middle passage, with humans stacked and chained. A living hell and more to come for those who survive the voyage.'

'She's bluffing! Take her, Harbury!'

But Charles, his eyes wide, didn't move.

Psyché let out a silent breath. She'd suspected that Charles was a coward, but she knew better than to taunt him with it. 'Good decision, Charles. Because after shooting Lucius I'd gut you like a herring and consider it a job well done.'

'C-cousin, I'm sure there's no need for—'

'Order the coachman to stop, Charles.'

He hesitated, glancing at Lucius. She could guess his thoughts. If they could keep her in the carriage, once they got her to the dock, no matter if she killed one of them or not, the odds were high she'd be overpowered and would end up on the ship. She had to escape *now*.

'Think, Charles. If we reach the West India Dock, I'll shoot you and take my chance with Lucius. Order your coachman to stop.'

Charles licked his lips, staring at the pistol.

'Damn it, Harbury! The blasted thing probably isn't even loaded!'

She simply smiled. 'Care to wager on that?'

His eyes never leaving the pistol, Charles banged on the trap. The coach slowed and the trap opened.

'My lord?'

'Stop the coach.'

'My lord?' The coachman sounded confused.

'Stop the damn coach, Bragg!'

'Yes, my lord.'

The trap closed and the carriage slowed further.

'When it stops,' Psyché said, 'you are both going to get out. Then, Charles, *you* will take the pistol out of Lucius's pocket and place it very carefully on the ground. Hold it by the muzzle. Understood?'

He nodded.

'Make sure it doesn't look as though you're going to try shooting me, Charles.'

The fear on his face suggested that was the very last thing on his mind.

The coach came to a halt.

'Out, Charles.'

His hand shaking, Charles opened the door and stepped down.

'Now you, Lucius.' She kept the pistol levelled at him as she shifted to keep them in sight.

'Disarm him, Charles, and remember who will get shot.'

Lucius stood utterly still as Charles drew out the pistol and placed it on the ground.

'Kick it away.'

'It...it might go off!'

She smiled. 'It might. But that's not my problem. See where my pistol is pointing?' Straight at Charles's chest. 'Kick that one away.'

He obeyed and it spun away with a clatter.

'Very good. Now, tell your coachman to throw his pistols down where I'll be able to see them.'

Charles gulped. 'Bragg, do as she says.'

There was a ripe curse from the box, but a pistol sailed through the air to land with a thump on the heath.

'And the other.' Most coachmen carried a brace of pistols. She could think herself lucky they had decided not to risk any more witnesses to a kidnapping and there wasn't an armed footman to deal with.

Another curse and a second pistol joined the first.

'Both of you, back away. Not towards any pistol.'

Lucius clenched his fists as Charles grabbed his arm and dragged him back. 'You're no better than an animal!' he spat.

'One of you would be dead already if that were true,' she said, slipping the knife back into its sheath in her muff. She stepped down and circled carefully to get herself between the pair of them and Lucius's pistol. Never taking her eyes off them or letting her own pistol waver, she crouched down to pick up the weapon.

'Carriage coming, my lord!'

Automatically she looked, saw the gig perhaps a quarter of a mile away…and heard the metallic click of a gun being cocked.

Will urged Circe on up the steep road over the Heath. The ground was muddy, but he was making good time. He'd driven out of Soho and on to the Edgware Road again as the sun rose, the mare's breath condensing as she settled into her stride and trotted easily along, hooves ringing.

He kept her moving at that swinging, mile-eating trot, well up to her bit. She was fresh and even the steep hill didn't seem to bother her.

The sun was well up now, banners of pink fading in the eastern sky, and the rising green of the heath in its cloak of golden daffodils around him. Ahead at the very top, among the greening trees smoke rose from the chimneys of Highwood where Psyché's uncle lay. The groom who'd brought the news had said she'd been in time.

'Mr Marney said as how they stayed with him and the master passed very peaceful.'

Eventually it would comfort her to remember that she had been there at the last for the man who had been there at the right time in her own life.

He hoped she wouldn't mind that he had driven out to bring her home. The groom had also brought the news of

Harbury's arrival and said that he was *'swinging his weight around'.*

He didn't doubt that Psyché could look after herself, but after what she'd told him about Harbury, he didn't like the idea of her having to deal with him. Even if Lady Harbury *was* there.

With Highwood's chimneys in sight, Will saw the carriage halted some way ahead. He eased Circe, wondering. Hold-ups were not unheard of, but in daylight? And there was no horseman—more likely a breakdown.

Two men were already out of the carriage, another stepping down… He frowned, squinting—that was a woman. Dressed in black, she took a few steps, then crouched and the rising sun fell on a dark face, the light glinting on something in her hand…

Two shots rang out and she fell.

He cracked his whip beside the mare's ear, dropped his hands and sprang her.

Chapter Twenty-Five

Psyché dropped and rolled as the coachman's pistol roared and her own discharged. Deafened, she scrambled into a crouch in the reek of gun smoke and Lucius—ten feet away—stopped dead in his tracks.

In the distance she could hear the thunder of hooves, but didn't dare look around. Lucius was too close.

Trembling, she levelled his own pistol at him, cocked it. 'No closer.'

The thunder of hooves drew closer.

'Harbury—quick! Circle around. We'll flank her. Say we're taking a thieving servant before a magistrate.'

Charles shook his head. 'It won't work, Lucius. She'll talk! And the servants—'

'Will hold their tongues if they know what's good for them and *she* can't talk if she's on a ship!'

She kept the gun steady, her heart pounding as she prayed whoever was driving the carriage would believe her.

Closer it came, closer. Until the horse, flanks heaving and breath smoking, halted beside her.

'Back off, Winthrop.'

His voice, so dear and familiar even iced with rage, nearly dropped her to her knees as relief roared through her. She locked her trembling legs, kept the pistol unwavering.

'You lose, Lucius.' Somehow her voice remained steady.

'Are you hurt, love? You fell.' Will's voice, not quite as steady. From the corner of her eye she saw the pistol in his hand.

'He missed.'

Will spoke with lethal softness. 'Where were they taking you?'

Psyché took a deep breath. 'Will, don't—'

'Where?'

If he lost his temper— 'The West India Dock.'

A short, vicious curse accompanied the click as he cocked his pistol.

'Will!'

'I should shoot you like a dog, Winthrop.' No longer unsteady, promise edged his voice and Lucius paled, taking a step back. 'Except I'd give a dog a quick death. You, too, Harbury.'

'I… I… It wasn't me!' Charles babbled. 'Bragg fired that shot! It was all Winthrop's idea!'

Will snorted. 'Perhaps a ball between the legs for you? At least you'd have one, then.'

Psyché backed up until she stood by the gig. 'Will, better if—'

'Any other guns you know about, Psyché?'

The calm, utterly controlled voice, as if he were merely asking if there were more coffee in the pot, had her blinking. 'The…the coachman threw down two. I didn't realise he had a third.'

'Fetch them while I cover you.'

She obeyed, seeing the sense of making sure they couldn't rearm. She brought the guns back to the gig, keeping it between Lucius and herself.

Will flicked them a glance. 'Set them on the seat for now and get in.'

She stepped into the gig, but kept her own pistol cocked.

A brief smile touched the corner of Will's mouth.

'You.' He levelled his barrel directly on the coachman. 'Get down from there. Leave the brake off.'

The coachman clambered down quickly as the horses stamped, restless with slack reins.

'Can you hit the coach, sweetheart?'

'Can I—?' She swallowed the insult. He'd never seen her shoot after all. 'Yes.'

'Do it.'

She put the ball straight into the front of the coach. The already nervous horses bolted down the hill, the coach rattling and jouncing behind them.

Will handed her his own pistol and steadied the mare as she huffed and sidled. 'Good shot. Take another pistol. Cover them until we're clear.'

'Think again, Barclay,' Lucius snarled. 'You think you're going to stop me walking back to my own house?' He gestured to Highwood, his expression smug.

Genuine laughter bubbled up in Psyché. 'But it's not yours, Lucius.' Fierce satisfaction burned through her as his jaw dropped. 'Uncle Theo left it to Hetty—tied up in a trust along with sufficient income for her to live there.' She glanced at Harbury. 'Not even you can touch it, Charles. He made very sure of that. And since you left her tied up, I somehow doubt she'll be inviting you to visit.'

'Off you go then, *gentlemen*.' Sarcasm dripped from Will's voice. 'You've a long walk ahead of you.'

He gave them a wide berth and set the mare into a trot. Psyché twisted around to watch, keeping the pistols cocked until they were well out of range. Then she uncocked them carefully and took what felt like her first steady breath in an eternity. Lucius, Charles and the coachman were trudging down the muddy road after the runaway carriage.

'Will?' Somehow just saying his name made her feel safer. 'Thank—'

'What are they doing?'

'Walking after the carriage.'

'Right.' He pulled the mare up before the gates leading into Highwood and set the brake.

'What—?'

His mouth silenced her. Fierce, desperate and demanding, as if something had ripped loose inside him and found an answer in her. Because she responded in the same vein, as though there were nothing else in the world, as if it had contracted to this moment and the space that held them.

There were no words. He was not entirely sure words existed to express what he'd felt on hearing those shots, seeing her fall. All his control, all the words had been used up getting her away. Now all that mattered was to reassure himself that she was alive, safe in his arms where she belonged. Her mouth, lush and sweet, burned against his, offering everything and demanding more. He took it, gave it, with a groan, wondering if he'd ever be able to let her out of his arms again, let alone out of his sight.

The thunder of hooves broke them apart. Freeing his mouth reluctantly, Will looked up to see half a dozen riders rounding the corner of the house, Caleb and Lady Harbury, the latter hatless and dishevelled, in their midst.

'Company.' He touched her cheek with shaking fingers.

'Caleb,' she whispered. 'He…he was on the box. He realised something was wrong and jumped. He must have—'

Her words were lost as the riders pulled up around them and Lady Harbury flung herself from her horse, weeping and laughing. 'That *pig*!' She dragged Psyché from the gig, hugged her wildly. 'He gagged me while I was still asleep and tied me up!'

Caleb leapt from his horse and ran to them. 'Miss Psyché! You're safe!'

Lady Harbury, one arm still about Psyché, reached out

and squeezed Caleb's shoulder. 'Caleb raised the alarm and found me. He's a hero!' She hugged Psyché again.

Psyché reached out and Will saw her hand tremble as it curved against Caleb's cheek. 'Thank you. More than I can say.'

Caleb hunched his shoulders. 'I knew it was all wrong when that Mr Winthrop got in.' He looked up at Will. 'I was coming for you, Mr Barclay.' He waved at the grooms. 'Her ladyship and the grooms were going after the coach.'

Will swallowed. Brains, courage and unswerving loyalty. 'My thanks as well, Caleb. I'll never be able to repay you.'

The boy shuffled a little. 'You beat us to it, sir.'

He gave a cracked laugh. 'Only because you'd asked the groom to stop at The Phoenix last night, you young idiot. And—' he wrung the boy's hand '—she'd already escaped the coach when I reached her.'

He had a woman who could look after herself and inspired unswerving loyalty in her friends. He wasn't sure what he'd done to deserve her, but he'd be grateful for the rest of their lives together.

Releasing Psyché, Lady Harbury took charge. 'One of you ride down to St John's and inform the Vicar that Lord Staverton has passed. He is needed here as soon as possible. Someone else is to take the carriage into London to bring my children back and ask my housekeeper to pack my clothes as well. I will be remaining here for the time being.'

'Hetty—' Psyché touched her cheek gently.

'He told me where they were taking you, Psyché.' Lady Harbury's eyes were wet. 'He *boasted* of it. And *then* claimed you'd offered to be his mistress. That he was doing it to spare me embarrassment.'

'Hetty, I—'

'And don't you *dare* think you have to tell me he was

lying! I'm going to *ruin* him!' She rounded on Will. 'When are you going to marry my cousin, Mr Barclay?'

Laughter welled up in him, as he pulled Psyché back into his arms. 'Next week.' He looked down at her. 'If that's what you want. I'm yours. Now. For ever.' He smiled.

Psyché stared at him. 'Can we? That fast? You have to apply for a licence.'

'I did that yesterday.' He chuckled. 'Huntercombe expects to give the wedding breakfast at Moresby House.'

'What does Lady Huntercombe think of that?'

Will grinned. 'She's delighted. I left Huntercombe writing to Selbourne on the very vexed subject of who escorts the bride down the aisle.'

'Excellent.' Lady Harbury gave a decisive nod. 'Uncle Theo did tell you not to keep him waiting.'

Psyché met Will's smiling eyes for a moment, then turned to Hetty. 'There's not the least chance of that!'

Epilogue

Will stretched his legs by the fire, sipped his brandy and wondered how long it took for a bride to ready herself for her wedding night. And was she going to sit out here by the fire and sip brandy decorously while *he* readied himself in the bedroom? In fact, what *did* a bridegroom need to do to ready himself? Beyond tearing off his own clothes and the bride's, that was. Because he was more than ready now and had been since they arrived back at The Phoenix.

Tomorrow they were going out to Chiswick for a few days. Cambourne had offered them a small house '...*for as long as you like, Barclay. Consider it a wedding gift.*'

But tonight, after spending the day surrounded by friends and well-wishers, both of them had wanted to return here to the apartment where they would live. He'd thought it a marvellous idea—fully intending, the moment he got Psyché upstairs, to take her straight to bed. After a week during which he'd been chaperoned more closely than any virgin, Will was more than ready for his wedding night and his bride.

It had been a wonderful day. They had married around the corner at St Anne's, then Huntercombe and Lady Huntercombe had given a wedding breakfast. Kit had arrived in London the day before and, according to Lady Huntercombe, society was reeling at the news that the one-time heiress had spurned her father, been disinherited and moved openly into her great-uncle's lodgings above his shop.

Hetty had come down from Hampstead with her children to attend. The scandal over the attempted kidnapping had forced Harbury to agree to a deed of private separation from Hetty and to leave the children with their mother. Even Lucius was persona non grata with a number of influential hostesses, Lady Huntercombe among them. Huntercombe had made it very clear that if it had come to an ordinary trial, both men would have very likely been found guilty.

'Unfortunately, they'd have to be tried literally before their peers—in the Lords. I couldn't guarantee the outcome of that.'

As it was, several members of the Lords, including Huntercombe and Cambourne, had publicly stated that if either Harbury or Lucius crossed their paths, a thrashing would be the least they could expect. Will had gone a little further, calling on Harbury to inform him that any attempt to force Hetty to return to him, or to take the children before the deed of separation could be finalised, would result in an immediate challenge.

He hadn't mentioned that to Psyché yet, not wanting to worry her before the wedding. Not that he thought there was much to worry about—Harbury had swallowed several times before assuring Will that he had no such intent... hadn't crossed his mind. That he would be leaving London directly the legal deed was signed.

Assured of Harbury's ongoing cowardice, Will had approached his wedding day with joy.

Even Will's mother and brother Rob had attended. They had been rather stiff and uncomfortable, but at least they had come, congratulated him, wished Psyché happy and welcomed her into the family.

He suspected that they were simply putting the best face

they could on what they considered an appalling situation, but his mother had thawed enough to say she hoped Psyché would soon visit them for a few days. Rob had reiterated the invitation, a little over-hearty, but they were trying.

And he still had a position. Foxworthy was retiring on a generous pension and Hunt had offered him the post. It would still involve some travel outside London, but he wouldn't need to accompany the Marquess all over the country.

But now all Will wanted was his bride. The woman who filled his life, his world and his heart with such joy and love that—

The click of the bedroom door opening behind him had him slewing around in his seat to see... Very carefully he set the brandy—a wedding night gift from Hunt—on the wine table.

Before he dropped it.

Psyché glided towards him, hips swaying, confident and utterly alluring. All that wonderful, spiralling hair tumbled about her shoulders and her smile promised every earthly delight imaginable.

'Do you like them?'

God help him! The low, sultry voice was temptation incarnate. And *like* was an understatement. A very poor choice of word indeed. He was fairly sure there wasn't a word in the entirety of the English language that would cover this. At least not one he could think of when every drop of blood had apparently drained into his breeches.

In the lamplight her bronze skin glowed against the dusky, rose-pink chemise—the exact shade of the gown she had worn for their wedding—veiling her curves. She stroked one hand over matching drawers that skimmed long, slim legs. But the coup de grâce... She might as well have hit him in the head with a brick.

'Ah…' He fought for coherent words. 'Are those *my* riding boots?'

'Mmm.' Her sultry smile lured him to insanity. 'I never did get around to trying them on.'

He rose from the chair. 'Do they fit?'

She came to him on a ripple of laughter. 'Not really. But—' a wicked glance assessed his state '—they do seem to have done the job.'

He grinned, scooping his bride, his woman, up into his arms, boots and all. 'I can assure you, that job was already accomplished.'

* * * * *

If you enjoyed this book, why not check out
these other great reads by Elizabeth Rolls

The Unruly Chaperon
Lord Braybrook's Penniless Bride
Royal Weddings
'A Princely Dilemma'

And be sure to read her Lords at the Altar miniseries

In Debt to the Earl
His Convenient Marchioness

Afterword

People always ask, 'Where do you get your ideas?' Usually I just make something up, because I have literally no idea. But with this story I know exactly where it came from.

Some time ago I fell down a virtual research rabbit hole and followed the River Fleet upstream to its source on Hampstead Heath in the grounds of Kenwood House, home of the First Earl of Mansfield. With an actual trip to London planned, I added Kenwood to my itinerary and started exploring the house and grounds online.

Lord Mansfield was a familiar name, but I read the story of his Black illegitimate great-niece, Dido Elizabeth Belle. Fascinated, I started looking for more information.

I found a fleeting reference to Dido in Hugh Thomas's *The Slave Trade*, which has been on my shelves for over fifteen years. Scouring the internet, I found the biography *Belle*, by Paula Byrne, which accompanied the 2013 film of the same name, starring Gugu Mbatha-Raw in the title role.

There is little direct information about Dido. She left no diary and she only appears, ghostlike, in various letters—sometimes snidely referenced by those who disapproved of her place in Mansfield's home.

Wanting to know more about her world, I looked deeper

and found other sources on slavery and the Abolition movement of the late eighteenth century.

On my trip to London I visited Kenwood House and looked back down the Heath to London and St Paul's, as Will does in the story. I explored Soho with a friend, learning the streets where Psyché makes her life. I should note that by the time of this story coffee houses were nearly gone from London—The Phoenix Rising was possibly the last of its kind!

Readers familiar with Dido's story will realise the enormous debt I owe to her for the inspiration for this book. They will certainly recognise Kenwood House in my story, thinly disguised as Highwood, and notice other elements of Dido's history that have made their way into Psyché's tale—not least in the way Lord Staverton uses his will to ensure Psyché's safety. Those are Lord Mansfield's words.

But this is not Dido's story by any means. That is not a story I feel I have any right to tell. I did bring her portrait home from London in the form of a drink coaster, which I keep on my desk for my water glass—Dido and her cousin, Lady Elizabeth Murray, have been my constant companions in this telling.

Slowly we are coming to see that London was never quite the homogenous society we imagined and perhaps now we are seeing further beneath the glitter and romance of the Regency period to some of the darkness that underpinned it. I hope that in telling a story that touches on this darkness, the brutal reality of slavery and its influence on society, readers will be encouraged to look further into how history continues to shape and inform our world today.